Spanking Yesterday

Oxbow Lake the 2nd
(with Ward A Bobb the 3rd)

If you don't laugh at our books,
you're probably dead . . .
or should be!

ShipWreckPublications.com

Unsolicited Praise for Oxbow Lake's
Spanking Yesterday

"Regardless of Mr. Lake's many requests, I refuse to make this novel required reading for my computer science courses at this university. However, I may buy a remaindered copy for myself when they're available provided the discount is substantial, of course."
-- Dr. Roger Grice, Professor, Something to do with Computer Science

"My place in literary immortality remains unthreatened by this source. It's too late."
-- Mark Twain (You Dead Tube)

"Is *Spanking Yesterday* a novel? Who wrote the damn thing? I find it all quite confusing, but then again, I'm dead. Hopefully those who are alive will be less confused, but I have my eternal doubts."
-- John Kennedy Toole (Giggle Beyond Internet Site)

"It appears that not only can't you keep a good man down, you can't keep a plagiarizing bastard down either."
-- Raymond Kennedy (scratched on a bar near Columbia)

"Well I can now say that Mr. Oxbow Lake's first novel is the second worst punctuated novel I've ever reviewed. The author or authors of this tome are even more obsessed with ellipses and remain out of their freakin'… elliptical minds!"
-- Lisa Lazzero (alias Lisa Lazzaro) Senior Freelance Punctuator

"It can be safely said that Dave Barry is now the second funniest writer alive (and quite possibly the third), and that Carl (stuttering a's) Hiaasen has dropped out of the top 10,000 behind an ethnic German graffiti scribbler named Sanas the Fakir from Jaipur, India, who spray paints jokes on bathroom walls about snake charmers who get bitten between their legs by their cobras!"
-- Kramer Killread, Editor (The New Tampa Guide to Sane Automobile Repair)

"The dirty parts are real good!"
-- Super Amazing Steve Nash (Poet of Ill Repute)

"Oxbow needed at least two sets of knee pads to get his first novel published. I hope for his sake that he kept or replaced them."
-- Senator John "Bluto" Blutarsky (Animal House séance)

"I find Oxbow Lake's second novel to be as vulgar and despicable as the first, and I haven't even bothered to read the first page this time."
-- Charles Dickens (channeled through Hugh Hefner)

Oxbow Lake: Possible Winner of the 2013 Costa Concordia

Every April 1st, ShipWreckPublications LLC is proud to award the prestigious Costa Concordia Award for Fictional Excellence to the author who best epitomizes extraordinary fictional excellence in the ever perceptive and discerning eyes, ears, nose and throat of the carefully selected judges on the awards committee who are appointed to that esteemed committee by the staff at ShipWreckPublications. These judges were chosen for their reputed excellence in the field of literature and for their independence from any external influence that would sway their opinion. They willingly agreed to become members of the awards committee and participate in the awards process... after given an offer they could not refuse, so to speak. (Sadly, the committee members have requested to remain anonymous to date. Only time will tell if they succumb to our rather vigorous request that we announce their names.)

These judges, reputed to be the best in their field, had a great deal of difficulty selecting who should merit the prestigious Costa Concordia award this year, particularly given the possibility that their names would be attached to the awarding of this great prize in literature. They considered a number of factors. However, after much profound and intense discussion with the staff at ShipWreck, they finally succumbed to choosing a winner for the prestigious 2013 Costa Concordia. While the committee has not announced the winner, we have it on excellent authority that it is possible that the winner will be Oxbow Lake the 2nd for his second novel *Spanking Yesterday*. Should this happen, Mr. Lake will be a two-timer so to speak when the award is formally announced given that he also won the award in 2012.

3

A premature congratulations to the possible winner, Mr. Oxbow Lake the 2nd!

Spanking Yesterday is Mr. Lake's best novel to date while still on a par with his first novel *The Adventures of the Posse of Little Horses* for which he won the 2012 Costa Concordia as well. *Spanking Yesterday* is available in paperback and Nook and Kindle ebook editions and can be ordered online from both the Amazon and Barnes & Noble internet sites as can *The Adventures of the Posse of Little Horses*. Go to our web site www.shipwreckpublications.com for links to the Amazon and Barnes & Noble sites to order the novels. While on our site, check out the ShipWreckPublications' special offer for signed copies of both novels.

Yesterday be made required reading for all computer science and technical communications programs as well as all literature programs in our colleges and universities. We can arrange sweet deals for Instructors and Professors (and you instructors and professors know what we mean)!

The ShipWreckPublications Speakers Bureau can livin' up any meeting of hoi polloi that you can muster into a conference room or hall, particularly if the projected audience can and has read at least one book in the last decade. Technical tomes of a scientific and mathematical nature do not count in this instance.

We realize that the previous condition might limit our sale of our speaker services, but we thought it appropriate to state since we want you to get your money's worth. For the most part, an audience of ill literates would not enjoy and/or profit from a healthy dose of one of our speakers' lectures as we incorporate very little slap stick in our lectures. However, for an additional fee, this situation can be easily rectified as we are fans and aficionados of the Three Stooges, both past and present.

There is one caveat to the above limitation concerning ill literates. We believe that older dyslexics, particularly if their dyslexia is severe enough to prevent them being able to read a book, can still attend one of our lectures and appear to enjoy and profit from it as they usually have developed coping mechanisms so as to appear to be well read and thus will also strive to appear to enjoy the lecture. As an added bonus, older dyslexics will probably rate your efforts at scheduling one of our lectures very highly as they want to appear to fully enjoy and understand the lecture and any negative comments would require an understanding of what was said in order to state specific reasons for their dissatisfaction... an understanding they are unlikely to have at least concerning specific literary references.

Younger dyslexics tend not to fall into this limitation as they most likely have learned to use audio books and thus in most cases are more literate in an auditory sense than their non-dyslexic peers.

For more information about our audio books, whether or not you're dyslexic, please contact the **ShipWreckPublications Audio Books Department** at be498ar@earthlink.net or visit our web site at www. shipwreckpublications.com

We guarantee that our speakers will be pretty much as advertised and always dress appropriately.

For the terms of our speaker services and to schedule a speaker, please contact the **ShipWreckPublications Speakers Bureau** at be498ar@earthlink.net or visit our web site at www.shipwreckpub-lications.com

Speaking of our web site, take a gander at it. You'll enjoy the topics, particularly if you have even a shred of humor in your bones and enjoy someone else's eye getting poked.

www.shipwreckpublications.com

Designed by Karen Mathis
Mathis Web Masters Unincorporated

Manufactured somewhere in the United States of America. Due to the structure of the internet, the exact location is difficult to impos-sible to determine but we're pretty sure that location is in the US of A.

Spanking Yesterday

Copyright © 2013 by Oxbow Lake the 2nd, Ward A. Bobb the 3rd, or Robert A. Ward III, take your pick.
v2.0
ISBN: 978-0-9839766-1-5
This edition is published by ShipWreckPublications LLC.
Cover design and illustrations by Karen Mathis
Photos by Lisa Lazzero (alias Lisa Lazzaro)
ShipWreckPublications LLC
9745 Fox Chapel Road
Tampa, FL 33647

Visit our website at www.ShipWreckPublications.com

PRINTED IN THE UNITED STATES OF AMERICA

Contents

A note to the reader on the publication of *Spanking Yesterday* from a concerned publisher

As the publisher of *Spanking Yesterday*, I feel ethically obligated to inform the reader of my concerns about this novel if indeed it is a novel… and the authorship of Mr. Oxbow Lake the 2nd. The ever mysterious Mr. Lake sent the manuscript to me last April… that is, April 1st of 2012. In the note that accompanied the manuscript, he wrote that he had just finished it and sought my opinion. He also gave me a bit of background on the novel's structure. In summary, he described the novel as written in first person in the form of a journal written by a fictional character that he named Ward Bobb the 3rd .

The naming of Mr. Ward Bobb the 3rd as the protagonist of *Spanking Yesterday* and the fictional author of the journal that was the novel confused me, for on the back cover of Mr. Lake's first novel, *The Adventures of the Posse of Little Horses*, a Mr. Ward Bobb 3rd was listed as the true author of *Posse* and Oxbow Lake was described as a pen name used by Mr. Bobb. I found this confusing since I had met with someone whom I thought to be Mr. Lake several times during the negotiations for the publishing contract that he signed with ShipWreckPublications… a contract that he signed 'Oxbow Lake the 2nd'.

Then when *Posse* was subsequently published, Mr. Lake provided the text and the picture for the back cover of that novel and in the blurb about the author that appeared on the back cover, he wrote the following: "Oxbow Lake the 2nd is a pen name used by Ward Bobb the 3rd which is an alias". Since I had a contract signed by an 'Oxbow Lake', I wondered if the contract could be invalid. I contacted Mr. Lake via the U.S. Postal Service regarding this concern and he replied in a hand-written note, again delivered by the U.S. Postal Service, that... and I again quote... "I use the name Ward Bobb the 3rd as a kind of reverse pen name to protect my anonymity. I am who I am and the contract is valid!" He did not sign the letter. I had never heard of a 'reverse pen name' and I thought it a rather odd concept but so much about Mr. Lake and his writings were... how should I put this... out of the ordinary... that I just chalked it up as just another of the idiosyncrasies of the world according to Oxbow Lake... but now I am not so sure.

In spite of my initial question concerning the name and existence of the central character in the novel and the authorship of the novel, I read the manuscript and was very impressed. While the novel is laugh-out-loud funny, it is also pointedly satirical to the extreme and deals with a number of rather serious themes... much like *Posse* which ShipWreckPublications published last year and which won the prestigious Costa Concordia Award for Fictional Excellence.

I was stunned by how real the journal felt. It was a jump up from the already high perch upon which his award winning *Posse* so comfortably sat. The setting, the depiction of mental illness, the time period, corporate life... it felt as though I were actually living and laughing and suffering in that time... in that setting with a Mr. Ward Bobb the 3rd, a fictional character who spoke to me through a journal created by Oxbow Lake, the author. I got lost in the novel. I identified with the central character and forgot that it was a novel written in the form of a journal by the supposedly fictional character, one Ward Bobb the 3rd. Talk about suspending disbelief... it all seemed so humorously and tragically real!

I penned a quick letter to Mr. Lake praising the novel highly and noting in particular how real it seemed… how it read like an actual journal written by a very disturbed, mentally ill individual who was at war with himself and the world around him. I sent the letter via the U.S. Postal Service to the return address on the manuscript. (Oxbow often refuses to meet face-to-face, is constantly on the move and rarely communicates through the internet as he considers that technology inhumane.)

My letter was returned to me with "return to sender, not deliverable as addressed, unable to forward, etc., etc." scrawled (not stamped, as is usually the case) across the front of the now ripped and pretty much destroyed envelope that I sent. I was shocked and dismayed. I later learned that Mr. Lake had again disappeared and gone into hiding. At least that's where we think he is as it has happened before.

A week later, much to my very great surprise, I got another letter through the U.S. Postal Service… this time from an individual who claimed that he co-wrote the novel and wanted to be listed as a contributing or co-author when the novel was published. (See a copy of that letter below which I urge the reader to read and read carefully!) It was signed 'Ward Bobb the 3rd', the fictional journal's supposedly fictional author and a so-called 'reverse pen name' used by Mr. Lake himself.

Could it be that the journal is not fiction and the Ward Bobb character is real? Could it be that Ward Bobb is Oxbox Lake's alter ego and that the fictional journal is so well written that it appears to be real? Could Oxbow Lake actually be the pen name used by Ward Bobb the 3rd as originally indicated on the back cover of *Posse*? The questions multiplied as I thought. I had no idea what or who to believe… still don't… but regardless of who wrote the book or claimed to write it or co-write it, there is one fact that I am sure of: it's a great read… entertaining, satiric, thought provoking, tragic, funny as hell in an Animal House kind of way… and culturally significant.

Since Mr. Oxbow Lake the 2nd or the individual reputed to be the author of this magnificent "novel" has apparently gone into hiding, I cannot communicate with him on this matter, and since I have this individual under an exclusive contract which the signer of said contract never bothered to read… which contract grants me certain powers concerning the publishing of his… novels?... I feel obligated to publish what I consider to be a great book… possibly a great novel… even if I must credit Mr. Ward Bobb the 3rd as a contributor and let the chips fall where they may.

However, I have taken the unprecedented action of publishing the manuscript exactly as sent to me, including the original art work crudely attached to that manuscript. I added only the front and back covers, a title page on which I recognize a certain Ward Bobb the 3rd as a contributing author, the front matter including this note to the reader, an updated table of contents, and the back matter. The rest of the book is the manuscript exactly as he author sent it to me.

As a responsible publisher, I thought it absolutely necessary to inform the reader of the situation which I believe I have now done.

CAVE CANEM MAGNUM!

Robert A Ward III
Publishing Mogul & CEO
ShipWreckPublications LLC

Date: July 11, 1965

To: Robert A Ward III
Publishing Mogul & CEO
ShipWreckPublications LLC

Subject: Co-authorship of 'Spanking Yesterday'

Recently you received a manuscript from Oxbow
Lake the 2nd entitled 'Spanking Yesterday'.
I am not sure how Oxbow presented to you the
manner in which that work was created since I
was not sent a copy of the letter which I believe accompanied that manuscript.

I worked very closely with Oxbow in the creation of this work using some material I had
written previously. The story of how this
came about is both interesting, illuminating
and very germane to this work's publication.

Oxbow and I are… or at least were… close
friends many years ago and actually worked
together in the late 60's as technical writers. We lost contact over the years when I
suffered a protracted illness, but we seren-
dipitously met last year at Disney World in
Orlando, Florida.

While visiting Fantasyland… I do so annually
to ground myself in reality… I saw this di-
sheveled man at the entrance to Cinderella's
Royal Table restaurant arguing with, of all

people, Cinderella herself… something about luncheon reservations that he apparently didn't have. He had hair down to his asshole and he looked more like one of Sleeping Beauty's unkempt dwarfs suffering from a terrible case of acromegaly, more commonly known as gigantism, and a very bad case of poor anger management.

He yelled "I shouldn't need reservations. I'm Oxbow Lake the 2nd, a famous award winning author." I took a quick trip down memory lane and sure enough an image of a young Oxbow popped into my head. I said to myself, "Why that's that ol' reprobate Oxbow Lake himself… I'm sure!" And sure enough… it was.

By now, things between Cinderella and Oxbow had reached the boiling point and it looked like Cinderella was about to call a posse of well-armed and muscular Prince Charmings to beat the snot out of what appeared to be an erstwhile insane acromegalical dwarf, so I interjected myself as a peacemaker. When I told ol' Oxbow who I was, his eyes lit up and he gave me a big bear hug like the Dancing Bear he used to be… thus diffusing the potentially dangerous confrontation with Cinderella and her posse of strong arm Prince Charmings.

I had reservations for Cinderella's Table. I make them for two just in case… always do. I hate to eat alone and there's usually someone around to accompany me on my annual grounding expedition to Fantasyland. This year I was alone, so I say, "Oxbow, I've got reservations for two. Join me!"… and he did.

Over a fine lunch of 'Pork Three Ways' at Cinderella's Royal Table, we chewed the fat. Oxbow had a hidden flask of whiskey… that reincarnation of ol' John Barleycorn he… and he liberally sweetened our cups of Cinderella's dreadful java numerous times during the meal making the java drinkable and the conversation smooth and deep.

We talked about his recently published award winning novel, "The Adventures of the Posse of Little Horses", which I later read and enjoyed. Actually, at lunch he gave me a signed copy, one of the last of the 137 copies that he has committed, I believe to you, to sign.

He mentioned that he was searching for material for his second novel and I suggested that he take a look at something I had written years ago and that perhaps we could work together on his next tome using this material. The long and short of it is that I sent him the material which greatly intrigued him and we worked together using the material as a base when we jointly created the manuscript which you recently read and praised.

Since I worked closely with Oxbow in the creation of this work and since this work is based on material that I originally wrote, I would like to be recognized as co-author or

at least a contributing author. I am not concerned about being compensated… at least for
now. While I am not a litigious man, I assure
you that I can become so. I have attempted to
talk with Oxbow about this but he has again
disappeared… which is why I am writing to you
directly.

Original signed by Ward A Bobb the 3rd

News Flash Concerning the *Spanking Yesterday* Imbroglio

April 1, 2013, New Tampa, Florida. ShipWreckPublications LLC harbors great concern in its corporate and literary heart concerning one Ward Bobb the 3rd and the creation and publishing of what has been purported to be Oxbow Lake the 2nd 's second novel *Spanking Yesterday...* so concerned in fact that I have expressed our corporate and literary concerns in two publisher's notes... one at the beginning of this "novel" and one at the end. If you've gotten this far, you've probably read the first publisher's note.

Originally I thought to contract the New York Times to investigate this imbroglio as they apparently do a lot of contract journalism. However, after reviewing that newspaper's investigative reporting and considering its motto "All the news that's fit to print", I've decided that my definition of "what's fit to print" is so different from that organization's that I could not trust the New York Times with so important a contract.

Instead , I have contracted the celebrated literary scholar, hard-hitting, and very inexpensive investigative reporter Dr. Kramer Killread the First, Esquire, to solve the mystery of this imbroglio. For an example of Dr. Killread's wonderful scholarship and investigative reporting, see Dr. Killread's first investigative report subtitled "Who Really Wrote *Spanking Yesterday* (A Preliminary Conjecture)" that appears in the back of this book.

The hard-hitting Dr. Killread is charged with piercing the mystery of this imbroglio and determining who's who and what's what as regards Oxbow Lake, Ward Bobb and *Spanking Yesterday*. He is free to go wherever and whenever his investigation leads him and to report what he finds to the citizens of this great republic as well as to the world at large. His reports will appear periodically on a regular basis in that well known internet journal *The New Tampa Guide to Sane Automobile Repair*, a highly regarded scholarly journal of literary and societal commentary and investigative reporting. The *Guide's* motto says it all regarding this journal's… and the good Doctor's… dedication to the truth: "A journal dedicated to the proposition that all fiction is true and all non-fiction is not" as compared to that of the New York Times which is more concerned with "fitness" (and a very intellectually flabby fitness, I might add) rather than with "truth"!

We encourage our readers to sign up for Dr. Kramer's investigative reports which will be published at *The New Tampa Guide to Sane Automobile Repair* (http://guidetosaneautorepair.wordpress.com/), and to visit the ShipWreckPublications website (http://www.ship-wreckpublications.com/) which is chock full of important information and entertaining stuff, including short stories and critical writings by someone whom we believe to be Oxbow Lake his very own self as well as reports about the goings-on of this rogue publishing house.

As noted above, Dr. Kramer has already written his first report, which appears at the back of this book. See "Investigative Report 1 Concerning the *Spanking Yesterday* Imbroglio: Who Really Wrote *Spanking Yesterday* (A Preliminary Conjecture) ". Unfortunately Dr. Kramer's first report was submitted to ShipWreckPublications LLC late in the publishing process and I could not incorporate the information into my publisher's notes. However, I was fortunate enough to be able to add this and several other short news flashes to update the reader even though we were very late in the process.

Spanking Yesterday follows. Enjoy, laugh and think as you read this great work, for just as it matters not who wrote Shakespeare's plays or Sam Clemens's and Mark Twain's novels in order to enjoy the great works attributed to these men, it matters not a whit or even a wit that an imbroglio surrounds this wonderful oeuvre extraordinaire. Bon Appétit!

Robert A Ward III
Publishing Mogul & CEO
ShipWreckPublications LLC

The following epigraphs are not to be confused with an epitaph even though an epitaph of sorts did appear as the "Dedication" to our first novel, *The Adventures of the Posse of Little Horses,* as an epigraph

Epigraph 1

"There is no accounting for human beings."

Mark Twain
A Connecticut Yankee in King Arthur's Court

Epigraph 2

"All fiction is true and all non-fiction is not!

Dr. Kramer Killread the First, Esquire
The New Tampa Guide to Sane Automobile Repair

Epigraph 3

"The past can be a dangerous place to go."

Ward A Bobb the 3rd
Spanking Yesterday

Dedication

I dedicate *Spanking Yesterday* to myself for without me, this entire effort would have been much more difficult to complete… Hell, it'd have been at least as difficult to even begin!

Signed,

Yours truly

More Spanks and Some Thanks

First and foremost, we still do NOT thank the many, many publishing agents of that debilitated, incestuous profession who rejected our wonderfully humorous, satiric and entertaining first novel, *The Adventures of the Posse of Little Horses*. In fact, we are so pissed off at them that we refuse to even give any of the bastards the opportunity to represent us for the publishing of *Spanking Yesterday*! We'd rather lose money than let any of them gain profit from our brilliant work.

We would, however, like to thank ourselves for our dedication and devotion to our craft, for as we note in our formal dedication above, without us, there would be no need for a "More Spanks and Thanks", and if there were such without us, it would be somewhat pointless, very short and quite possibly... irrelevant!

We like to thank that great publishing mogul Robert A Ward III ahead of publication for publishing this novel through his Ship-WreckPublications LLC as we're sure he will do. In our opinion, he will remain a man of great vision and taste and our high opinion of him will not change as long as he actually publishes our novel.

And we believe that we still owe a debt of gratitude to Alan R Beebe and Tom and Sue Wolfe for reading the manuscript for *Spanking Yesterday* and not saying they didn't like it any less than they did our first, *The Adventures of the Posse of Little Horses*, which we also encourage you to purchase even if you've already done so. Mr. Beebe and Mr. Wolfe also make cameo appearances in the novel... or at least their names do... and for this we also thank them.

We use several other names that may be considered real in some circles, such as the name "Gregg (two g's, two z's) Lazzaro" even though I invented the "two g's, two z's" part myself. This acknowledgment is probably unnecessary anyway since it is very unlikely that Gregg (two g's, two z's) Lazzaro will bother to read the novel. There are probably others but I've tired of this whole exercise and therefore am stopping this particular form of acknowledgement.

We owe a debt of gratitude to Morgan Lazzaro-Smith-Unterberger-Bridger, who has the tuition bills to prove her expertise, for her astute analysis of the character of the protagonist of *Spanking Yesterday*, and we quote: "After a careful reading of the novel and an in depth analysis of the character Ward A Bobb the 3rd, considering all the possible traumas and life experiences that character has obviously suffered, it is my carefully reasoned opinion that Mr. Bobb is crazier than a loon, psychologically speaking."

I guess we should also thank published authors Steve Hamilton and David Silverman who after reading the manuscript said... blah, blah, blah, etc., etc., etc. Much like Mr. Beebe and Mr. Wolfe, Mr. Hamilton also makes a cameo appearance in the fictional sense of that word. Thank you, Steve.

Then there's a prophylactic "thank you" for Lisa Lazzero (alias Lisa Lazzaro), who, if past history is any guide, will probably send us another quote to use to advertise the novel as she apparently gets off through acts of implied denigration. Ms. Lazzero did take a series of pictures of the author, one of which will probably be used on the back cover although we would like the other photos that she took to be destroyed or at the very least be kept extremely private until all of us are dead and thus no longer care. We will formally thank her for the picture that we'll probably use when she presents us with evidence that she's destroyed or safely hidden the others.

Finally, we'll thank ShipWreckPublications' brilliant Creative Director, Karen Mathis, who will undoubtedly design and create a wonderful cover for the novel and do lots of other stuff that is equally brilliant enabling us to eventually get the book published.

Perhaps I should also thank Gordon Gensler, whom we believe may have edited *Spanking Yesterday* although we're not sure. So we offer him another 'thank you'… more a prophylactic act in this case, but a 'thank you' none the less.

And really, really, really finally and perhaps most important, I thank Rick Haughey, handyman extraordinaire, for unclogging my toilet… which may, in the end, be one of the most important tasks enabling me to complete my wonderful novel, *Spanking Yesterday*. Thanks Rick, for what is very likely a major contribution to the future of American literature in particular and world literature in general. Nobel Committee… here we go!

At this point, we feel obligated to acknowledge that John Robinson finally did return the manuscript of *The Adventures of the Posse of Little Horses* that we chastised him for not doing in the 'Spanks' portion of the 'Spanks and Thanks' section for our first novel. However, his comments on said manuscript were so thin as to be perilously close to non-existence (consisting primarily of accusing the author of being inebriated while writing, which, even if true, did not affect the quality of said writing and may have actually improved it! William Faulkner, anyone?), and so we did not send him a copy of the manuscript for *Spanking Yesterday* to critique for to do so would be, in our judgment, a waste of our precious time and the cost of the postage.

Then there's Colin Lazzaro-Smith, who did not bother to return the manuscript for *Posse...* uncommented or otherwise. And to increase his debt of ingratitude, he still owes us $19 for the signed copy of that novel which he ordered, which we imprudently sent to him unpaid for and in which we wrote a very pertinent, appropriate and personal inscription. Needless to say, he too did not receive a copy of the manuscript of *Spanking Yesterday* to not comment on.

A Stranger in a Strange Land

It's only been five years... at least I think it's been five years... sometimes it's hard to tell. Maybe it's seven or eight... hell, maybe ten. Anyway, seems like a bad dream now... but I can still remember like it was yesterday standing at my cubicle door... squinting into the Hudson Valley's early morning summer sun... watching those fuckin' engineers and fuckin' programmers park their god damn cars with such sinister precision... inside those god damn carefully defined white lines... as if the god damn white lines were unbreakable rules, their unbreakable rules. Then, having successfully conquered their day's first great challenge, these two groups of ravenous techno-turncoats then march into the lab for another day dedicated to consuming society for their own pleasure and sustenance. Hell, they chomped away at my life every day like I was beef tartare.

I could tell the engineers from the programmers. Anybody with two eyes and half a brain could. The engineers always wore high-water pants, white sox and pocket protectors. Not to be outdone, the programmers also wore high-waters and pocket protectors but being more self-centered, they usually did not wear white sox. In fact programmers did not wear white sox at all. They displayed their faux individuality by wearing pairs of cotton sox that were either light brown or light blue. Occasionally, like a ray of sunshine, a wild card pair of argyles would sneak into the programming mix, something that absolutely never happened with the engineers. Ironically, with the sense of dented pots and banged up kettles, engineers and programmers made fun of each other for the way they dressed and acted. To normal folks like me they looked and acted like creatures from another world. The ravenous idiots.

31

Oxbow Lake The 2nd

Sprinkled amongst these two onrushing cacophonous marching bands of well-paid traitorous geeks… geeks employed by the world's largest and most nefarious computer manufacturer… were some misfits… some slovenly dressed 'sore thumbs', some with hair down to their assholes as our third-line manager, an engineer turned programmer by profession, so poetically put it. These sore thumbs were members of a third group, more like a tribe than a marching band… called Technical Publications or just plain Tech Pubs in the vernacular of those times. Many members of this tribe of sore thumbs did not wear any sox at all. They probably meant to, but forgot. If they had remembered, their sox would have been unmatched and most likely of inappropriate colors, one purple and one red for example, as had actually happened on at least two occasions.

The members of this tribe of misfits were my people, the maggot infested hippies, who didn't belong but who were a necessary evil in the eyes of the programmers and the engineers, both of whom agreed on little else other than that they had to put up with these stupid pubs assholes because the documentation they produced was required to get their insidious creations out of Product Test and into the eager hands of other idiot geeks whose employers paid dearly for the privilege.

I remember thinking to myself, "Kronos Technologies International, better known as KTI. Who'd a thunk? In college I majored in English Lit. Turned down two engineering scholarships because I was convinced that science would destroy mankind and here I was, years later, toiling away in the belly of modern technology's most efficient and destructive engine, managing a bunch of technical writers, many of whom hated the work more than I did… probably because they still had to actually do it…

they were my own tribe of outliers who toiled away each day documenting the latest mainframe software creations of KTI's bastard creatures so that these poor devils of mine could continue writing the great American novel late into the night while still supporting themselves and their families if they happened to still have one."

By then I wasn't writing the great American novel any more. I had given that up a long time ago. Instead, I managed my tribe of maggot infested hippies... herded is probably a better description as in herding cats... and the only things I wrote back then were performance evaluations and other official management type documents for and about these misplaced souls who were sentenced by life's inexorable necessities to work in the belly of this dreadful all-consuming beast under my semi-watchful eye.

At 8:12 AM on the button, the official starting time for my little tribe at KTI, the attendance bell buzzed and my phone rang simultaneously... and both very annoyingly so I might add. I could hear that KTI punch clock chugging away in the main hallway as the non-exempts jammed their time cards into that infernal time clock of a machine to be, appropriately, punched in for another day of work that would challenge their very sanity. I knew who was calling... my manager James Jankowski, the Polish fuckin' Prince, all six-two of the bastard. He was as crazy as my maggot infested hippies only in a different way. He had been an electrical engineer turned technical writer. He wore white sox, was very disciplined but goose-stepped to a different drummer than did his former peers. He was not only my second-line manager; he was my friend... in a Polish Prince sort of way... which is to say I was allowed to be his friend.

Oxbow Lake The 2nd

He wrote too, short stories, early every morning in his office before the dawning of the work day. When he wrote, he wore an accountant's green eye shade, the kind with a brim and no top to cover his slowly balding head. When he was finished writing, he drank a cup of that dreadful vending machine coffee… black… and smoked a long maduro cigar. Back then, you could smoke whatever and wherever the hell you wanted to as long as it wasn't mary jane. Hell, it was your patriotic duty to smoke and smoke whatever you wanted wherever you wanted.

James's short stories were sad, tidy little pieces about bad relationships with women… something about which he had a lifetime's worth of experience. He wrote well in a soap opera kind of way. Many years ago the first story he had ever written got published in The New Yorker, a real tear jerker, and he hadn't managed to get anything published since. However, he kept toiling away for the decades since, writing in No. 2 pencil on legal-sized yellow pads trying to recreate his early and only success… so far fruitlessly… while steadfastly maintaining his long held tradition of bad relationships with women as he did so.

I let the phone ring a couple of times before picking up the receiver. I held the ear piece a half a foot from my ear and James's infernal voice blasted the air between me and the phone's ear piece.

"Ward, get yer ass over to my office… and quick. We got ourselves a real problem."

About the dialogue and the writing… I was advised to start this journal as part of my… let's call it personal introspection. It's really not a journal since it's not about the day's events. I'm writing about whatever pops into my head and it's usually the past that pops into my head since my days here are pretty vanilla… not much happens… but I'm not sure what else to call it other than a journal. There are no dates, at least current ones, attached to the entries and I can't remember most of the dates from the past anyway. Time passes slowly up here in the mountains as Judy Collins used to sing, and the past can be a dangerous place to go, but what choice do I have. So be it.

To help trigger my memories, I have been allowed to keep a box of mementos, memos and other such items from my old office. My buddy the Flake threw my personal stuff into the box when he cleaned out my desk and brought it to me. Back then I wasn't allowed to keep the box as its contents were thought to upset me after what happened. Maybe they did upset me. I don't remember exactly. I'm surprised the powers that be didn't just shit-can the box years ago, but since I began this journal-type business, they gave the box back to me. Like I said, it's full of mostly personal stuff… stuff I wrote, notes I took, even some sketches I drew, some that our technical illustrator back then, Frank "Shakes" Voltonne, drew, and some stuff I should probably have thrown out to be on the safe side… there were some KTI confidential documents and copies of official papers that I kept in my private files… stuff I wasn't allowed to keep but did anyway thinking that they could come in handy should the shit hit the fan, which it did in spades.

This is my first entry and it isn't about today like I said. It's about several years ago, but it's what popped into my head today. I was looking out the window of my room watching the sun rise and bam… up came this memory that I'm writing about today. I was told to distance myself from the events that I write about so as to be able to better observe and understand them… you know, remove my personal involvement from my own personal life. Nice trick. It's kind of hard to do since I'm writing about a 'him' which is really a 'me'… and when I write, I'm writing to a 'you'… which as it turns out is actually a 'me' too in a strange sort of way since I'm the only person who's going to read this journal. At least that's what was implied although never stated outright, but I have my suspicions so I plan to hide the journal every night. But it's hard to figure out how I'm supposed to write. My 'I' becomes a 'he' and my 'you' becomes a 'me'. At least I think that's how it works. It's very confusing.

Anyway, all this I-me you-me stuff has gotten me so bollixed up that I've decided to just write what pops into my head, which is what you, meaning me, will eventually read and think about in that introspective sort of way. I was told to leave lots of space and write comments about my thoughts when I read the entries later so I am only writing on the odd numbered pages of my journal. I guess it's a journal within a journal. To aid this process, I was told to be as specific as possible. I'm concentrating on what happened at KTI at least for now. The rest of my life is still kind of a blur. Since I can't write about what I can't remember, I'm writing about what I can. Maybe writing about my life at KTI will trigger other memories of the rest of my life. As to all the details that I do remember, I think they're supposed to help me see what really happened. Not that it matters much. What's been done has been done and someone else holds all the cards and regardless of what I really think, I've gotta pretty much do what I'm told.

To clarify myself to me about the dialogue as I recreate the previous events of my life at KTI, I have a pretty good memory when it comes to conversations but who knows after what happened. Anyway, I include conversations in my journal…

again from memory. They may not be word-for-word what was actually said, but it's a good bet they're pretty damn close. And I do have that box of memos and other memorabilia… a kind of archeological trove of my life at KTI… to help me remember and even to quote from when the mood strikes me. It's kind of like writing that novel I never wrote, only it's true or kind of true depending I guess on your point of view. But the truth of the matter is this ain't horse shoes, Mr. Ward Bobb: it's hand grenades. Just pretty close is more than good enough! Anyway, I'm pretty sure I say to James a rather prosaic, "Right, what's up?"

And then he says, "You're not goin' to believe what happened last night. It involves one of your people."

Then I say, "Let me guess who. Lurch. Right?"

And he yells into my unprotected ear, an ear-drum piercing "Bingo!"

I shoved my flashlight into my jacket pocket and 'hustled' over to James's office, stopping along the way to pick up my second cup of that dreadful vending machine java with artificial powdered cream wondering what the hell could have happened last night that involved Mr. Richard Tadd, called Lurch by his tribal peers, for Tadd never stuck around after that 4:42 end-of-shift bell buzzed, which, while welcomed, still managed to be quite annoying. As ol' Lurch had put it so succinctly, "When the bell rings, I go home." Getting between Tadd and the exit was a dangerous thing to do when that bell buzzed. There was a rumor that he had worked overtime once two years ago, but I could never find any documentation to verify that fact.

Hold it... flashlight? Perhaps you'd care to illuminate... you know, shine some of that light on that flashlight of yours. Why, my paragon of sanity, are you carrying a flashlight? Has there been a power failure... an unexpected eclipse? And why, my friend, are you no longer allowed to have that precious flashlight? In fact, your flashlight privileges were cancelled years ago.

Who the fuck are you and why are you writing in my journal? What, cat got your tongue? Two days and no reply. This is quite annoying. Speaking of annoying... more than annoying... the very name Kronos Technologies should have set off warning bells in my head when I first applied for the job. The KTI corporation began manufacturing clocks... you know, those industrial-type clocks on the walls of offices, factories and other institutions... hell, there's one here in the cafeteria with that distinctive KTI logo on the clock's face. The corporation even dabbled in punch clocks, meat scales and other commercial business machines. I think that they even manufactured cash registers at one time... and rumor has it they're doing it again... only this time the damn things have been computerized. Early on the corporation had the temerity to call itself an international and now I know why.

Lots of people think that Kronos just means time like the time kept by clocks and watches... the measurement of time... but I looked that bastard Kronos up and the ancient Greeks, being no dopes, understood time a lot better than we do, for them Kronos's time was an all-devouring force that ruthlessly destroyed everything... like when you get old and pretty much fall apart. Inexorable... inexorable... inexorable.

Just in case anyone thinks that this whole Kronos business is a figment of my fevered imagination, take a look at this propaganda post card with that distinctive KTI logo that the ravenous bastards used to give away for free. I was going to send it to my brother Donnie when I first got the stupid job at KTI, but somehow it got lost in my initial corporate two-step shuffle and I never did send it. I found it in that box of stuff. Kind of ironic I used a "Liberty" stamp given where I got the job and what happened.

KTI produced lots of propaganda stuff like this and gave it all away... tons of the stuff. Take a gander at that catchy official corporate motto on the post card: "timely technology for tomorrow." Why's that clock faded in the background? Timely technology? For what? What exactly do the bastards have planned for tomorrow? ...and what the hell is the meaning of all those barely visible blue men lined up in the background anyway?

39

Oxbow Lake The 2nd

I was in a hurry but not that much of a hurry to get to James's office… for he had some god damn emergency every morning. Besides, as was my habit and need back then, I required a lot of caffeine to jump start another day at the 'ol' bom-bor factoree', as the old timers would say, particularly when my day began with a meeting with god damn James, second-line manager extraordinaire. I remember thinking to myself, "What the hell could that asshole Tadd have done that would upset that other asshole? I'd bet my balls against a huge bogartable joint that the bastard wasn't even here once that go-home bell buzzed."

Upon my arrival, James was seated behind his large mahogany desk, one of the signs of his exalted status as a second-line manager. His floor was carpeted and his "cubicle" was a real office, for it was totally enclosed with solid walls… that is, his walls reached the ceiling… unlike the cubicles occupied by grunts such as myself and the rest of the tribe, for the walls of our little piece of the lab were six-foot high, the top third being glass, bottom half frosted, top half clear… our desks and other odds and ends of used furniture, a metallic grey and our floors bare… like our souls. Igor, our Polish Prince, was still wearing his customary green eye shade and smoking his customary maduro cigar. He motioned me forward into his sanctum sanctorum with his left hand in which he held a cup of that dreadful vending machine coffee… black.

"What's up chief?"

"Get yer ass in here and close the door. Take a look-see at this."

I did as instructed, swung the door to his office closed, and took a seat in the chair of organizational subservience, my usual place, on the opposite side of his imperial desk awaiting news of the latest tragedy that was about to rock our management boat. James blew a huge smoke ring in my general direction and pushed a tabloid newspaper, open to the center fold, across his desk towards me.

"What's that look like to you?"

I studied what appeared to be an infrared photo of some sort. At first I thought it looked like a picture of a rough, barren landscape with tufts of brush around a ravine. Knowing that such a photo was very unlikely to cause an early morning emergency call, I squinted my eyes and studied the photo more carefully. Then it struck me.

"Shit, James. It's a life-size close-up of a pussy. It's a woman's pussy... an infra red picture of a woman's pussey... in all its glory. Self-basted and ready for cooking. Where the fuck did you get this?"

James closed the tabloid newspaper and there on the front page before me spread the banner headline: Screw Magazine.

"At 2:23 AM last night KTI security officer, one Steven Hamilton, discovered this newspaper, open to that centerfold on the desk of one Richard Tadd. It was easy for him to spot in the darkness since Tadd left his desk lamp on... a god damn spot light of fuckin' depravity. Our esteemed third-line manager chewed my ear off this morning. Apparently the outraged Officer Hamilton just happened to be a born-again Christian and this photo offended him to his very soul, the prick... all that Christian sanctity of women bull-shit. He called the manager of lab security right then and there, who rushed into the plant to see the outrage for himself. When he saw the outrage, he was... well... morally outraged as well and met the Lab Director when that asshole arrived this morning.

41

Oxbow Lake The 2nd

The Lab Director, after viewing the moral outrage, bucked this fuckin' rag to our fourth-line manager, who bucked it to Jerome… who bucked it to me… the bastards must have had a good buckin' time… and now to you. There's a yellow buck-slip stapled at the top of the front page. What's it say?"

Expecting some subtle, esoteric point, I carefully observed each entry on the buck slip and counted them on my fingers. Able to see only the obvious, I said, "Please handle. Three times… each 'please handle' initialed by someone in the management chain above you and if you add yours, that'd be an even four." I knew that the bastard wouldn't put his initials on that buck slip unless he was forced to. Turns out there was no esoteric point. Subtlety from James? What was I thinking? He rambled on.

"Right, please fuckin' handle… three times, starting with the Lab Director. Moved pretty fast down the management chain. Seems like no one wants to have that fuckin' rag stuck in his in basket. I'm not goin' to put my initials on the god damn thing. I'm just gonna ask you what the fuck YOU'RE goin' to do about it?" He placed great emphasis on the word 'you're'. I knew what he was doing. Like I said, he was keeping his initials off that buck slip, James being James and all.

I got pissed. "Me? What am I going to do about it? James, you're not Tonto and I'm not the Lone Ranger here as in one of those 'what you mean WE white-man moments'. Listen, kemo saabee, this is a 'we' and not a 'me' situation, and here's how we ought to handle it… WE... and I do mean we as in YOU and ME... get a bunch of the programmers that work with Tadd (James was all ears)… I'm sure they'll volunteer… take the bastard out to the parking lot and have that bunch of programmers beat the living shit

42

out of the bastard… something I'm sure they'll enjoy a great deal, and then have Marsha, our local militant feminist, castrate him."

In spite of my bravado, I actually didn't give a shit if Tadd ogled nasty pictures… even today I don't give a fat rat's ass… even after all that's happened. Where Mr. Richard Tadd chooses to focus his eye balls is his business. Hell, I enjoyed good porn too… a lot. But what did piss me off was his getting caught. How the hell could he be so stupid? It wasn't like security ran some kind of anti-porn sting and trapped him. Sometimes I think he did stuff like this on purpose… a kind of kamikaze rebellion against KTI and all its corporate conventions and bourgeois rules. But because of his kamikaze run, the prick was forcing me to do something which I found distasteful, annoying, difficult and organizationally dangerous since whatever I did would be under the ever watchful eye of upper management. A person in my position never wants to be under the ever watchful eye of anyone or anything, particularly KTI upper management. No good can come of it. If it does happen, you pray for a tie and corporate anonymity… and it could be downright dangerous!

James smiled grudgingly at what I thought was an outrageous suggestion and said, "That's a pretty good plan of attack, but we won't be able to replace the son-of-a-bitch. My headcount's frozen again. We gotta think of something else." The idea actually appealed to him, but even he knew we couldn't get away with it and then there was the problem of replacing Tadd if we canned the bastard. In truth, James's caution had nothing to do with a cunning business move, good sense, what happened to me or Tadd and least of all what was right. It had more to do with his workload and his anonymity and thus his ease and safety. Looking back, I realize that he was a real siren of a self-centered prick.

43

Oxbow Lake The 2nd

You should have realized it a long time ago.
He works the shit out of you and you just
handle his problems and kiss his ass. You're not
his friend; you're his ass-kissing mule... your his
god damn donkey man!

you better get more serious, asshole

Getting more serious,ˆI thought for a minute and said, "How about we cite Tadd with a violation of some sort... something that sounds real official and I write a scathing memo of reprimand to place in his personnel jacket. You can buck a copy of the reprimand back up the management chain and every one will be happy."

Hold it. Hold it, damn it! Whose writing is that?

"I like it." Of course he would. This way he had almost no involvement in the problem or the solution.

I rambled on, "We can cite him for a security violation. The management chain always likes that. Shows we're diligently protecting KTI's family jewels."

James thought for a minute and then yelled a self-protective, "Hold it! No can do. No security was involved in this situation. Security violations are for leaving out confidential or registered confidential KTI information. Ain't no way Screw Magazine falls into either category. Hell, one of the assholes up the chain might even take the use of this code as a violation of management protocol on our part... in other words bad management. We gotta think of somethin' else."

The 'we' thinking of something else was 'me': "Well there's safety.

44

We could tag him with a safety violation, but that seems a real stretch."

I reached over to James's mahogany bookcase and pulled out the hefty, red loose-leaf binder that was the KTI management bible. I flipped through it until I got to the tab labeled 'employee violations'. I quickly skimmed the page before placing it on the desk before James. "Take a look-see at our choices."

James read and then said, "Apparently we only have three violations to choose from: 'security', 'safety' and this last one, 'industrial incident'. The first two are out... that leaves 'industrial incident'."

He looked up at me and asked, "You ever heard of an 'industrial incident violation' before?"

"Never."

"Says here an industrial incident is, and I quote... and I remember the damn quote word for word... 'any act by an employee which is deemed by management to be detrimental to the product development processes as defined in the KTI Product Development manual, SY69-6969-69F for 'fuck the employees' (I can't remember the actual number but it really doesn't matter)... or to the employees that perform the tasks of those product development processes as defined therein'. Can we shoe horn it?"

"Sure. The definition is as ambiguous as hell. All we have to do is deem what Tadd did as detrimental and it is. I'll bet the assholes up the chain never heard of an industrial incident violation either. When those ass holes read the memo of reprimand that I write, they'll think the bastard is the reincarnation of Adolph Hitler. Hell, they'll probably want to know why we didn't take him out into the parking lot, beat the shit out of him ourselves and have Marsha rip his balls off with those sharp carnivorous teeth of hers."

You're a clever bastard, aren't you!

There's that god damn writing again!

James had second thoughts based, of course, on James: "Could you nuance it? I don't want to have to fire Tadd. I can't replace him and besides, I'd hate like hell to have to fill out all those separation forms. And he does serve a semi-useful purpose. No one notices the other idiots that work for us as long as he's around. Takes the pressure off everyone else, including us." The 'us' in this instance, being primarily 'him'.

What the hell did you expect him to say?

Fuck, more writing.

"OK. Suppose I make him sound like the reincarnation of Mussolini. Il Duce's evil in a clownish sort of way and fascism is pretty much passé."

James thought his self-protective thoughts and said, "Anybody you know of up the management chain Italian?"

I didn't have a clue, but said an emphatic "Nope."

Good move!

Damn.

James smiled the smile of the uninvolved and yelled, "Il Duce it is!"

Thus it was decided to officially cite Mr. Richard Tadd with an industrial incident violation, write an official memo of reprimand for his personnel jacket and buck a copy of the memo up the management chain to show how tough we were with the undisciplined hippy assholes who populated our organization.

I folded the copy of Screw Magazine, tucked it under my arm and turned to leave when James yelled, "Hold it. Where you goin' with that filthy rag?"

I turned facing him and replied, "I was planning to put it in Tadd's personnel jacket."

"Leave it here. In case I get a call from Jerome. I may need to refer to it and I want to be accurate. Besides, we don't want our secretary or one of those personnel bitches coming across this filthy rag. I'll give it back later when you need it. Close the door behind you."

Right, like Jerome was going to call him and ask for a verbal description of some detail of that pussey picture over the phone… a picture by the way that Jerome had already studied, probably in great detail, and then having sated his… let's say 'curiosity'… moved it off his desk as quickly as was humanly possible. As to James's 'worries' that some secretary or personnel bitch, as he put it, would see the "filthy rag"… ain't gonna happen. I kept all the personnel jackets in my office under lock and key as per KTI regulation which he knew. I flashed fuckin' Igor, our Polish Prince, a wry smile, handed him "the filthy rag" and left, gently closing the door to his sanctum sanctorum behind me.

Why that Monster of Technology Gave Me Heebie Geebies

I read what I wrote… I think it was yesterday… to see if I was making sense to me and I found something very disturbing: comments written by someone else, that's what… comments scribbled between the lines and in the margins and on the facing pages. Someone else is reading my journal and writing comments that aren't exactly compliments. It might be the Doc, that nosey obnoxious prick. I've got to hide the damn journal better. Well at least the part I'm writing makes sense. Reading yesterday's entry got me to thinking about Kronos Technologies International and my hatred… no hatred's not the right word. No… more like fear… fear and trepidation… of that all consuming monster of technology and its minions. The fear and trepidation started a long time ago. Before I knew that KTI even existed… way back even before high school and it only got worse as I got older and learned more.

That's the ticket. Now you're concentrating on reality and what really happened to you. It's working, you're memories of life at KTI are triggering other memories.

Listen, you asshole intruder, you have no idea what's going on in my mind! There's more here than meets the eye, particularly your eye!

Way back in fifth grade I belonged to this paperback book club. Everyone had to so I was in, like it or not. Every month my teacher, Miss Bateman (she was one of my all-time favorite teachers) passed out a pamphlet with a list of paperbacks. We could order one of the paperbacks and use it for a book report. Each book had a little description and the number of pages. Miss Bateman kind of frowned if you weren't ordering a book that month, so being no dope and knowing which side my academic bread was buttered on even back then, I usually ordered something. I always chose the book with the least amount of pages which was usually the cheapest one so it had two advantages. It was November, I think. Anyway, I chose The Time Machine by H. G. Wells. With the stupid introduction and the short bio of Wells, it was barely a hundred pages and it had a neat cover. Ideal and for only forty cents. What a bargain! (I still have that copy of the novel and have read it many times.)

If you ask me, you've read it too damn many times, and with the way your mind works, once was probably too many... but then again, knowing you as I do, you'll probably read it again. By the way, Miss Bateman hated your guts.

There it is again. More writing. Whoever the hell you are, mind your own god damn business. I knew I shouldn't have even mentioned Miss Bateman before.

I read The Time Machine for my book report and it scared the shit out of me. From my fifth grade perspective, this guy who didn't even have a name built a time machine and traveled way ahead to the future, the year 802,701 AD to be exact. He found the place populated by people who called themselves Eloi. They were short stupid creatures… real dweebs… which wigged out this time traveling guy. Even back then, I pretty much understood that if in thousands of years we became those wimpy Eloi, we were pretty much done for and what I couldn't figure out for myself, the stupid introduction to the book told me what to think. Thank god for stupid introductions since what they tell you to think is what the teacher… and later professors… want you to think, say and write. Saves a lot of time. A valuable lesson well learned. Hell, it even worked at KTI… give'em what they want!

Well these Eloi were actually like cattle, meat, for the Morlocks, the creatures who lived below the ground and ran the machines that produced all the stuff the Eloi needed. These Morlocks were dreadful looking creatures who had adapted, evolved if you will, to living underground. White, hairy creatures with big eyes who couldn't stand the sunlight since they lived in darkness. At night they'd round up the meat supply they needed, Eloi on the hoof, and take them below for butchering and consumption. They couldn't come out during the day because bright light blinded them. At night, this time traveling guy used the light from matches as a weapon to blind the ugly bastards.

What's this obsession with Eloi? Are you out of your… The real beast stands before you.

There's another comment. What the fuck's going on. Whoever's writing this stuff, stay the fuck out of my journal! Who's the real beast? I'm beginning to think it's you, you prick.

This whole flesh-eating creatures living in the dark business reminded me of our cellar. The door to the stairs down to the cellar was right next to the door into our first-floor apartment. I always ran as fast as I could passed that cellar door, for our cellar was a place to be avoided if at all possible… a creepy place, even in the daylight… at night it was downright terrifying. The floor was dirt. There were only two dim bulbs hanging from the rafters at each end to light the whole place. An old coal furnace, converted to oil, dominated the center of the cellar. It was huge and when that sucker fired up, it sounded like a growling explosion… rattled the entire house… scared the living shit out of you. In the back, there was this old coal bin that we didn't use anymore. The place was just plain creepy. I was reluctant to go down there alone in the warm weather even during the day and didn't dare go down there at all once the weather got cold unless I absolutely had to… to get a hammer or something. And I set some kind of land-speed record going down and then up those stairs. You never knew when that furnace was going to fire up and scare the living shit out you.

The back of the cellar was a crawl space and I imagined all kinds of creatures lying in wait back there… waiting for a chance to grab me and if the furnace was roaring away, no one would hear me screaming for help. Reminded me of the Morlocks. I thought that that crawl space would be an ideal place for Morlocks to hang. Our Morlocks must have been cheap lazy bastards since they never produced anything, but maybe they were smarter than Wells' Morlocks since we pretty much took care of ourselves, kind of like free range Eloi. The question in my mind was when would the bastards get hungry and when they got hungry, would they climb the cellar stairs to round up some meat… the meat being us in general and me in particular. I guess I thought of us as Eloi dweebs without realizing it.

Once, on a double dare from my younger brother Donnie, I

51

ventured into the cellar after sun set. It was a matter of pride and honor. No one refused a double dare… just didn't happen. I crept down those steps one careful step at a time. Each creak of those old steps gave me the willies. When I got to the bottom, I peeked around the corner to be sure that those two dim lights were on and they were. It was already dark outside making the whole adventure even more risky and terrifying. In the back of the cellar in front of the crawl space, there was a bunch of huge jars of peanuts and what looked like Chiclets gum. Donnie and I saw them for the first time earlier in the day from the cellar window. My quest: to grab some of those Chiclets from the back of the cellar to prove I had been there, the Chiclets being proof that I completed the dare and a sort of treasure or prize for doing so.

I could hear my heart pounding. I crept to the back of the cellar where the crawl space began. Looked to me like our Morlocks were finally getting into production which meant I had to be very careful, for the next thing they'd do after being productive was round up some meat… meaning me in this case. I prayed like hell that the furnace wouldn't kick in as I carefully crept over to the crawl space. I gently grabbed the lid to one of the jars of what I thought were Chiclets gum and turned it slowly so as to make as little noise as possible. I felt like my stomach was about to jump out my throat. I didn't want to wake up any of those Morlocks. I lifted the lid ever so gently, grabbed a handful of… yes… Chiclets! I stuffed the handful into my back pocket. As I did so, the furnace roared. I looked up and into the crawl space and I swear, two big round eyes were staring back at me. I jumped up and took off like a bat out of hell for the stairs. In my panic I knocked over the jar and Chiclets poured onto the dirt floor. I thought: "Boy would those Morlocks be pissed now!" I tore up those stairs and when I reached the hallway I slammed the cellar door shut and collapsed against the opposite wall. It took me a while to catch my breath. Donnie's eyes were bugging out of his head. After what seemed forever, I pushed my back against the wall and slowly rose. I said nothing, reached into my back pocket and gave Donnie a bunch of Chiclets which he crammed into his mouth. I reached into my pocket a second time and grabbed what was left and shoved the remaining Chiclets into my mouth.

The whole Morlock production thing turned out to be a false alarm. My Uncle Louie had started a vending machine business and the jars of peanuts and Chiclets were his. He went on the hunt for who dumped his jar of Chiclets. I don't know why he was all that pissed. All he did was scoop the Chiclets up from the dirt floor, blow off the dirt, dump them back into the jar and use them on his vending machine route like nothing happened. Nobody squealed on me because I was a hero for performing that most daring of deeds and the mystery remained unsolved until today. I considered myself lucky for I was sure that our Morlocks, as unproductive as they were, were still lying in wait beneath that crawl space.

Well I was giving my book report to Miss Bateman's class. We had to give one oral book report to the class each semester. It was getting close to the end of the year and for me it was now or never… never being an "F" and I didn't need another one. I had just got to the juicy part where the Morlocks are gathering up the Eloi for holiday roasts. (It was close to Thanksgiving so the class could identify with the Morlocks in a strange sort of way.) I had the class on the edge of their chairs when the fire alarms went off. Brring… Brring… Brring! Everyone, including me, jumped out of our skin.

Miss Bateman marched us out into the hallway and had us face the wall and yelled "Kneel, duck and cover!" We all squatted against the wall and covered the back of our heads with our hands. It was our first atomic bomb drill. Scared the crap out of all of us since we had no idea what was going on. Miss Bateman had warned us about the drill earlier in the year, but no one paid much attention. At least I didn't. We were always getting warned about something. Then it dawned on me and a bunch of my classmates. It was for an atomic bomb attack. Back then even fifth graders knew that an atomic bomb blast would blow you to smithereens. We'd all seen the A-bomb go off on TV. Well we didn't get blown up because it was only a drill… a surprise drill. I remember peeking down the hall and all the kids from the other classes had ducked and covered too. The whole damn school. Yeah, turns out it was only a drill… right… a fuckin' drill! A drill that scared the living shit out of us!

And it was only a drill for us dweebs. None of the stupid teachers had to duck and cover. After what seemed an eternity, Miss Bateman marched her bunch of scared shitless fifth graders, including yours truly, back into our classroom.

It took a little while, but finally the class settled down and I resumed my report of the Morlocks munching on the Eloi like they were Thanksgiving turkeys and how it wasn't such a very good thing for humanity. One kid, Gregg two g's two z's Lazzaro, asked me why the Eloi put up with the Morlocks eating them and I said because according to the introduction they evolved into meat and the Morlocks controlled the machines and evolved into the workers who ran the machines and needed the meat. I wasn't sure of what "evolved" meant but I could tell Miss Bateman was very impressed. Everyone else was afraid to ask what it meant and so I slipped through. All the kids pretty much agreed that if they had a choice they'd rather be Morlocks although eating Eloi seemed pretty icky.

That first duck and cover drill still gives me the creeps... even today... a living fuckin' nightmare. Seems like just yesterday. The very fact that we had to practice those atomic bomb drills made it all too real and terrifying. And who the fuck were those terrifying Soviets? Some kind of country of monsters who existed for one purpose... to kill us? Now it seems rather silly to duck and cover if you get hit by an atomic bomb blast.

As I grew older, I learned more about the cold war with the Soviets and the Cuban missile crisis. Technology marched onward bringing us ever more accurate missile systems and ever more powerful nuclear weapons, thanks in large part to the advances in computer technology and software development. I came to the realization that all this technology was making us less safe and less human. By my senior year of high school, I was determined to not become an engineer or scientist even though math and science were my best subjects and I had two scholarship offers to prove it. I decided to stick with the humanities and this is why I turned down those nice juicy engineering scholarships. And in spite of all that principle and dedication, all that concern for the future of humanity, there I was toiling away at KTI, the center of 20th century computer technology. I worked in the belly of technologies most ferocious beast. Gives me the Heebie Geebies just thinking about it. It's like I was a traitor Eloi helping the Morlocks devour us. A god damn Judas goat Eloi!

You chicken shit! Is that a flashlight shoved in your pocket or do you like me?

Shit, there's some more of those god damn comments.

55

The Tables Are Turned

I can see that arrogant bastard sitting there… Mr. Richard Tadd… staring at me from across the table casually sipping his coffee… black coffee if memory serves me… and smiling that supercilious smile of his. I can see him like it was yesterday. He was always smiling no matter the situation… smiling like some fuckin' bemused Olympic god looking down at the goings on of us mere mortals… a pock-marked Olympic god at that, for one side of his face was badly scarred from burns he had suffered as a boy… his unkempt hair down to his asshole. When he stood, he was tall, thin and angular… all asshole and elbows when he moved any of those gangly limbs of his… his drinking his coffee involving these signature herky-jerky gangly movements and thus instilling fear in those around him with each sip … fear that they'd be victims of splashed hot coffee at any awkward Tadd moment.

Droplets of coffee clung to his scraggily mustache in a most unappetizing way as he sipped his black swill. Every now and then he raised his left arm, while precariously balancing his stupid coffee cup in his extended left hand, and ran his left shirt sleeve across his mustache to wipe off those droplets of coffee that still clung to the unruly whiskers above his upper lip. It was by unanimous consent that our tribe of pubs creeps had christened him 'Lurch', his tribal nom de plume. He looked like a Lurch. He moved like a Lurch. He ate and drank coffee like a Lurch. Hell, he probably slept and fucked like a Lurch.

This nom de plume business is interesting stuff… kind of my own little study in corporate cultural anthropology. Say that three times fast, buddy boy. It all started with my old buds the tech writing subcontractors that KTI buried deep in the bowels of the plant along with yours truly. We kind of adopted the practice from them. It's their legacy to our tribe today... well not today, but yesterday, meaning a long time ago. Most of those subies have long since gone into technology's metaphorical happy hunting ground in the sky since their contracts were terminated many moons ago... and some of them... at least one of them... has presumably gone into that real happy hunting ground in the sky having been permanently terminated from life as in dead... luckily for her fully equipped with an adult nom de plume... but just maybe the trip she took to that happy hunting ground wasn't all that happy and initiated by forces outside of herself.

I think our practice of giving a nom de plume to each of our tribal members is kind of like what the American Indians did when they named their little papooses. I've read that American Indians were given two names: a unique name that they got as a child... all those little Indian munchkins couldn't all be called 'Little Brave' and 'Small Squaw'... and one that they got as an adult. When the time came, some tribal elder held some kind of tribal naming ceremony when an Indian had reached adulthood. It's unclear to me how it was determined that the Indian about to be re-named had reached adulthood, but when it happened, a tribal elder gave the newly minted adult Indian a new name... a name that reflected some outstanding characteristic of that individual... and since the Indian being renamed had lived a while, it was now pretty obvious to the tribal elder and even his fellow Indians what that characteristic was. Thus the tribal elder bestowed an adult Indian name on the newly minted adult tribal member and that name reflected who the Indian really was or at least who the tribe thought he or she really was and not some name chosen at the whim of parents who pretty much had

57

no idea who their little Indian munchkin would turn out to be. Well our little tribe at KTI did pretty much the same thing. These turkeys showed up at our tribal doorstep with names their parents had given them... with the exception of a black guy, Jeremiah Smith, who had four alias, but that's a whole different story... and we got to observe those turkeys gobbling around our tribal hunting grounds and after a while, us tribal elders gave the new gobblers our equivalent of an adult name... a nom de plume... that reflected their unique gobbling... who they really were... at least in the eyes of their tribal elders and fellow tribal members... meaning us. Sometimes the nom de plume wasn't all that complimentary, but a person is who he is. Let the nom de plume chips fall where they may! And our tribe improved upon the Indian practice taking it a couple of steps further. Hell if we got the nom de plume wrong, we'd re-nom de plume the bastard and if the previously nom de plumed bastard changed, we'd re-nom de plume him... or her, can't forget the 'her'. And sometimes a guy can hoist himself on his own god damn nom de plume of a petard.

How'd the blast from that ol' petard feel, buddy boy?

My local tribe of scribes gave Mr. Richard Tadd the nom de plume of Lurch because he was the spitting image of that TV character Lurch sans the hair, the butler in a television show that was popular back then... I think it was The Addams Family... so they christened him Lurch and Lurch he remained ever after, for the tribe had its own customs and culture... its own way of enforcing its code of behavior, and finding the right nom de plume for each member of the tribe was the first step of initiation into the tribe. Thus 'Lurch', which Tadd not only accepted but wisely gloried in. The tribe had accepted him and he had accepted the tribe in a tentative and odd sort of way, oddness being the norm for both the Tadd and the tribe.

I pushed the recently retrieved copy of Screw Magazine across my desk toward Tadd and opened it to the center fold.
"Look familiar?"

"Sure does!" This conversation is very easy to remember given the speaker and the circumstance.

"Well? What is it?"

"That's a photo of a very close friend of the family… Cynthia Osterhoudt… goes by the stage name Twyla Twatly. She does performance art down in the Village. See over in the corner… she's autographed it for me. How'd you get it? It's my personal property."

Sure enough, there, written in the corner of the photo, were the words 'With All My Platonic Love, Twyla Twatly'. James and I had been preoccupied with the center of the picture and thus had missed the signature off in the corner as probably had the management chain above us, an understandable oversight given the subject of the center of the photograph and the makeup of those observing said subject.

I looked sternly at Tadd, giving him my most intimidating your-ass-is-in-deep-shit management stare. I pounded my index finger down on the picture for emphasis and said, "A security guard found this magazine opened to this picture on your desk last night."

"So?" He was quick with his response and unintimidated, like the parry of a left jab by a confident challenger. It was like we were in some kind of rhetorical boxing match.

I jabbed back with a "So it's inappropriate for a professional work environment."

He remained unintimidated and parried my jab again. "What's one of the company screws doing nosing around my cube anyway?"

I shot back "His job." Then I jabbed back a third time looking for an opening for a knockout blow. "Besides, you made it easy for him. You left your desk lamp on. He was probably checking to see if someone was working late… like that's going to happen in your cube. Like I said, this photo… in fact this whole damn magazine… is inappropriate for a professional work environment."

He slipped my jabs with ease and jabbed back. "How so? Cynthia's a professional, a nationally recognized performance artist. That photo's ground breaking art. Is KTI against ground breaking art? You'd think that a company creating ground breaking technology would be all for ground breaking art."

The interrogation was not going as I had planned!

Right, buddy boy.

Instead of me intimidating Tadd, Tadd was doing a pretty good job of intimidating me. I felt like it was me being interrogated, so I swung a mighty uppercut that I hoped would connect and end the fight. "Look, Tadd, we're citing you with an industrial incident violation and placing a memo of reprimand in your personnel jacket."

He looked bemused as he easily parried my upper cut. "What the hell's an industrial incident violation?"

I danced and looked for another opening. "Any act that management deems detrimental to the product development process and to the employees working within that process. It's a serious violation."

Tadd smiled that damn bemused Olympic smile of his and threw a round house punch at me. "Sounds phony to me what with all that management deeming." He pointed down at the photo with the same determination that I had, and possibly more, and said, "Even if I left this copy of Screw Magazine on my desk open to this ground breaking work of art and with my desk lamp on... none of which I admit to... it didn't involve any product development process and hell, no one saw it but a company screw and the screw sure wasn't involved in developing any products whether or not he saw my copy of Screw Magazine." His round house punch connected, sending me reeling against the proverbial ropes.

I'd been stunned. Tad's multiple uses of the word 'screw' were starting to confuse me, probably his intention, for I had dropped my rhetorical gloves for a split second and he then smacked me squarely on the button. He smiled and took another herky-jerky sip of his black swill and said, "I want to speak to my personnel rep. I'm getting shafted here with this industrial incident bull shit." Bam... bam... bam!

The bout was much more difficult and punishing than I had anticipated. I was losing on points, moving toward the wrong end of a TKO with the distinct possibility of being just plain KOed. Tadd was no tomato can but it began to look like I was. I had planned to intimidate the bastard by reading him the memo of reprimand that I had written, have him sign it, and be done with it. Put a satisfactory end to the entire incident, but given Tadd's self-righteous protestations and vigorous defense, I thought better of reading him the memo as I'd written it. I'd have to rewrite the damn thing, this time more carefully, now that a personnel rep would be involved.

He looked at me with his most annoyingly bemused 'who-the-hell-do-you-think-you-are-to-censor-great-groundbreaking-art' stare and asked, "What's the memo of reprimand say, anyway?" Bam!

I parried his punch… lied to him: "I haven't written it yet. I wanted to speak with you first."

There's that ol' integrity of yours shining through.

What'd you expect me to do? Grab my ankles and pray for vaseline!

And then he staggered me, hitting me squarely on the button, hard… very hard… with a left hook. He had me on the ropes and he knew it: "How do I contact my personnel rep?"

I wrote the name William Whitcomb on a buck slip and an extension number. I knew the name and number well. He was the personnel rep for our area and it was his job to make sure that all employees weren't getting screwed by management. I remember thinking that things were going to get very interesting in a Chinese curse sort of way.

For years James had been dueling with Mr. William Whitcomb, whom he dubbed All-Wet Willie. Whitcomb was James's mortal enemy and I was about to participate in another of the grudge matches between our own fuckin' Polish Prince and a certain Mr. All-Wet Willie, this time my role being the tennis ball that they would smash across the net at each other, a prospect that I did not look forward to, particularly given the pummeling I had just received in my metaphorical boxing match with Tadd.

As I heard it, the two first faced off a decade ago when James had taken a management personality profile test, which Mr. All-Wet Willie championed and administered to all employees in the lab whose career development plans indicated that they wanted to be managers. James's test results indicated that he was psychologically unfit to be a manager according to the all-wet one, who put the test results and a written recommendation that James never be promoted to manager into James's personnel jacket. James protested vehemently, ironically, through his personnel rep, and All-Wet Willie's manager ordered the all-wet one to remove the information after a long and very contentious battle… a battle which also forced the wet one to terminate his pet testing project. James never forgot the incident and neither did Mr. William Whitcomb.

Maybe All-wet Willie and that test of his weren't all that wet.

I gave Tadd the official management death stare, which he didn't even bother to ignore, and covered up. "Call Whitcomb in personnel. He's the personnel rep for our area."

63

Oxbow Lake The 2nd

Tadd wasn't done punching. He took the buck slip, read it and said, "I want my magazine back. It's valuable and has a lot of sentimental value for me and my family." Bam!

I continued my unacknowledged and now feeble death stare from the far corner of the ring. Leaning against the ropes, I muttered, "It'll be returned to you when this matter is resolved."

Ya know, you're the real pussey. And you were going to save civilization as you want to know it?

Tadd smiled that very annoying bemused fuckin' Olympic smile of his again, realizing full well that he had me on the ropes and said indignantly, "Well that photo had better not have any stains on it when it's returned to me if you know what I mean… and I don't mean coffee stains." I knew full well what the bastard meant. He slammed his almost empty coffee cup onto the corner of my desk, knocking it over as he did so. Coffee splattered onto my desk as he stomped out of my cubicle. So ended a punishing Round 1. Tadd ahead on points.

If this were a real boxing match, you'd be in the hospital barely clinging to life. Maybe you should have blinded him with that stupid flashlight you're so crazy about.

You're a meal about to happen, asshole. I'd be a little more circumspect, if I were you.

An Historical Problem Arises from the Depths of the Hysterical Past

I'm seeing red! Someone's still writing comments, the bastard. It's none of his damn business… whoever the hell it is. If it's the Doc and he wants to read my journal and talk about it, all he's got to do is ask. He holds all the cards any way. His wish is my command like I said. It's probably one of his god damn experimental techniques. As far as I'm concerned, he can shove his experimental techniques up his queer ass like this whole journal business is going to do me any good anyway.

To get back to what I wrote yesterday, after my pummeling at the rhetorical fists of one Richard Tadd, I staggered over to James's office slamming his office door behind me and startling the shit out of our Polish Prince, who was engrossed in the sports section of the New York Daily News.

I blurted out, "That problem with Lurch just got a lot more complicated. He's refused to accept that industrial incident violation bull shit and is officially protesting. He's asked to meet with his personnel rep and you know who that is."

And, of course, James did: "That fuckin' All-Wet Willie! Someone ought to plaster that bastard all over the bumper of his car some morning… he'd be doin' the world a favor… probably make that asshole's wife ecstatic too." James took a moment to compose himself and continued, "What'a ya mean Lurch won't accept the industrial incident violation. Ram it down his fuckin' throat."

I felt the slam of a tennis racket against the most tender parts of my already bruised and battered career. "James, he's contesting the violation. I've already rammed it down his fuckin' throat as you so poetically put it and he spit it back at me. He's not going gently into that good night. We got to strategize about what we do next. You'll be getting a call from All-Wet Willie any minute to set up a meeting about this whole mess."

"Well I'd like to see him defend Lurch's right to have life-size pussy pictures plastered all over his cubicle. That's a slam dunk."

Someone had to remain sane. I had to keep James centered and not let his Polish rage determine my fate, "James, Wet Willie's a smart guy. That's not what he'll do. He's going to question our ability to manage. He's going to ask how such an event could have ever occurred. You know that great ambiguous bullshit question: 'What kind of a professional business culture have you established?' and then all that 'What kind of counseling have you been providing?' bullshit. He won't give a shit about Tadd's rights, pussy pictures, management counseling… none of that crap. What he'll want is your head for a trophy to hang above his desk and he's going to run the personnel bus over me to get it. I do not cherish the prospect of becoming KTI road kill."

James came around, his instinct for self-preservation overcoming his rage: "What the fuck do we do?"

"Well we got to establish that Tadd has been counseled many times about all kinds of stuff. That he's never really fit into the system. That'll be easy to do. All they've got to do is look at him. Then we throw him under the bus in order to keep me from that fate and your head from becoming a trophy hanging on the wall over Wet Willie's desk."

James could be irrational but he was no dope. He puffed on his maduro and stared into the distance thinking and then said, "Looks pretty simple. Wet Willie will try to get the focus of the investigation… and if he's involved there will be an investigation… on us… management… you and me. What we gotta do is keep the focus on Lurch. Have you counseled the bastard about professional decorum and not displaying pictures of women's pussies at work?"

"Well kind of, but who the hell would counsel an employee specifically not to display pussy pictures in his cubicle?"

"What do you mean 'kind of'?"

Then it struck me. "James we've got another problem… an historical one going back a couple of years… before Lurch was even hired." My slate wasn't clean either as I realized. Back then, a big problem; today, as I write these journal entries, the whole thing seems inconsequential given the vicissitudes of my life… but I'm writing about… what, five years ago… maybe it was a lot longer… I'm not sure.

Well, was it five years ago? Ten? Get a handle on it. So the light now shines from that dim bulb!

Look, who gives a shit about the exact date? Stay the hell out of my business.

Anyway, I don't know why I hadn't thought of this historical problem before… or James for that matter.

Oxbow Lake The 2nd

Maybe because both of you are assholes.

Bells should have gone off and yellow lights blasted my brain, but the day-to-day work at KTI was like being submerged in warm pea soup. There was no yesterday or tomorrow, only the problems that appeared on your desk in the morning and had to be buck-slipped to someone else's desk before that annoying bell sounded at 4:42 in the afternoon. Who did that bell toll for? Well if that problem stayed on your desk, it tolled for thee.

Look, you've been swimming in pea soup your whole life. It's not some recent crazy vegetarian aquatic experience.

There's a lot that you don't know about, whoever the hell you are. I know things that no one else knows... things that would scare the shit out of even assholes like you. If you knew them, you wouldn't be writing the crap that you do.

Back then, I was a lead technical writer, actually a lead programmer-writer analyst in the corporate-ese of that time. My little tribe of programmer-writer anal-ists, as we called ourselves, maintained the Program Design Information Publication, or the P-DIP, which we pronounced, appropriately, the pee-dip. Everything was hardcopy back then... very primitive. We took the crap that system designers gave us... the stuff they called design documentation and, as one idiot design manager we called 'the Banana' put it, 'The job of yous guys is to pubs it up'... his quaint way of saying that our job was to make the inane scribblings of his inarticulate designers intelligible and in a set format.

Each designer was responsible for one component of the system

68

and each component was a chapter of the P-DIP. We'd 'pubs up' the chapter when a designer updated it, get the updated chapter repro-ed over night and distribute it in the morning to the designers and the poor program developers who had to code the stupid design. There were literally hundreds of designers and programmers involved. The P-DIP was the technical bible for the project and we were always updating the damn thing.

The trick was to get the designers and programmers to pick up the updated chapters when we had updates... which was at least once a week. They were pretty self-centered, lazy bastards who spent most of their professional lives communicating through and with computers. The problem I had was how to get these P-DIP updates distributed and I sure as hell didn't want to be a package delivery service for the bastards. Besides, they could use the exercise, the fat bastards.

At that time and unrelated to my actual work, I was maintaining a private hardcopy lending library of sorts, one that several members of the tribe had helped me setup. We called this library 'SYS-ONE dot PORNLIB' in programmer-ese. I kept the library locked up in my desk since it consisted of quite inappropriate material, all sorts of books, magazines and pictures, pretty much pure pornography, for the horny bastards who worked on my team and those others in the tribe who wished to participate... no women of course. I wasn't stupid enough to leave a sample of 'SYS-ONE dot PORNLIB' on my desk overnight... and in a spotlight no less. But looking back, what I did was probably just as stupid, but at least it was kind of clever and based on a legitimate need.

You know, you're a perverted asshole!

Hey Doc, cut the comments. Your tough love's become a cruel cudgel. You're beating the shit out of me here... violating your own rules.

There weren't many women working in the lab back then, most were secretaries. Sure there were a couple of skirts working as programmers, a couple of subcontractors, a couple of writers, but damn few. There was the dirty dozen... that bevy of 12 beauties that worked as key punch operators in our organization, but that was it for the whole development lab. Other than those few exceptions, the lab was pretty much an all-male world and what do males think about when they aren't working, eating or talking sports... right, they think about sex... mostly with women but not exclusively. The writers on my team loved 'SYS-ONE dot PORNLIB'.

$10   *Satyric Enterprises*   **$10**

SYS-ONE dot PORN-LIB Division

Share Number: 11

Number of Shares: 11

The owner of this share of stock is entitled to full borrowing privileges from the SYS-ONE dot PORN-LIB administered by the official librarian, Ward A. Bobb the 3rd. This share is not transferable and all library contents, lending rules and enforcement are at the discretion of the librarian.

Issued to: Harlan Gore

To get the money to buy the porn, I sold shares of stock in the enterprise for ten bucks a share. I even had Frank "Shakes" Voltonne, our Senior Technical Illustrator, create these really neat looking stock certificates which I then issued to my investors. I had eleven investors in the project, including myself. One of the investors was Harlan Gore, our production scheduler. He salivated at the prospect of joining. His favorite saying was 'Women are for breeding. Little boys are for pleasure.' He was a sick bastard. He also had a corollary to his previously stated principle on breeding and pleasure: 'If a girl's old enough to bleed, she's old enough to breed.' Like I said, he was one sick puppy. Tribal name: Perv. Anyway, you only got borrowing privileges from 'SYS-ONE dot PORNLIB' if you were an investor. Here's a copy of the stock certificate. It's Perv's. He paid his ten bucks but never bothered to pick up his stock certificate, so it ended up in my box of KTI archeological wonders. He was too busy being first in the borrowing line.

Clever devil that I am or was… and this is the really stupid part… I got to thinking: "How could we motivate those lazy designers and programmers to hustle their asses down to my cubicle to pick up the latest P-DIP update?" Then it struck me… programmers were mostly male and somewhat human. Whatever motivated my grunts would probably motivate those geeks. What was that motivator… pornography, good old fashioned pornography… so I set up this distribution system where the first designer or programmer to pick up his P-DIP update would get a prize, a fine picture of some obscene sex act that I liberated from 'SYS-ONE dot PORNLIB'. Clever, huh, but like I said… cleverly stupid.

Amen, brother! Is this the beginning of self-realization? Will miracles never cease?

Oxbow Lake The 2nd

It's none of your fucking business. Get out!

Back then porn was hard to come by… excuse the pun Bobbo, my man… and most of those horny geek bastards had no idea how to get their sticky fingers on the stuff. I did. The first designer or programmer to pick up his P-DIP update got a nice piece of liberated porn, compliments of yours truly. Later I had to modify the system and also give a second prize to a randomly chosen individual who had picked up his update after numero uno so that the fat bastards would keep coming… again no pun intended… after that first asshole had already won his piece of men's room delight for being the afore mentioned numero uno.

The system worked like a charm. As soon as I hung the sign up outside my cubicle announcing that a new update was available, those designers and programmers were elbowing each other down the hallway to my cubicle to win their own little piece of heavenly delight… for it was good, well chosen porn if I do say so myself, being somewhat of an expert on the subject. And the system worked like the aforementioned charm for several months until one of the losers complained to his manager that my unique pee-dip distribution system favored those programmers who sat closest to my cubicle. His manager, one of the naïve ones, is reported to have said, "What unique distribution system?" and the porn was out of the plain brown paper wrapper, so to speak. Scared shitless, I got called into the third-line system manager, one Mr. Tim Fortunato whom we nom de plumed Timmy Tough Nuts. Ol' Tough Nuts made his designers cry like baby girls during his status meetings. Well, ol' Tough Nuts grabs me by the back of my metaphoric neck and tells me to ditch the porn and find another way to motivate those assholes to pick up their P-DIP updates.

Ol' Tough Nuts wasn't performing an act of charity. He didn't know the meaning of those words. Hell, he didn't know the meaning of lots of words. Lucky for me, he wanted to bury the whole matter for his own reasons… keep everything hush-hush because so many of his people had willingly participated in the porn-driven distribution system. If it ever came to official light, I'd take a lot of his very important technical people with me along with several of his managers. And he knew it. His project would be in deep doo-doo. At his gentle encouragement, I ditched my sex-driven distribution system and went to a food-driven system. We gave cafeteria chits instead of porn… everyone likes to eat too. The new distribution system worked but not as well. There were no written records of the incident that I knew of and all who participated kept their mouths shut, their silence driven by an embarrassed self-interest… AKA the fear that they'd get fired. But to this day, I think that someone was keeping tabs on me and that whole porn distribution imbroglio. They didn't squeal on me, but I knew they were there, had the goods on me and would get to me… eventually.

Maybe it was one of those god damn Morlocks, you turkey.

Igor, our Polish Prince, was a first-line manager for a different project back then, but since we were buddies in that Polish Prince sort of way of his, he knew about 'SYS-ONE dot PORNLIB' but in that unacknowledged way of his. Typical for him, he wanted plausible deniability should the existence of the porn library ever come to light and in this instance, I really don't blame him. In his shoes, I'd have done the same thing. But he never knew about my 'unique' porn-driven pee-dip distribution system as far as I could tell. I explained the events surrounding the system in excruciating detail. He sat there stunned. When I finished he said, "So the rumors were true. (I guess he had heard something.) Were you out of your fuckin' mind?"

"Yeah, but so were a couple of hundred other people. You know what things were like around here back then. There weren't many colleges or universities even teaching software design and development as a discipline. We were pretty much self-taught and made it up as we went. It was the Wild West of technology. Hell, the lead designer had a degree in archeology. Great times!"

James chomped on his maduro for several minutes thinking, then said, "No written records?"

"Right. No written records that I know of." I had no idea whether or not some manager or personnel snitch or even one of the loser programming nerds had any written records of what I had done, but I sure as shit wasn't going to tell Igor. And there was the problem of being kept tabs on, which I sure as shit wasn't going to bring up now.

James remained stunned, "That you know of?"

"Right. There were plenty of rumors floating through the Lab, but even if All-Wet Willie had caught wind of it, he has no proof… no written records of the great porn distribution system imbroglio… no proof it ever existed. Besides, no one wanted to cross Timmy Tough Nuts and get squashed like a bug. I'm pretty sure we'll be OK, but maybe we should do everything we can to bury this thing as fast as we can with Lurch just to be on the safe side." I was scared shitless but kept my mask of confidence on. Things like this just never turn out right and I knew it, even back then.

Spanking Yesterday

James, obviously worried about protecting his own precious skin, mumbled "Burying this pile of shit is going to be difficult now what with All-Wet Willie involved." And I feared that we wouldn't be able to bury it fast enough or deep enough.

The Tribal Elders' Lunar Celebration

In those days we celebrated on the last Friday of the month… a kind of lunar madness… and I remember thinking, "TGIF, TGIF, TGIF baby… THANK GOD IT IS FRIDAY!" … for it was time for what we called NB2P, our Night of Beer, Pizza and Porn… a celebration when we, as tribal elders, embarked on our monthly lunar trek into the wild forests of the local cinematic erotic beast… a time to feed our stomachs, free our brains from worry, and recharge our libidos… and this celebration was an opportunity for me to forget all about my potentially Lurch-induced impending doom, which I was desperate to do in order to maintain my… sanity? Even back then, the double irony of the situation did not escape me.

Boy, you're boiling in your own primal juices now. You'd make a great dish for All Wet Willie to feast on.

Look, back then KTI was a technological asylum. When you're in the middle of it, it seems normal, but when you're not, you realize how fuckin' crazy that place was… and probably still is.

You're talking about that place being crazy? Pretty ballsy given your present, shall we say, accommodations.

75

Oxbow Lake The 2nd

I drove my old dilapidated and besmirched white delivery van up to the house of Dr. Franklin C. Baker the Third and honked the horn, having already picked up Magic Mike and the Flake, both of whom were sprawled out in my van's cargo space, drinking beer. I had bought the van used… very used… it was all I could afford after my financially catastrophic separation… divorce?… from what-cha-ma-call-it… purchased it from a dry cleaners in Saugerties last year so there were no seats in the back, just a rug and a long lock box that I bolted to the floor.

Magic Mike? What are the particulars of a certain Mr. Michael Mosley becoming Magic Mike? If memory serves me, when ol' Magic first joined my writing team, being the new guy, he got the shitty end of the pee-dip stick, that much dreaded component, the Memory Management Supervisor. The damned designer was updating the stupid component hourly. Making sense of his idiot scribblings and then rewriting them so that they made sense took forever. Late one Wednesday I dumped over 50 pages of hand-written updates on the future magic one's desk and left for a department softball game. The following morning the 50 some odd pages, rewritten and neatly typed, were on my desk ready for repro. I asked Mike how he got all that work done. His reply: "Magic!" Thus the new guy became Magic as in Magic Mike. He had inadvertently nom de plumed himself. Sounded like some kind of tribal nom de plume onanism to me, but no one could come up with a better one so it stuck.

As to the Flake, his story is a little more complicated. His real name is James Sullivan. The tribe initially defaulted to the rather prosaic 'Sully' for want of another tribal name… a disastrous retreat from creativity in my opinion given the fertile field upon which the tribe had to plow. Then one Sunday, Sully is Best Man at a very formal wedding… tux, top hat, the whole nine yards. At the reception he gets very snookered as was his Irish want.

About 2 AM Monday morning he gets stopped for driving erratically down 9W in an apparent and perhaps even valiant attempt to get home. The local constabulary forces him to the side of the road and into the Caldor's parking lot right across from the Bridge Circle. Since Sully's family is well known in the community, the cop offers to drive Sully home and forget about the DUI that Sully has so justifiably earned. He tells Sully to leave the car. He can pick it up later after he sobers up. Ol' Sully must have cut quite a figure in his formal tux as he donned his top hat and stepped out of his car

No pushover he, Sully spies a phone booth alongside the road not far from where he's parked. This was long before cell phones and there were actually phone booths all over the place. He demands his right to call his lawyer and staggers to this phone booth. He fumbles with several coins and finally manages to deposit enough of them in the pay phone to get a dial tone. He dials a number but apparently gets no answer, not surprising, given that it is now after two in the morning and, with the added impediment of advanced inebriation, that he quite possibly dialed the wrong number. In disgust, he slams down the receiver and staggers back to the parked police cruiser. By now the cop is furious. As Sully staggers toward the police cruiser, he is overtaken with the urgent need to relieve himself, so he whips out his johnson and pisses on the trunk of the police cruiser… obtaining bladder relief and some twisted form of revenge for the inconvenience that the local constabulary was causing him.

The cop, now furious, jumps Sully as he's tucking his johnson away and wrestles him to the ground, knocking off Sully's now battered top hat in the process, handcuffs him and stuffs him in the back of the cruiser for a quick ride to the Ulster County jail. The whole incident gets written up in the Police Blotter of the local rag, The Daily Freeman. In the police blotter, the arresting officer is quoted as referring to Sully as a real flake. Bingo, Mr. James Sullivan is transmogrified from the prosaic 'Sully' into then incredibly descriptive 'Flake', right before our tribal eyes and ears…and justifiably so!

Back to Dr. Franklin C. Baker the Third. Not to worry, Mr. Ward Bobb, I'm not lost in my memory banks quite yet. Even in my present condition I can still remember my place in this sordid tale of introspection. Well, Franklin's the only member of the tribe who looks and acts like a well-mannered engineer, if you can imagine such a being… a fastidious dresser, neat as a pin. Hell, he even wore pressed white socks. He's our human factors engineer, a human factors engineer before there were human factors engineers… one of the first, so he in fact is part engineer technically speaking. He has the unenviable task of testing both the technical publications and the system they describe to make sure that both are usable from a human standpoint, a daunting task given that the manuals describe unusable software written by barely human programmers, piled on unusable hardware developed by barely human engineers, and the manuals themselves written by technical writers, most of whom would rather have bamboo shoots shoved under their finger nails than write the god damn manuals he tests. He then sends his reports on usability to executives who are Attila the Hun clones and who only care about reducing expenses, making product release schedules and maximizing profit.

However, none of this bothers Dr. Franklin C. Baker the Third, for he is insane. On the inside, he is crazy as a loon… granted, an extremely well organized loon… but still a crazy loon. He carries a series of logic tight compartments encased between his ears… one being of his professional duties… so that the absolutely ridiculousness and hopelessness of his work never bothers him, which in my book is the very definition of professional insanity. What appears outwardly to be a well-organized sanity is in actuality a well organized and very neat internal insanity. The tribe dubbed him "Doc Frah-ken-steen"… "Doc" for short… given that he worked on a monster in the supposed name of humanity. The door to his house swung open and the esteemed Doc Frah-ken-steen appeared, turned, kissed Lady Frah-ken-steen goodbye, and trotted to the van in his neat and evenly measured strides. For very personal but never stated reasons, the prim and proper Lady Frah-ken-steen encouraged her hubby to participate in NB2P and looked forward to his return with great anticipation and enthusiasm.

Doc Frah-ken-steen jumped into the death seat and yelled over the rhythmic banging of my van's rusted muffler, "Hear about Lurch?"

Magic Mike yelled from the back of the van, "Heard he left a life-size picture of a female pudenda on his desk Thursday night." (Magic prided himself on his knowledge of the scientific terminology for all things sexual.) "One of the screws found it. Caused quite a panty twist in the organization."

Doc Frah-ken-steen turned and yelled, "Heard Flashlight Bobb up here"… Flashlight Bobb being me… "tried to tag ol' Lurch with something called an 'industrial incident violation' for leaving that risqué picture of a rather sensitive area of a woman's anatomy in plain sight on his desk. What in heaven's name is an industrial incident violation?"

Flashlight Bobb... I didn't used to be Flashlight Bobb, but I am now. I used to be Dancing Bear... I still remember being stuck with that tribal nom de plume. Dancing fuckin' Bear! Thanks to that perv Harlan Gore... that was back when I first joined KTI. I couldn't shake it. I was a brand new Editorial Assistant or EA back then. The job title was really a misnomer like most of the job titles at KTI since I didn't really edit anything. I coded the text for the manuals so that the stupid manuals could be poorly formatted by a computer program. Back then I was the new kid on the block and very anxious to strut my stuff, so I showed Harlan my text coding and know what that perv says? He says 'You are a true dancing bear.' So I naively ask 'How so?' And that fuckin' perv says 'The wonder is not how well the bear dances but that he dances at all.' That's how I became fuckin' 'Dancing Bear', a name that I 'earned' not because of my ability to dance and hardly a compliment. Some things you just gotta accept and live with if you can. For reasons that shall remain undocumented, the other tribal elders decided to re-nom de plume me. Now I'm Flashlight Bobb.

Flashlight Bobb! Now there's a nom de plume for the ages. Why didn't you write about how you got that nom de plume?

This whole commenting thing is getting aggravating, in fact more than aggravating. First I write a journal entry. Then I re-read it later, usually the next day, so I can tell that queer doc that I've done it and get some brownie points. Then later I find these stupid comments which I think the Doc is writing. He vehemently denies it... sometimes with a smile, the queer prick. Then the next day I find a comment written about my comment about a previous mysterious comment. Well here goes again:

there's a good reason I don't write about my Flashlight Bobb nom de plume and since you know so much about me, you should be able to take a pretty good guess as to why. I don't have to write about anything I don't want to write about. It's my god damn journal. End of story.

So I turned and yelled at Doc Frah-ken-steen, "How the hell did you come across this bullshit rumor about Lurch, anyway?"

Doc, that is, our tribal Doc, as unflustered as always, yelled back, "It is distinctly more than a mere bullshit rumor. It is an actual bona fide rumor of the highest order. The words came from Lurch's lips to my ears. He told a bunch of us at this afternoon's coffee break and it spread through the Lab like wild fire. Is it true?"

"Guys, I can't talk about it. It's a confidential managerial thing. Did he say anything else about that photo?"

Magic Mike chimed in, "Yeah. Said it was a great piece of art work tastefully executed. Kind of a bad choice of words… tastefully. Think he was implying that cunnilingual activity of some sort had occurred before the photo was taken to account for the moisture excreted about the labia majora of the exposed pudenda?" You could always count on Magic to keep the conversation on a high plain.

I was stunned by Magic's detailed knowledge of the photo in question: "How the hell did you know about the details of that photo?"

"Bought a copy of Screw Magazine…"

Oxbow Lake The 2nd

"So you've seen the photo in question."

"Yes, we all have. It's a great photo… ground breaking like Lurch said."

Wanting to end what was quickly becoming a very tense discussion and move on to tonight's entertainment, my relief from the very subject we were discussing, I yelled, "Guys, we gotta drop this. It's a confidential management issue and I can't talk about it. Let's hit the road. North or south?"

From the back of the van, the Flake yelled, "North… to Saugerties. The pizza in New Paltz sucks the biggone (tribal-ese for 'the big one')."

I yelled, "What's playin' in Saugerties?"

Flake yelled from the back, "Does it fuckin' matter? Porn's porn…" and the magic man added "but a good pizza's somethin' you can cunnilingually necrophag, to coin a phrase… that is, lick and eat to your satisfaction all that pizza covered with toppings that are well cooked and presumably already dead." Like I said, you could always count on the magic man to keep the conversation on a high plain. The Flake, not as appreciative of the magic man's creative and pseudo hyper-scientific sexual terminology, interrupted his interrupter and yelled, "For Christ's sake Magic, don't talk that shit before we eat." Then he yelled at me, "Hey, I'm goin' hoarse back here from the racket your fuckin' muffler makes… and it stinks of carbon monoxide exhaust fumes. This piece of shit is an Auschwitz on wheels! Oh bright and shining Flashlight Bobb, when you gonna fix the fuckin' muffler?"

Damn, I just realized it. That was a first... The Flake had nom de plumed an inanimate object, my van, by christening the piece of shit "Auschwitz on Wheels".

I yelled, "Never. The van isn't worth it and neither are you two assholes. As to your statement that porn's porn, say it ain't so, Joe, say it ain't so! Some porn can get pretty boring and seeing the same porn flick twice is definitely boring, my cunnilingual necrophagist pizza eater. It's like cunnilingually necrophaging used pizza with your eyes and ears and even possibly your brain. Perish the thought. Watching a good porn flick is what turns a night of pizza and beer into NB2P. That last 'P' is very important and it shouldn't be used porn so to speak."

Doc Frah-ken-steen opened the newspaper I had thrown on the dash and after carefully perusing the pages of that local rag The Kingston Freeman, yelled, "Our choices are Think Dirty of Me, Part 1... at the Orpheum up in Saugerties... an Think Dirty of Me, Part 2... down in New Paltz. Anybody seen either one?"

No one replied.

The Flake yelled from the rear of the van, "Well that pretty much settles it. We can't see Part 2 until we've seen Part 1. Gotta be Saugerties. Head north!"

Voices of assent spread through the van, agreeing with the unassailable logic that viewing a porn movie subtitled Part 1 had to precede the viewing of a porn movie of the same title subtitled Part 2 what with the importance of character and plot development and all, so I turned north onto Route 9W and chugged towards Frank's Hunting Lodge, home of our favorite pizza.

After the torturous ride north on 9W which included several sharp turns through a series of 90-degree corners just south of the village and then over a bridge that looked like it was about to collapse, my old van chugged up the steep hill into the friendly confines of the self-proclaimed 'friendly' little village known as Saugerties. I pulled into a parking space in front of Frank's Hunting Lodge and me and the other tribal elders piled out.

Beer, Pizza, and Aristotelian Ethics

Frank's Hunting Lodge was full of two kinds of heads back then… the kind that hung above the bar reflecting the dead denizens of the local forests… and the kind that hung out in front of the bar reflecting the undead denizens of the village, mostly blue collar workers… hunters to their very core… ready, willing and able to kill anything on four legs and occasionally on two… sometimes on purpose… sometimes not. The atmosphere at Frank's Hunting Lodge was unique… Frank's pizza very unique. The beer was… well beer… an often boiled with a shot of cheap whiskey to give it enough character to approach uniqueness. This was Saugerties before it got overrun with Woodstock wanna-bees from the City, who gentrified the village so that they could drive north on the Thruway to spend their weekends relaxing "in the country" after working hard all week on Wall Street screwing some unsuspecting investor out of his retirement… and in so doing becoming week-enders in the village… driving the real estate values there so high that the locals couldn't afford to live there anymore and had to move out.

Hell, if memory serves me, I heard that Frank's ain't Frank's no more. Has some French name now and all the trophies are gone. Now it's just a pizza joint. I think that Frank has succumbed to Kronos's march to eternity, for father time marches on inexorably and inexorably for the worse, particularly in this case for Frank.

Back when, hunting trophies, ranging from well-racked deer to fierce black bear, stared down at us as we scarfed Frank's unique pizza and guzzled his quite un-unique beer. There was even a moth-eaten old wolf protecting the bar under the watchful eyes of other not as easily identified and just as poorly preserved furry heads hanging from the walls above. A pheasant, a turkey and two ducks guarded the bottles of liquor arrayed behind the bar. The tribal elders liked the atmosphere at Frank's as well as the unique tasting pizza, which was particularly greasy. We always ordered a couple of extra-large garbage pizzas piled high with cheese and whatever else Frank had laying around the kitchen… as well as a bunch of pitchers of beer.

Magic Mike finished off his fourth piece of garbage pizza and exclaimed to no one in particular as he patted his belly, "That's excellent pizza. No other pizza tastes like Frank's pizza. What do you think makes his pizza so deliciously unique?"

The Flake waved in the general direction of the trophy heads staring down at us and said, "Besides the grease? Well what do you think happened to the back halves of all those stuffed creatures staring down at us?"

Magic looked up at the trophies and asked, "What's the back halves of all the trophies got to do with the unique taste of Frank's pizza?"

The Flake smiled wryly, "Well, you're eating them, asshole. I heard that it's the back half of those trophies that give Frank's garbage pizza its unique and meaty taste."

Magic stared up at the trophy heads and, having lubricated his brain with a dozen or so beers, took the Flake's fantastical statement to heart, and said, "These taxidermied trophy heads have been hung up there for a long time. Surely Frank has run out of back halves by now."

The Flake, entering into what was fast becoming a serious tribal discussion of the nature of Frank's pizza and its relationship to the décor of the establishment, replied, "I heard that Frank supplements the back halves with road kill. Nothin' wrong with that! Had to be fresh road kill of course, much of it donated by his loyal patrons, those Saugertarians at the bar."

Magic Mike slumped back in his chair and stared at the brigade of dead beer pitchers spread across the table and loudly pronounced, "Road kill! I'm not sure I like Frank's ethics here. He's got to be violating an Aristotelian ethical definition or principle of some sort. This place isn't called Frank's Road Kill Lodge… it's called Frank's Hunting Lodge. I'm not so sure that we should patronize this establishment. This unethical behavior on Frank's part should not be encouraged, condoned or even tolerated… particularly by us."

Doc Frah-ken-steen, who had been pretty much silent, concentrating on his drinking and then his eating and then his drinking, said, "Look, Magic has a good philosophic point. If Frank advertises or even implies, as I think he's obviously done, that the unique flavor of his pizza is the result of adding hunted meat as a secret topping to his pizza, he's violating the

86

very definition of Aristotelian ethics… in this case, the bond of understanding that he's created between his customers, such as us, and himself, such as him. He's being quite unethical and his customers may not even realize it."

I doubted that the Doc knew much about Aristotle and I was pretty sure that until tonight there was a good chance that the magic one believed that Aristotle was an ethnic Greek who played second baseman for the old Boston Braves. Hell, he probably thought that before, during and after the discussion. I had no idea what the Flake knew and there was a good chance that he didn't either… but in the present circumstances, it was pretty clear that actual knowledge was unrelated to the discussion at hand as is often the case with the tribe. The boys were on a roll Blutarsky style, as they say.

I had refused to participate in the discussion… not because I knew what I didn't know and had the integrity to not act upon that realization but rather, honestly, because of the lack of a high level of alcohol coursing through my veins. As the driver of the Auschwitz on Wheels, I had to remain relatively sober so that if my passengers were to die while in my van, it would be a long slow process not involving physical violence of any sort and most likely related in some way to inhaling carbon monoxide. I was proud of myself for showing such restraint. Besides, the tribal talk seemed inane, harmless and even humorous.

However, I noticed that the Flake was now nodding his head in agreement. The three drunken tribal elders were moving to a consensus through some strange interpretation of Aristotelian ethics as it applied to Frank and his pizza, which just happened to be the best pizza in Ulster County with or without road kill or hunted meat. Hell, there was a good chance that this whole road kill business was a figment of Magic's alcohol addled off-center brain, but even if he made the whole damn thing up… knowingly or otherwise… there was a better than even chance that he now believed it.

As the discussion proceeded, I feared that the three tribal elders' would conclude that we had to boycott the place because of Frank's perceived violation of their insane interpretation of Aristotelian ethics, thus depriving me of my favorite pizza. I had to think fast. Then it struck me smack between the eyes… a metaphorical 2x4 so to speak. There WAS a way out of this ethical dilemma. All I had to do was move the discussion from the Aristotelian to the Socratic: "Look guys, we may not have an ethical problem here at all. We may have a semantic problem. Answer me this: how does one usually hunt?"

The threesome thought for a long moment. Then the Flake put forth, "With a weapon of some sort, maybe a rifle, but probably a shot gun."

I asked "What's the weapon do?"

Magic replied, "Kill. It kills what you're hunting."

"So to hunt you have to use a weapon to kill what you're hunting, right? Does it matter who has the weapon and who does the hunting, vis-à-vis Frank… ethically speaking?"

Doc Fran-ken-steen joined in, "No. I guess not."

"Well what kills road kill?"

Again, Magic, "A car or truck, usually, right?"

I now had them right where I wanted them Socratically speaking, "So if someone is driving a car or a truck and runs over an animal and kills it, he or she is, in essence, using a weapon and is thus hunting. Granted it's a sort of four to 18 wheeled random kind of hunting, but it fits the definition of hunting. Right?"

Magic smiled from ear-to-ear, "Right! So road kill is actually a hunted and killed animal. Great! Puts Frank in the clear ethically-wise. We don't have to boycott this establishment. We can continue to patronize Frank's Hunting Lodge and consume his fine and unique pizza!"

I sighed a sigh of great relief and figured out the tab. It was time to head for the Orpheum and the second P of NB2P after a quick trip to the men's room after all that beer… a good move, for back then, it was always best to avoid the men's room at the Orpheum if at all possible.

Pretty clever. Seems to me that those buds of yours should not be out and about. To say that whole tribe of assholes of yours is a little off center doesn't do them, you or the meaning of 'off center' much justice. I can't tell whether you're a bad influence on them or they're a bad influence on you… not that it really matters all that much now.

It's none of your fuckin' business. Stay the hell out of my life. As to Frank's pizza, looking back, I wonder if Frank wasn't using something higher on the evolutionary scale to give his

89

pizza its unique meaty flavor. Wouldn't surprise me in the least. Had I thought about it back then, I'd a probably spent the evening barfing in Frank's rest room. Se la vie, mother fucker, as they say.

An Evening of Great Cinematic Art with Surprising Credits

Another day, another entry. Where was I? Ah yes, we left Frank's Hunting Lodge and strolled around the corner to the Orpheum. It's different now being a legit movie house and all. I think someone converted it to a three-plex. Back then, it was a one-screen porn palace. There's that temporal inexorability again. The lights were already dimmed when we entered the place. Oddly enough, the theatre smelled like a church… you know, that old rug smell… which it obviously wasn't, for unlike a church, this church-like smell was spiced with the aroma of a horny humanity, not a reverent one, and of buttered pop corn, not old hymnals. The two venues… a porno palace and a church… in spite of any aromatic similarities, were obviously different; the humanity occupying them was, for the most part, however, not.

I pulled out my trusty flashlight from my belt holster and blasted that baby down the aisle to light the way. Someone in the back yelled "Douse the fuckin' illumination" but I ignored the prick.

We carefully shuffled down the aisle to an empty row about a third of the way from the front, making sure that the rows in front and behind were empty. Thank god for my trusty flashlight. Choosing a seat at a porno flick is something that has to be done carefully and wisely, believe me. Sometimes the floor gets quite slippery, thus caution has to be exercised with each step, particularly as you shuffle along a row of seats. As to choosing the location of your seat wisely, not all the clientele appreciate the movie as an art form and refuse to exercise the discipline of delayed gratification. This lack of self-discipline causing in some cases surreptitious self abuse, sometimes not so surreptitious, affecting not only the floors as previously noted, but possibly affecting those sitting nearby. Thus it was also best to keep at least one empty row between you and any of the other patrons if at all possible.

Too bad you weren't as careful with the rest of your life, ol' Flashlight Bobb.

I doused the illumination and snapped that baby back into my belt holster. We settled in, large buttered popcorn containers in our laps, for an evening of hoi polloi entertainment. The Flake elbowed me in the ribs and whispered, "Look over there, that guy two rows up to the left. Isn't that Mr. Natural?" Mr. Natural, AKA Tommy Tompkins, was an old-time editor in Tech Pubs, a loner and not an active member of the tribe. His longevity gave him, if not acceptance, at least benign neglect... a neglect he had both earned and desired.

I squinted and sure enough, it was Mr. Natural sitting next to a young woman. I whispered, "Looks like him. Who's the young babe he's sitting next to?" It was rare for a woman of any age to attend a porno flick. If there were two in the audience, it was a lot, so a woman, and a young one at that, sitting next to Mr. Natural would bring notice.

The Flake moved forward in his seat and squinted into the darkness, awaiting the reflected brightness from the screen to flash a few moments of light. As the light flashed he said, "Shit, looks to me like his daughter… what's her name. Maybe we should call ol' Tom Tom, 'Mr. Unnatural'. Why the hell would a guy bring his own daughter to a porno flick?"

I shrugged my shoulders and said, "Who knows. It's his business… not ours. Watch the movie."

To my surprise, Think Dirty of Me, Part 1 lived up to its title. Since a pussey cat is a pussey cat, as they say… and there's only so many ways to skin a cat, pussey or otherwise… virtually all of which I believe we'd seen… the voice-over thoughts of Miss Pussey Cat and her skinning partner Mr. Tom Cat were the novelty. There were the usual groans and joyous howls of 'Oh my God!', both bass and soprano, with the occasional erotic metaphor… read 'dirty talk'… moaned and screamed out loud for good measure. Sometimes the groans and howls and the moaned and screamed erotic metaphors seemed to be out of synch with the action.

At the time nobody seemed to care, including us, but thinking about it now, it seems really strange. The voices seemed real and the action seemed real, but the two realities were out of synch… begging the question "Which one was really real?"

But the real genius of this erotic masterpiece… the thoughts expressed by the well-endowed Mr. Tom Cat who apparently thought a lot during the skinning ritual with Miss Pussey Cat… and those of Miss Pussey Cat, who was also very good looking and extremely well-endowed in her fashion, and who matched the skinning Mr. Tom Cat thought for thought… their thoughts expressed as voice-overs… spoken words… as they prepared for the skinning of the cat, the actually skinning of the cat, and recovery from the skinning of the cat… the recovery the prelude to yet another skinning of the proverbial cat. All in all, a most satisfying flick.

As the credits flashed, Mr. Natural and his daughter hustled up the aisle to the exit, obviously wanting to escape before the lights went on in order to avoid being recognized. He saw us as he passed by, put his hand up to shield his face and turned, grabbed his daughter's hand and dragged her up the aisle to hasten their exit as unobserved as possible as she looked around without care in the world apparently bewildered by it all.

As aficionados of the art form, we always stayed to read the credits. After the flick, we'd critique this much maligned but well attended cinematic art form over coffee at the Village Diner just down the street. As I read the credits, the Flake grabbed my arm and shouted, "Shit… did you see that, 'Script written by Mr. Richard Tadd'."

The credits rolled on. 'Female voice-over groaning and dialogue by Miss Twyla Twatly'… the credits continued… 'Male voice-over groaning and dialogue by Mr. Richard Tadd'… All of us saw it. Although I wasn't sure how I could use this information in my dealings with Lurch back at the ol' bom-ber-factoree, it seemed to me that there had to be a way. Back then it was bare knuckled organizational combat… for all I know it still is… so my thoughts were as natural as Mr. Natural's… that is normal given me and my situation in our little world at KTI.

If I were you, I'd be very careful about using the word normal in any context.

Well you ain't me, thank god.

93

Thoughts of being Mau-Mau-ed in the Tribal Critics Corner

Me and the other tribal elders sat in the Village Diner around the large odd shaped table in the corner which we called the critics corner, sipping coffee and scarfing Danish as required by NB2P ritual. I loved those prune Danish… sure do miss them. I don't miss the coffee much now. I used to love the aroma of fresh brewed coffee, but now it turns my stomach. Might be the medication.

I could hardly contain myself with what we'd read as the credits for Think Dirty of Me, Part 1 flashed by, "Can you believe that? Lurch wrote the script, and it was damn good dialogue. The boy can write porn." I, of course, was also trying to think of a way I could use this information back at the Lab to throw our porn-script writing, moaning and groaning Mr. Richard Tadd under the bus, flatten the bastard and have him moan and groan for non-erotic reasons.

Magic Mike smiled, "And the boy can moan with the best of them although his speaking parts could use some work." I thought, "Surely, I can use this info too."

The Flake added, "I thought the male voice-over sounded familiar. And how about the female voice-over… Miss Twyla Twatly? Made you want to butter your own popcorn." I thought, "There's got to be a way to tie the moaning and groaning Miss Twyla Twatly into my battle plan."

Doc Frah-ken-steen raised his hands in protest, "Please… I find your metaphor of buttering your own popcorn quite inappropriate, particularly while we are eating. Don't get me wrong. I'm not suggesting that we change the topic. I'm merely suggesting that we be a little more discrete with the language we use to describe and critique our evening's cinematic experiences. After all, are we not Pubs Creeps?"

The Flake, to mollify Doc Frah-ken-steen and his sensitivities to provocative metaphoric language for all things sex-u-al, said, "Well Doc, I understand. We're 'word people', Pubs Creeps to our very core. Words matter. For us, a thousand pictures are worth a well chosen word or two. Not that I'm denigrating the place that pictures play in our little world as our recent cinematic experience obviously indicates."

It was true. We were 'word people' and Pubs Creeps, by definition… which is why Think Dirty of Me, Part 1 was such a hit with us, and why Think Dirty of Me, Part 2 was now a must see and, I might add, hear… for all those thoughts were expressed with words. It's also one of the reasons our tribe stuck out like a sore thumb at KTI. Engineers did circuits, programmers did code, and we did words, the invention used by humans to communicate with each other over the millennia. True we did supplement our words with a diagram or two, but even the diagrams had words and were a supplement to words, for we were a tribe known throughout the Lab as The Pubs Creeps.

And how did we become Pubs Creeps, Mr. Lotus blossom? Well, our job was to communicate with humans while engineers communicated primarily with machines and programmers communicated primarily with software. Ironically, engineers had to use software to build more machines and programmers

95

had to use machines to build more software. Engineers and programmers had two common bonds, machines and software. True, the machines changed and the software changed, but both marching bands always played their cacophonous music with, to and through machines and software. They communicated poorly with each other within their marching bands and hardly at all without... one geeks' music being another's noise. When it came to playing songs for non-machines and non-software, AKA humans, both bands played unbearable and sometimes unhearable cacophonous music as they marched along. Instead of 'AKA humans' when referring to the bastards, I could have said 'AKA other humans', but that would have been through implication a grievous insult to humanity. Unlike those marching bands, the Pubs Creeps always communicated with other humans although it must be admitted that most of that humanity outside the lab with whom we communicated professionally shared many of the characteristics of the engineers and programmers within the lab. The music these lab assholes composed and played would make your ears hurt if it was hearable! Don't believe that music of the spheres bullshit that so-called scientists always espouse!

Patience, dear alter ego, we're almost to that Pubs Creeps business... which you should remember. While programmers and engineers looked with daggers at each other, they both looked down on the aforementioned Pubs Creeps, another characteristic they both shared which I failed to mention earlier. We were KTI's first tier humans, outliers in their eyes, who had to communicate with other more distant humans... flawed though those other humans might be. These other outliers... these humans outside KTI's asylum of technology... were KTI's second and third tier outliers, some of who were full humans... some of

96

who were not... and these other outliers were called in common parlance 'customers'... individuals representing organizations that paid a great deal of money for the privilege of using the hardware and software that our cacophonous bands of engineers and programmers created... something that did not seem to matter much to these two cacophonous marching bands of idiot geeks, for from their point of view, outliers were outliers, mere annoyances to be tolerated at best as these two bands played their self indulgent painful music. In their minds, playing their music being its own raison d'être excluding both KTI and those other outliers, i.e., customers.

Now for that 'Pubs Creeps' business, my sweet boy. Patience rewarded, rules obeyed! I have had to resist the urge to get ahead of me to myself and jump right to the end, but I was told to be as ordered as possible in my comments... that everything has a beginning, middle, and end... that I should be as specific as I could... thus the need for patience. But now Lafayette, we have arrived! In order to get our source material to write the software manuals and to get those manuals reviewed for technical accuracy, we had to literally haunt the cubicles of the programmers. Our starting point was that dreadful design document, the pee dip... the Program Design Information Publication... but that was only the starting point. I'm not sure what the starting point was for the hardware manuals since I had never written one of them. I do know that the hardware writers complained as much as the software writers and pretty much about the same things. Since programmers hated to write or 'do the doc' as they put it, we had to literally harass them to get the latest updated source material and the technical reviews we required.

In frustration, the software designers and programmers dubbed us 'Pubs Creeps' since, from their point of view, we creeped around the Lab bothering them with inconsequential questions which any omniscient professional, like themselves, would know the answers to. Our inexcusable ignorance took time away from their real jobs, designing and coding software systems that were impossible to understand and use. The dubbing was not meant as a compliment. However, being slightly off-kilter word people, the tribe gloried in the insult, much to the dismay of those who sought to insult us. We realized that an insult was only an insult if the insulted party was... well, insulted. We knew words and how they worked and the programmers did not. Thus we adopted the name 'Pubs Creeps' as our tribal name, the insult becoming a badge of honor. We became that mighty tribe, 'The Pubs Creeps'.

The post-NB2P critical review moved on, requiring another cup of dreadful diner java for all present. The Flake observed, "You know, I think that Lurch is stealing ideas from us. Granted, he writes porn well, but the whole idea of knowing what someone thinks while having sex... like in Think Dirty of Me, Part 1... that's really my idea. A bunch of us were bull shitting at one of our coffee breaks... had to be well over a year ago... and I asked, 'Wouldn't it be interesting to know what someone thinks when they're getting banged, particularly the woman?' Our minds wandered and we ended up wondering about Mollie Mau-Mau and what she thought when she banged."

Specifics, you idiot... specifics! The Mau-Mau was one of the few female programmers in the Lab and a good one to boot. She was also known for three other things as well: a great ass, short skirts and a willingness to fuck. Rumor had it that she was quitting to go back to school to get her PhD in mathematics… some school out on the west coast… in Oregon, I think. She was real smart but had a screw loose in the sex department. Her recently stated short term goal, as the aforementioned rumor would have it, was to fuck every gas station attendant who would pump gas for her from Kingston, New York, to Eugene, Oregon. I guess she thought that if a gas station attendant pumped for her, she'd pump for him.

One had to admit it was an ambitious goal, but most of us thought she would give it the old post graduate college try and given her proclivities and talents, we thought she had a pretty good chance of succeeding. All agreed it would be quite interesting to know what the Mau-Mau thought as she banged away, for it was quite clear that she had many opportunities for such thought and, given her many proclivities, shall we say, would have many interesting things to think about.

Her name had become a verb in the parlance of the tribe: to be Mau-Maued, that is to get royally fucked, as was about to happen to me if I couldn't throw ol' Lurch under that personnel bus Wet Willie was driving 100 miles an hour at yours truly. Back then, such possibilities scared the shit out of me.

Our cups were now empty and our words few as the conversation ground to a halt. Doc Frah-ken-steen broke what had become silence, "It's time to hit the road, boys." He was always the one who was anxious to return home after one of our NB2P rituals for obvious yet unstated reasons.

Round Two: Wet Willie Attacks

That boxing match with Lurch became a tag-team affair. I've never heard of tag-team boxing, but here it was: in the near corner Igor the Polish Prince and Flashlight Bobb (i.e., Dancing Bear… me) versus, in the far corner, the ever-dangerous Wet Willie and the deceptively powerful Lurch. Now that I think about it, it seems more like Friday Night Wrestling stuff, but it really wasn't since the blood would be real… in an organizational sense… and the outcome was far from predetermined.

James and I sat at the long mahogany conference table across from Wet Willie and Lurch. We were on Wet Willie's turf, for he had called the meeting and scheduled it for Personnel's conference room. Turf was important for both psychological and physical reasons. It was like that Greek legend about the ogre asshole who Jason or Hercules or some other Greek hero had to beat the crap out of. As long as that ogre asshole's feet were on his home ground, Jason or Hercules or some other Greek hero like that couldn't beat that ogre asshole, but if the ogre asshole's feet were lifted off the ground, the Greek hero could beat the crap out of him. Metaphorically, we had to get Wet Willie's feet off the ground and then beat the crap out of him or get him onto our ground, which was the same thing, and beat the crap out of him there. We knew from the outset that this battle was going to be hand-to-hand fisticuffs of the most vicious organizational kind with no holds barred or punches pulled.

Lurch smiled that aggravating bemused Olympic smile of his and Wet Willie stared at us as if we were Nazis being prosecuted at Nuremberg and he of course was the chief prosecutor. Richard Widmark couldn't have done it better. He opened the meeting:

"This case is a lot more complicated than the immediate facts would indicate. In order to get the full picture of what happened, we must delve into the kind of professionalism that was promoted and maintained in your organization…"

Just as I thought, Wet Willie was going for the management 'created or at least tolerated an unprofessional culture' attack… the unprofessional culture being created and tolerated primarily by me and James. He continued, "… and the kind of counseling that the employees in your organization received regarding professional conduct," part 2 of his attack to destroy James after throwing me under the Personnel bus.

James turned red with rage. I slammed my hand down on his arm to keep him from compounding our problems with an angry, ill advised reply and said, "I think it best if we first establish the facts of the case before delving into any other aspect of what happened and why." I wanted to get the discussion to center on Screw Magazine and that picture of a woman's nether world, the nether world of one Twyla Twatly to be precise. I also wanted to get that name into the discussion. If the first things discussed in the memo documenting this meeting were Screw Magazine and a dirty picture of someone named Twyla Twatly, I thought we had a pretty good chance of burying the entire matter. Sure as shit, Wet Willie's manager wouldn't want to go to a meeting with the lab director and have his good offices appear to be defending Lurch's right to display a photo of a female's naked pudendum in his cubicle… and with the name Twyla Twatly attached to that female pudendum… as one of the central "facts" of the case! All other factors would pale in significance.

Wet Willie knew what the game was and parried, "Let's keep the cart behind the horse. Before this incident occurred, we have to be sure that there was nothing that could be interpreted in even the slightest way as having, if not encouraged or condoned this behavior, at least tolerated it." The battle was joined.

I placed the folder that I had brought with me on the table and opened it. There for all to see was the Screw Magazine in question. I attempted to open it to the center fold and Wet Willie reached across the table and slammed the palm of his hand down on the magazine covering the magazine's title and preventing me from opening it, saying rather forcefully, "No need to display that…" using the indefinite 'that' so the exact nature of the central 'fact' in question was not identified and openly stated… he continued, "we can all stipulate as to its nature"… again an indefinite… this time the word 'its'… the clever bastard. I never trusted the man. He had… How should I say it?... an evil glint in his eye.

Before I could say or do anything, he then yelled, "Shirley!" and his secretary entered the conference room. Shirley was a rather matronly elder woman, as straight-laced as they come. Wet Willie turned to us and asked, "Would either of you like a cup of coffee?" His strategy was now obvious. As long as matronly Shirley was in the conference room, that photo could not be displayed and I was sure that he'd have her popping in and out for a series of flimsy reasons. Could you get this memo? Could you get my copy of the KTI Managers' Manual …and so on. Matronly Shirley entered the conference room on cue.

Wet Willie asked again, "Would either of you like coffee? We brew our own. It's not that terrible bilge from the vending machines." We declined… I was losing my taste for coffee… even good coffee started to taste like shit… smelled like shit too… but both he and Lurch asked for a cup, no cream, no sugar. After the matronly Shirley left, I tried to push Wet Willie's hand off the magazine to open it to the center fold. He pushed down more forcefully on the magazine and he said, "I believe that it would be very inappropriate to display the photo in question given that my secretary will be in and out of the meeting. Let's just stipulate that the photo can be considered inappropriate and leave it at that. In fact, I think that magazine should be turned over to Personnel during this investigation. After all, this is a Personnel investigation."

Lurch smiled that Olympic bemused smile of his as James turned three shades of purple. The issue now was not whether or not we could display that picture, but whether or not we'd be able to keep possession of the whole damn magazine. Once that magazine entered the bowels of Personnel's bureaucracy, Wet Willie would make sure it never saw the light of day again, believe me.

Shirley reentered the conference room holding two cups of black coffee. The smell turned my stomach. Wet Willie reflexively lifted his hand off the magazine and turned to take the cup that the matronly Shirley offered him. It was enough for me to slam the folder shut and slip it off the table onto my lap. We would live to fight another day. A disappointed Wet Willie led a discussion of the process for the investigation, the rights and responsibilities of the employee, the role of management, etc., etc. He never discussed what had actually happened and pretty much prevented us from entering the actual facts of the case into the discussion.

After an hour of dithering and posturing, he realized that there was no way short of assault that he could pry that folder from me so he proclaimed the meeting over with, "I'll write the minutes," which he had every right to do since he had called the meeting. This was very bad news for us. It was a lesson that I had learned the hard way. Years ago, I had negotiated an agreement with a programming manager and when I read his memo documenting the meeting, I confronted him, "Irv, your memo doesn't reflect what really happened" and he smugly replied, "You don't seem to understand. The memo is reality," placing great emphasis on the word 'is'. And sure enough, as far as the organization was concerned, it was. Another organizational lesson well learned.

Well there's a bunch of lessons that you apparently never learned.

And there's one very important lesson you never learned, much to your own peril.

In the hallway outside the conference room, James whispered to me, "We can't let that asshole write the minutes. When he's done, Tadd will have committed the grievous sin of farting after we force fed him beans. The stink will all be our fault."

"James, we can't stop Wet Willie from writing the meeting minutes. It's management protocol. I'll have to write a report to you about the whole incident and put it in Tadd's departmental personnel folder, the one I keep. You know, one of those preliminary reports on the status of our investigation. I'll include all the juicy details in it, very graphic but in as a polite a way as possible. No one can fault us for writing a status report. In fact, it's expected. I can date it the day you got the 'please handles' and I first interviewed Tadd. I'll sign it. You can initial it and write a note on it saying something about how you agree that we're proceeding as required by management protocol and that you agree with the

PERSONAL AND CONFIDENTIAL

Date: July 4, 1960

To: J. L. Jankowski
     Senior Manager
     Systems Publications

Subject: Initial investigation of inappropriate
           display of picture of female anatomy in cubicle
           of Richard Tadd

I have verified with Security Officer Steven Hamilton that
while investigating a light burning in Mr. Richard Tadd's
cubicle at 2:23 AM this day, Officer Hamilton was
surprised, upset and offended to find a certain publication
on Mr. Tadd's desk opened to the centerfold of that
publication.

The publication bears the potentially offensive name of
Screw Magazine and the centerfold contained an enlarged
close-up picture of the anatomical area of a female where
the subject female's legs come together although in this
instance the legs were quite apart.

I have met with Mr. Tadd and he has confirmed that the
subject publication is in fact his. However, he refuses to
confirm or deny that he left the light on and the
potentially offensively name magazine open to the certainly
offensive centerfold.

I am convinced that Mr. Tadd is responsible for this and
recommend that he be cited for an industrial incident
violation and that a letter of reprimand be placed in his
personnel jacket.

Ward Bobb the 3rd
1st Line Manager
Core Publications

*Letter on investigation
of Richard Tadd
-WB*

105

preliminary findings. Send a copy to Wet Willie and buck a copy up the management chain. I'll get on it PDQ. If we get it out before his minutes get distributed, he'll be on our turf and his minutes will look like he's avoiding the problem." So ended Round 2, a draw… which for us was a win given that the match took place squarely in his ring.

I've attached a copy of my preliminary report below. Thank god for my box of KTI archeological treasures!

Fearful Swimming in Organizational Pea Soup

There was this tribal gathering of five or six, including Lurch, in Frank Voltonne's production area… the largest and only open area in our organization… as often occurred during the work day. All the usuals were there… most of who were quite unusual. They were sipping that terrible vending machine coffee during their 15-minute… let's stretch it out as long as we can… morning coffee break. Since I had gotten the report of my initial investigation of the great Lurch imbroglio written and distributed to all concerned including our entire management chain before Wet Willie got his minutes written and distributed, the incident had mysteriously disappeared into that great organizational black hole in the sky… that black hole that swallows all matters great and small which the organization does not wish to address.

The Polish Prince was still the Igor; I was still the Flashlight Bobb; Wet Willie was still the Wet Willie, and Lurch was still the Lurch… and the entire management chain was still the entire management chain. And no one was openly denying that Lurch

106

had committed some untoward act, defended his right to do so, or attacked us for supposedly allowing it to happen. As I said, the entire incident had disappeared. Let sleeping dogs lay, or lie as the case may be, was the apparent order of the day. We were again swimming in the KTI's pea soup of forgetfulness, a warm, soothing, forgetfulness that blocked all unpleasant memories, and we had been doing so by my rather shaky calculations for over a month.

I stayed on the periphery of the tribal coffee clotch, far enough away so that I could not be considered a part of the group. That way I wouldn't have to enforce any rules and yet could hear the conversation. Besides, given my position as manager and my involvement in the recent Lurch imbroglio, I thought it best to maintain a buffer zone of plausible deniability between me and the rest of the tribe while in the ol' bom-bor factoree… at least for now. I guess you could call me a cautious swimmer in that organizational pea soup of forgetfulness. Sometimes swimming in that pea soup of forgetfulness is a good thing… a real good thing.

As was their habit, the little tribal coffee clotch palavered about all things sexual, a preoccupation that they never seemed to tire of while slowly sipping their putrid smelling vending machine swill. Today the topic of discussion was the impending and physically odd matrimonial pairing of one of our male technical writers and his female bride-to-be. Lurch, having returned to his oblivious self with the threat of the "dreaded" industrial incident violation apparently gone, asked, "Do you think the Funkster has banged Freddie yet… the Funkster being George Funkel, one of our technical writers… all 5 foot, 90 pounds of him… and Freddie being Elfriede Hollenstein, his bride to be… all six foot, 190 pounds of her. The blonde, blue-eyed and very Germanic Elfriede, an apparent native of one of Wisconsin's Germanic tribes, wasn't bad looking either in an "I could beat the snot out of any two of you guys" sort of way.

The Flake observed that in all probability such a banging had not yet occurred and the two were most likely very close to sniffing virgins. As proof of his assertion, he put forth the following. Again, what follows may not be an exact quote, but it's pretty damn close: "If such a banging had occurred, with the Funkster being the banger, and thus on top, and Freddie being the bangee, and thus on the bottom, the Funkster would have placed himself in great physical peril and in all likelihood would now be in a full body cast, for in response to his initial cherry popping bang, ol' Freddie would have responded with a counter forward and upward thrust of those powerful hips of hers and plastered the poor bastard, all 90 pounds of him, onto the ceiling above them." The Flake proceeded to illustrate his statement with a very aggressive thrust of his hips and then continued, "The result: an emergency call for an ambulance, an extended hospital stay, a full body cast for the Funkster and the forced imposition of a long and frustrating period of celibacy upon the about to be nuptualated couple… in other words, lots of pain and suffering, and no satisfaction… a truly inhumane situation!"

The tribal clotch pretty much agreed with the Flake, believing that this fellow brave… as diminutive as he was… and his planned matrimonial pairing… as odd as it was… still deserved better. In fact, humanity demanded it. If the Funkster was to avoid what would surely be a honeymoon tragedy when he made his initial jump into Freddie's saddle of love, he'd need an innovative technique, a device of some sort, or a new body to insure his safety and prevent great bodily harm to himself and great psychological damage to his beloved Freddie. The tribal clotch, motivated by its humanity and sensitivity to the needs of others, particularly in all matters sex-u-al, quickly came to the realization that: 1) the chances were quite slim that the Funkster could acquire even a semi-new body and 2) given his present body, there was no technique, sans an unacceptable "coitus chastitus beltus abstinitus", to prevent the much feared and impending honeymoon tragedy. Thus the tribal gathering concentrated its discussion on a series of devices that the Funkster and his beloved Freddie could employ to prevent the necessity of that emergency ambulance call and still bring smiles of satisfaction to the faces of both, smiles that would surely fade into a duet of exhausted snores of relief… so the tribe thought along the lines of an a kind of anti-chastity belt.

After much discussion, the braves came to favor Magic Mike's solution to this vexing human problem and potential tragedy. The magic man proposed the utilization of a device made of strong elastic belts, a kind of double harness. The harness would attach the Funkster to the Freddie so that every time ol' Freddie thrust those powerful hips of hers up in response to a Funkster's banging thrust down and thus catapulting the diminutive Funkster into the air, the harness, being elastic, would slam the Funkster back into Freddie's saddle of love, the loss of contact in the process being viewed by all present as minimal, most likely erotic, and easily controlled by having four sizes of the harness available (large, medium, small and very small… the Funkster presumably requiring the very small). Magic Mike named the device "the Sexual Safe Re-entry Reverse Catapult" or, for short, the "2S-2R-Cat".

Doc Frah-ken-steen, our Human Factors guru, immediately raised objections to the use of the word 'reverse' feeling that the term implied that the device was also an aid to anal intercourse, which the group agreed it could under certain circumstances. However, since that was a secondary use from a product and thus Human Factors point of view, the term 'reverse' should be dropped. True the device did catapult the catapultee back into the action and not away from it, thus, technically speaking, reversing the catapultee's trajectory and direction making the term 'reverse' descriptive of the device's functionality when used as originally planned. However, the implication of doing so for a rear re-entry was definitely not the intended primary use of the device and to use the term 'reverse' would, in the commercial world, require a whole new level of human factors testing to work out the usability kinks and to avoid sticky safety and legal issues as well. The rest of the clotch liked the term and thought that it was far too descriptive and appropriate to be dropped.

The tribal collective mind clotted and ideas stopped flowing. In frustration the Flake knocked a coffin nail from his packette of Camels for a smoke to relieve the tension. Back in those days, smoking was OK. Hell it was your patriotic duty and an American right. I used to smoke like a chimney myself. Boy I liked to puff away! Made me feel… well, calm… took away the tension, but I gave it up… couldn't afford it.

Anyway, as Flake tapped his own personal coffin nail against the side of his packette of Camels to more tightly pack the tobacco, he looked up and said, "Hey, it says right here on my packette of cigarettes 'Caution: cigarette smoking may be hazardous to your health'. Just put a warning on the device. That way anybody that wants to use the '2S-2R-Cat' for rear entry can. Expands the potential market, but we're covered legally which is all that counts. Nobody really cares about anyone else's safety unless they can be perceived as not being so and are sued for damages. If a warning can cover the tobacco industry, sure as shit, one can cover us."

A discussion followed about the reason for the warning on a packette of cigarettes, the tribal clotch pretty much concluding that the situation with the 2S-2R-Cat was not analogous since the warning on a packette of cigarettes was required by law and apparently designed to protect the smoker and not the cigarette company.

Then Frank Voltonne, who hardly ever whispered a syllable, held up a package and said, "There's a warning on my pack of Speedo Knife Blades. It says, 'Only to be used to cut paper, wood or cloth. Not to be used to perform circumcisions or autopeotomies'. I know what circumcisions are. Got no idea about autopeotomies. But it's a warning. Maybe something like this one would work."

The magic one, with his vast knowledge of all terminology sexual, all but yelled, "Oh, autopeotomies… they're self castrations. Strange kinda warning. Who the hell would use one of their knives to perform circumcisions and autopeotomies?"

And the Doc chimed in, "Well someone must have or there wouldn't be a warning not to. However, notice that both terms are plural. That implies that their knives could be used for one of each without violating the terms of the warning… even stranger! If that rather poorly written warning covers the Speedo Knife company, surely we can come up with something even better for the 2S-2R-Cat"… which the tribal clotch, after much discussion, did: "This device is not designed and/or tested for rear re-entry activities of a carnal nature. Any individual or individuals using the 2S-2R-Cat for such activities, does so at his or her own risk". Thus the term

111

'reverse' received the Human Factors seal of approval.

With this sticky safety, legal and terminology problem resolved, the 'tribal clotch-idea-clot' broke and the discussion again flowed. All present pretty much agreed that the "2S-2R-Cat" would do the trick, but then another safety problem reared its ugly head. Suppose the Funkster, as the catapultee, being slung back into Freddie's saddle of love, didn't hit the bull's eye. Several members of the tribe expressed great concern that such a miss could cause the Funkster to damage his arrow of love as the "2S-2R-Cat" slammed him back into that love saddle.

Doc Frah-ken-steen suggested that the harness be modified so that it would hold the position of the catapultor's legs (in this case the powerful Freddie and from a usability and safety standpoint more than likely our worst case scenario) raised and bent at the knees and thus keeping the catapultor's thighs at a belly squashing 45-degree angle to the platform of love, i.e., the bed matrimonial. He believed that by so positioning the catapultor's legs (one Freddie, the participant causing our worst case scenario), given that her target was quite large, and given that in all probability the other participant, the Funkster, with an arrow of love that was in all probability quite diminutive as was the rest of him… that is quite small… that the chances of a damaged or a broken arrow were well within acceptable levels of risk tolerance from a human factors perspective. He believed that a user audience definition exercise should be done to verify the physical characteristics of the potential user groups, but for the purposes of initial planning, the present scenario, which came to be known as 'the broken arrow scenario', would suffice. The word 'adjustable' was added to the devices name so that it became "the Adjustable Sexual Safe Re-entry Reverse Catapult" or, for short, the "A-2S-2R-Cat". The tribal clotch gave the device its universal seal of approval. I had to admit that the proposal was ingenious, quite humane and even conceptually human factored. Viva la tribal innovation in the name of all humanity!

With those annoying draft schedules coming due for those dreaded software manuals, the tribal clotch unclotched and returned to their cubes to continue slogging away in the belly of technology's fiercest beast. I thanked my lucky stars that I didn't have to. If memory serves me right, I quietly and unobtrusively retreated to my cubicle to review the schedules and progress reports that my tribe of writers had submitted.

I've attached a sketch of the A-2S-2R Cat drawn by Frank "Shakes" Voltonne, our previously mentioned Senior Technical Illustrator. Remember, he attended the tribal coffee clotch and read that neat Speedo Knife Blade safety warning. Well, as the tribe discussed Magic Mike's proposed harness, ol' Shakes did what he always did at KTI: he illustrated what was for him another inane technical concept… in this case the A-2S-2R-Cat.

Several days after the coffee clotch in question, a plain gray envelop mysteriously appeared in my inbox. It contained the sketch of the A-2S-2R-Cat that I've attached. My guess… Frank didn't want to keep possession of the damn drawing, but thinking it too important to destroy, forwarded it to me for safe keeping… me being the person who had him create those SYS-ONE dot PORNLIB stock certificates and thus someone he could trust under these particular circumstances. Frank being Frank and all…

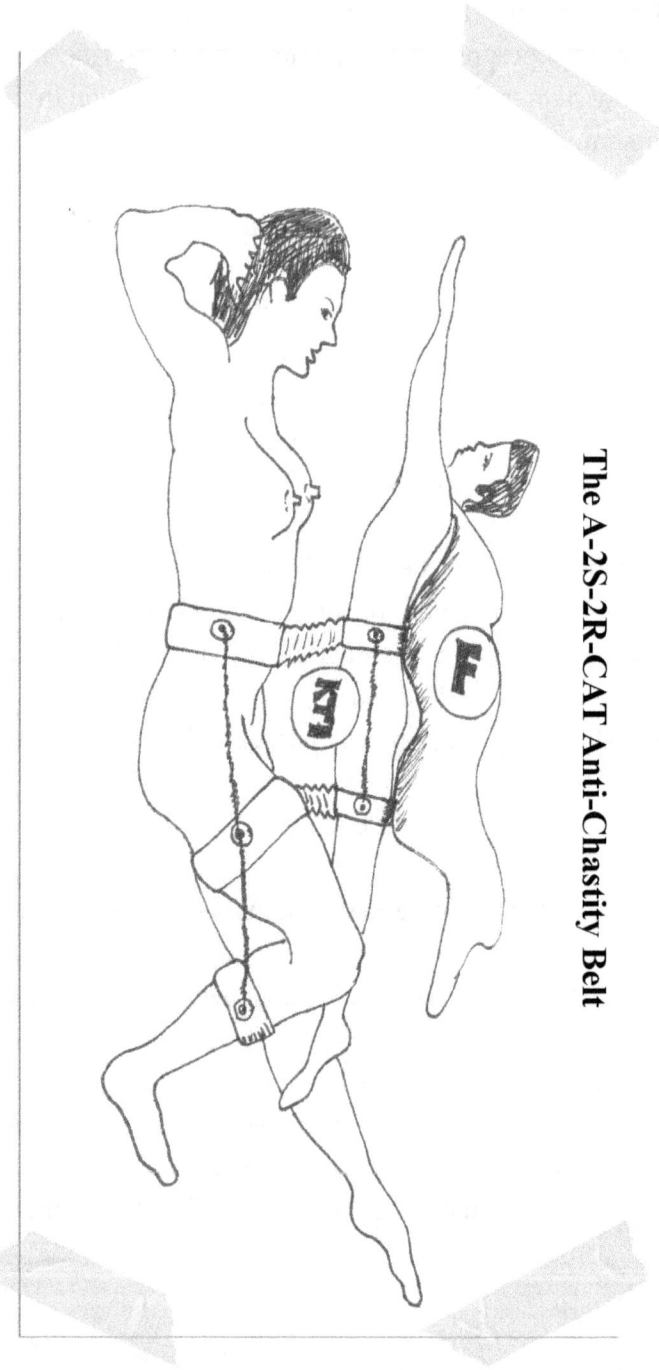

The A-2S-2R-CAT Anti-Chastity Belt

Here's a little question for you to ponder given your ever present fears! After all, what would be the end result of the first successful use of the reverse catapult? Mutually satisfying orgasms, right? Which would lead to more use of the A-2S-2R-Cat... which would lead to what? More babies, potentially lots of babies, right? Did someone in your so-called tribe have an ulterior motive for increasing the stock of humans available? Hmmmmm...

I have thought about this since... well you apparently know since when... but yes it has occurred to me. Why would someone be promoting the creation of more babies? Was there a Mr. Judas Goat in our midst? Could it be Magic Mike or the Doc or even the Flake? These thoughts were just taking form at the time and slowly but surely I was getting scared shitless and even fearing the dark again.

Singing the Auto Accident Blues

Back again, Bob-bo, for another whack at my bank of memories of things past... hopefully minus the smell stuff. After witnessing the latest chapter in that long series of scintillating tribal coffee clotch discussions, I slunk back to my cubicle and closed my cubicle door behind me for some semi-privacy, the 'semi' limitation being imposed by the walls of my office which were semi-high. I plopped into my chair for a morning of progress reports and schedules. The only thing that made such a morning look good was the prospect of me not having to make the progress that I was reading about, namely in writing those stupid manuals. I checked through the reports and the associated schedules and noted a problem here and there, nothing unusual… nothing that would threaten meeting the product release schedules. Then I came to Lurch's very short progress report, which consisted of one very succinct declarative sentence, "No schedules missed." I thought to myself, "Hell, brevity is the soul of more than just wit. It also prevents boredom and eyestrain." Still, it sounded too good to be true. I turned the page to his schedule and found out why it was in fact too good to be true: he hadn't committed to any. His schedule page was blank. Apparently he had deleted all the dates our beloved project planner had initially set and had not bothered to replace them. Thus technically he had not missed any dates on his schedule since there weren't any.

This was not good since he was writing what we call 'pseudo technical news letters' or as one of the more articulate programming managers called them, 'pa-suado' TNLs. The term 'pseudo TNL' sounds complicated but it really isn't. Lurch was writing the proposed changes to other manuals, many written in other KTI labs, to reflect the code changes that our new software would require in other components of the system. Pseudo TNLs were just a series of requested changes to manuals written elsewhere… some in the Kingston lab, some in other labs. In our case, many of these other labs were located all over Mother Earth.

I felt that a disaster of nuclear proportions was impending and immediate management action was required. The Lurch Screw Magazine imbroglio was a pimple on the ass of my career, comparatively speaking. Missing schedules was a whole different matter. If Tadd missed the release schedules for those pseudo TNLs and caused the delay of the release of the product, I'd be taken down to corporate and defenestrated from the 50th floor of our belov-ed headquarters, my career splatting all over the sidewalks of Manhattan.

The truth was that the most important thing for any manager, including a lowly Pubs manager such as yours truly, was to meet those sacred schedules. Sure it'd be nice if the manuals and the pseudo TNLs were complete and technically accurate and even nicer if the information could actually be used (a rare accomplishment), but incomplete and inaccurate technical information could be corrected later and if the technical information was unusable, all the better, since KTI could then sell the customers some more education and technical support for a very pretty penny. But missing schedules caused a delay in the release of the product and a delay in the collection of revenue. Your ass was grass, as they say, if you missed a schedule and caused a delay in the collection of revenue. No one cared much about the other stuff, at least until it caused other problems like an increase in maintenance costs. But it'd be many months and maybe even years before that happened and the perps would have moved on long ago, probably with a nice juicy promotion.

As far as I can remember, KTI had never held up the release of a product because the information package was inadequate or even grossly inadequate. And as to usability, you could tell it didn't count for much, for when management had to cut expenses, it always cut the human factors group first. And if you really didn't think it counted for much, you organizationally placed this easily and quickly cut group under tech pubs management, the smallest and weakest organization in the development lab… which is where it now was in the form of one human factors engineer, our own Doc Fran-ken-steen, and two co-ops who changed every six months, supporting a development effort of many hundreds of programmers all over KTI's technology creation.

With great fear and trepidation, I called Tadd and asked him to bring the drafts of the pseudo TNLs that he'd written to my office for review. He said he couldn't do so since he had a very important appointment with his personal automobile mechanic and couldn't miss it. There then occurred a telephone conversation that dragged me into Tadd's own personal twilight zone when I yelled in disbelief, "Your what?"

"My personal automobile mechanic, Buddy."

"Your personal mechanic Buddy?"

"Yes, Buddy. I have to confront the unscrupulous bastard. He's holding my old Mercedes hostage."

"Hostage?"

"Yes. And he's threatening to push her over the cliff behind his shop if I don't pay him."

"Why the hell don't you just pay him? Do you have the money?"

"Yes, but I'm refusing. It's a matter of principle."

"Principle?"

"Yes, principle. Insurance should pay. Not me."

"Your insurance won't pay?"

"No, someone else's. The kid's who hit me."

"You got hit by another car?"

"Yes, at the light at the cutoff to the Thruway in town… last month. The bastard ran a red light and slammed into me. He asked if I'd be willing to take cash rather than have the accident reported to his insurance company. He assured me he'd pay for everything in cash. Since he already had points on his license, he wanted to avoid getting it suspended and then having his insurance triple. Seemed like a good kid at the time."

"And your Mercedes?"

"Well it didn't seem like all that big of a deal. My front door on passenger's side was smashed in but the automobile was drivable."

I was hooked, "Did he pay you? Seems like no insurance company was involved?"

"Well I drove to the address on his license to collect and it was his father's business address. His father owned an auto body shop. When I went to collect, the kid said to me, 'I've never seen you before. What accident?'"

"He said, 'What accident?'"

"Yes. He took me out to his automobile and it was completely fixed. After he smashed into my Mercedes, the front end of his automobile had been smashed in and had to be towed away, but now there was no evidence of damage. So I submitted a claim through my insurance against his and took my car to Buddy's."

119

"And?"

"Buddy repaired my Mercedes, but the kid's insurance refused to pay claiming that no accident had been reported and as far as they were concerned, no accident had occurred… which is a crock… and my insurance refused to pay."

"Don't you have collision?"

"No. I forgot to get it. But it really doesn't matter. As a reputable business man, Buddy has a professional obligation to be patient and wait for the insurance payment to come through. I got to get over there. He says if I don't pay him $1,942.17 cash by high noon today, over she goes. I've got to get over there."

The phone went dead. I slammed down my receiver and ran over to Tadd's cubicle which was three aisles away. I turned the corner and breathlessly entered his cubicle. No Tadd. At least there wasn't a copy of the latest Screw Magazine displayed on his desk. I thanked God for small blessings and walked slowly back to my cubicle.

Tadd was technically a genius. He had one of the highest scores ever recorded on the P-A-T, the programmer aptitude test, and back then, you had to score well to get an offer from KTI… even to be a technical writer. He scored off the charts. Not only did he ace the test, he aced the KTI programming school. Got an 'Outstanding' as his final grade, one of only two in the class of 60 plus, most of who were to be programmers. But like Mollie Mau-Mau, there was a screw loose somewhere in that genius brain of his and that loose screw made him unable to function in the world at large where almost everyone else existed and even in KTI's world where lots of dysfunctional people functioned quite well.

I still remember Tadd's first day. Seems like ancient history now. I wasn't a manager then… just one of the grunts schlepping away, writing those soul deadening manuals, those SRLs, Software Reference Library manuals, for those of us unfortunate enough to be in the know. This tall and somewhat gawky and quite poorly dressed individual entered my cubicle. He offered his hand, which I reflexively shook, and he said, "Hi, I'm Richard Tadd, the new guy." I swiveled my chair to face him as he sat uninvited in the visitor's chair to my left. I gave him a quick visual once over. I noticed three things about him immediately. First, he could use a bath. Second his teeth could use a good brushing and third, he was wearing those low cut jet boots on his feet and apparently no sox.

Not one to beat around the bush, he said, "Could you lend my fifty dollars?" carefully pronouncing each syllable as would, say, a lecturing college professor.

Initially, I was stunned and blurted out, "What?"

He continued, "I can repay you in two weeks when I get another paycheck. I didn't realize that it'd be so long before I received my next check."

I said, "Mr. whatever-your-name-is…"

"It's Tadd, Richard Tadd."

"Well Mr. Richard Tadd, I don't know you from Adam. Why the hell should I lend you anything?"

"Of course, you know me. I've already introduced myself. To repeat and augment my initial introduction, I'm Richard Tadd, a newly minted technical writer fresh out of programming school. We're assigned to the same department. There. Now we know each other much better. Could I borrow fifty dollars from you?"

I said, quite distinctly, pronouncing each syllable very carefully, "Fuck no. Not just fuck no, but a flying fuck no. Besides, even if I were to consider your rather cryptic self-introduction adequate, I have a policy of never lending money to someone who doesn't wear sox, and you're not wearing sox. No loan!"

That unperturbed Olympic smile of his spread across his face as he leaned over and said, "But I am wearing sox" and he pulled the tops of his sox up, carefully and one at a time, above his jet boots. They were those thin stretch sox and they were frayed and filthy. One was purple and the other red, both with some inane design in black thread decorating their tops. If he threw them against my cubicle wall, chances were they'd stick.

I had to admit that I knew him better than I wanted to now and he was wearing in fact sox, so I said, "How about ten bucks?"

He beamed "Sold!" as I reached into my back pocket to retrieve my wallet, extracted a ten dollar bill and hand it to him. He grabbed the ten dollar bill and abruptly left without so much as a 'thank you'. I could hear him say to Magic Mike in the next cubicle, "Hi, I'm Richard Tadd, the newly minted technical writer in your department."

He never did pay me back. It seemed like he was always broke. As the Polish Prince said, "Lurch means well. He'd give you the shirt off his back, but he never has a spare shirt." Pretty much sums it up. The magic man never got paid either. And here I was, now a manager, still holding the bag for one Richard Tadd. The more things change…

Maybe things don't change as much as you think.

A-men, brother!

Texas Hots at George Kanockapopulous'

To pick up where I left off yesterday, with Lurch off to save his Mercedes from the clutches of his personal mechanic, the evil Buddy… there wasn't much I could do until later in the afternoon, so I wandered over to James's office to see if he was up for lunch. As they say, it's Wednesday so it must be George Kanockapopulous'. Excuse the spelling. I never could get that Greek miser's name right. Too many letters arranged strangely.

George was very old and gnarled… a god damn Greek Oppa Loopa of the Texas hot weiner… a veritable maestro of that precious and addictive culinary delight… but the bastard was stingier than an unreformed Christmas-hating Scrooge. Every Wednesday, the Polish Prince and I would drive into town for a lunch of George's Texas Hot Weiners, the best in Kingston, perhaps the best in the universe. Like I said, the damn things were addictive. George's hot sauce was a heart-burning, indescribable treat, particularly when covered with diced onions. I laid off the chili topping… you know, the beans… the weiners and buns were just an excuse to taste that sauce. Just thinking about those babies makes my mouth water even today. The damn things were so tasty they actually gave you a buzz. God, what I'd give for a couple of those babies now.

George's Texas hots ain't the only hot thing you can't have anymore.

Go fuck yourself!

Back then, the Polish Prince and I consumed four and sometimes six of George's culinary delights every Wednesday. Sometimes this guy named Larry joined us. I didn't know Larry or much about him since he never spoke. Most of the year he dressed in this long dark blue overcoat, a fedora, and… get this… gloves. Ever see a guy eat Texas hot wieners… actually ONE Texas hot weiner since he only ordered one… with gloves. With his fedora pulled down close to his eyes, all you could see of him was the lower two-thirds of his ashen face. He was an old-time KTI-er and James's friend from his hardware days. Larry was older than we were and James said he had joined the Marines at sixteen and fought the Japs in the Pacific. He looked it. He died of a heart attack a year later and thus did not join us for his single Texas hot wiener after that.

As the story goes, a fast food chain had offered to pay George a small fortune for the recipe for his sauce but he had steadfastly refused. The two guys who worked the counter for him, James the Counter Guy and Jism, his faithful companion, kept urging George to take the deal. Their encouragement wasn't all that altruistic since George had no living relatives that they knew of and they believed they were in his will. When they couldn't convince George to sell the recipe, they decided to steal it and sell it on their own. George was as wily as Odysseus and pretty much knew what James the Counter Guy and Jism, his faithful companion, were up to from the get go, so he made his sauce late at night when no one was around, thus jealously guarding his secret recipe.

James, Larry and I grabbed seats at the counter since the back tables were full of very loud teen agers. The high school was just up the street. From behind the counter, James the Counter Guy yelled over the noon time din "How many?" I raised four fingers as did James and James yelled, "… and Larry will have his usual."

James the Counter Guy yelled back, "A solo for the fedora? Right?"

James yelled, "Right… one solo for the fedora. Where's George?"

James the Counter Guy yelled back over the teenage din, "The greedy bastard went home this morning. He was here all night making another batch of sauce."

We knew of the attempts to steal George's recipe since both James the Counter Guy and Jism, his faithful companion, spoke openly about their plans with us. I yelled "Got the recipe figured out yet?"

"Not yet, but we're close. Hell, we all know that George is a greedy bastard and that fast food chain still wants to buy his recipe… for a small fortune. They called him again last week. Told him he could use his recipe here at the shop after he sold it to them. Just as long as it was used only here. Why the fuck won't he sell? He could make a mint and still keep selling his Texas hots right here. Anyway, we're close to figuring out the recipe."

"How close?"

"Got all the ingredients except one. We know about all the usual stuff and all he does is cook the damn stuff in this huge pot. But there's this secret ingredient that makes the sauce George's sauce

125

and we can't figure it out."

"Got any ideas?"

As he placed two paper plates of George's Texas hots before both James and me, he yelled "We're pretty sure it's a spice of some kind and it's something that you wouldn't suspect. Jism and me have tried making the sauce at home and the damn stuff never tastes like George's. It's good, but it ain't George's. We figure we're one spice away."

James and I inhaled our four Texas hots and waited for Larry to finish his solo. Larry was a very fastidious masticator and he rushed his mastication for no man. As he slowly chewed away, I watched several teenagers come up to the cash register and pay for takeout orders. It was a ritual I'd seen many times. The bags of orders were lined up along the counter alongside the cash register. One of the pimply bastards came up to the cash register and handed James a ten dollar bill and a five. James took the ten and put it in a cigar box on the counter behind him, rang up the sale and gave the teen ager change from the five. The teenager then chose a packette of cigarette papers from a rack alongside the cash register and left with two bags.

The rack held all kinds of cigarette papers, all kinds of flavors. Banana seemed to be the favorite. As I watched, James the Counter Guy gave me one of those knowing 'there's more here than meets the eye' wink and smiled, "Choose any pack of papers… on the house."

I took a packette of banana flavored papers and thanked James the Counter Guy as I stuffed the bright yellow packette in my shirt pocket.

The Polish Prince nudged me with his elbow, leaned over and whispered to me, "What the fuck was that all about. You'd think these kids could afford a pack of cigarettes instead of rolling their own."

Later, on the ride back to the Lab, I explained to James that George's sold another very popular product, this one strictly vegetarian in nature. I smiled at the Polish Prince and said, "That Mary Jane that James the Counter Guy is always talking about in such loving terms, is not his girl friend. When he says Mary Jane fucked him up last night and he sounds like it's a good thing, that's because it is. He ain't complainin', James me boy. He's braggin'! Mary Jane ain't his lady refusin' to put out... it's weed... you know... marijuana, that mary jane!"

I thought to myself "Maybe I've found a good supplier who could sell to me in bulk". I didn't smoke weed much what with my asthma, but I needed another source of income. The garnishee was taking a pretty big chunk from my pay check making it close to impossible for me to exist. I was considering selling mary jane to the growing number of recent new college hires who definitely pranced to a different drummer. The market was there... lots of customers with a need, no ready supplier to meet the need, and lots of cash to spend. A dumbfounded and oblivious James yelled, "Well fuck me and the horse I rode in on!" as he drove toward the Lab... sentiments that echoed through that addled and desperate brain of mine.

Later that year George died. Fell deader than a door-nail onto the floor at his shop while making his famous sauce late one night. James the Counter Guy and Jism, his faithful companion, arrived at work and found the bastard lying face down behind the counter in front of the stove where a huge pot of his famous sauce bubbled away. Here's the kicker. Know what they found clutched in his grubby Greek miserly fist? A big bag of marijuana! A fuckin' bag of marijuana! Explained everything. No wonder we got a small buzz from his Texas hots and thought the damn things were addictive… because they were! And ol' George couldn't sell his recipe to that fast-food chain, not with his secret ingredient being a fist full of mary jane. No way, Jose, and neither could James the Counter Guy and Jism, his faithful companion.

It's been a long time since I last visited George's and occasionally on Wednesdays I stare down at my Mac and Cheese institutional lunch and thirst for a couple of George's Texas hots… even a solo… even just one of those gourmet delights, Fedora style. The joint… that is George's Texas Hots Weiners… stayed open after George died and James the Counter Guy and Jism, his faithful companion, continued making that addictive sauce for those Texas hots now that they knew George's secret spice. I heard that their first couple of batches of sauce sold out in hours. The dynamic duo adjusted the recipe PDQ to avoid the attention of the local constabulary, but that was years ago. I'm not sure ol' George Kanockapopulous' even exists anymore. Probably not. C'est la vie, mother fucker. Inexorable time marches on!

Come on, Mr. Flashlight Bobb. Write about how you went to ol' George's funeral to be sure that there was a body.

Look, you prick, I went out of respect for George Kanockapopulous. No other reason. Igor went with me too… out of respect for ol' George. If you want to think about something, think about how time marches on like a god damn Nazi storm trooper destroying everything in its path.

128

Lurch Unspent So Over She Went

On the way back to the Lab, we had to pass the evil Buddy's Auto Repair Shop, which was across the street from the Lab's largest parking lot. James slowed down as we passed three police patrol cars and a group of people standing on the street-side of the evil Buddy's garage.

I yelled to James, "Pull over! Pull into Buddy's. There's Lurch." I could see his bushy unkempt head sticking up above the crowd. He was yelling something as a policeman pushed him back. James parked his car and we jumped out and ran toward the crowd. Lurch was yelling, "That n'er-do-well pushed my Mercedes into the ravine," and sure enough, as we got closer, I could see the grill to Lurch's Mercedes sticking into the air just above a steep embankment.

The evil Buddy was pointing at Lurch and yelled, "Pay yer fuckin' bill, you asshole, and you'll get yer fuckin' piece of shit Mercedes back."

Lurch reached over the much shorter policeman, pointed at the evil Buddy and yelled, "If you were a reputable businessman, you'd follow accepted business practice and await payment from the insurance company."

The evil Buddy yelled back, "Reputable my ass. Pay up. You owe me $1,942 smackaroos plus interest and the cost of that window you busted! I'm pressing charges, Billy,"… Billy apparently being the first name of the policeman restraining Lurch and whom the evil Buddy knew well enough to address by his first name.

Officer Billy spun Lurch around and pushed him face first against the shop's exterior wall. He pulled Lurch's arms behind him, handcuffed him and yelled, "You're under arrest for assault and vandalizing private property." He then started reciting ol' Lurch his Miranda rights. Lurch yelled, "I didn't assault anyone! I didn't vandalize anything! I'm the victim here! Buddy assaulted me! He broke his own window when he pushed me through the door! He not only assaulted me, he used me as the vandalizing destructive object that broke his window! He vandalized his own window! I made no conscience attempt to break his precious glass."

Officer Billy ignored Lurch and continued reciting him his Miranda rights, including the part about saying anything that could be used against you in a court of law. When Officer Billy completed his recitation, he yelled at Lurch, "You just admitted to breaking that window, wise ass. You're a god damn vandal, that's what you are. You assaulted a private citizen and vandalized his property!" and then he perp walked the unsteady Lurch over to the closest patrol car, opened the rear door, shoved him into the back seat, banging Lurch's head against the patrol car's exterior above the cruiser's rear door as he did so, and then he slammed the patrol car's door.

Officer Billy walked back to the evil Buddy and said, "See you tonight… eight… bowling." The evil Buddy grinned from ear to ear and shook his head 'yes'. Officer Billy returned to his patrol car, jumped in and took off, rear wheels squealing, lights flashing and siren blaring. I was pretty sure that I'd seen the last of Lurch at least for today.

That whole police business still makes me queasy… just writing about it makes me feel like blowing chunks. Brings back lots of very bad memories. But I was told to write it all down, so write it down I do. Somehow it's supposed to help, but it pretty much scares the shit out of me and makes me feel bad. Feeling bad is good? Sounds pretty fuckin' stupid to me, but what I do know is I'm in here and they're out there. And I ain't gettin' out any time soon with or without this fuckin' journal.

Anyway, to get back to feeling bad, once those bastards in blue got your ass, your ass is grass. Fuck Miranda and the horse HE rode in on! Like some god damn legalese chant mumbled by an asshole as he beats the shit out of you is going to protect you from getting the shit beat out of you by that bastard… the same one who's beating the shit out of you. And as to that pen is mightier than the sword crap. Tell me this… would you rather be stabbed by a pen or a sword? Fuckin' justice is as fuckin' justice does! Whoa, there Mr. Ward Bobb my man, slow down. Catch your breath. All that's in the past… and long gone. You have other more pressing worries.

Anyway, to get back to someone else getting the shit beat out of him by the cops, later I learned that Officer Billy was the evil Buddy's cousin, William Vander Meer, and that the evil Buddy was related not only to Officer Vander Meer but to approximately half the police force, many of whom shared the same last name. Things did not look good for Lurch, but then again they never did.

When I got back to my cubicle, I called Lurch's lead writer and the planner for the project, Dick "Cardinal" Clemens, and asked him to meet me at Lurch's office. Why the "Cardinal" nom de plume? Because as the lead writer and planner, his blessing was required before a scheduling commitment could be made or changed by one of the grunt writers… like a sinner seeking dispensation for a mortal sin he was about to commit. To change a schedule, you had to kiss his metaphoric ring, so to speak. I liked the Cardinal but was annoyed by his laissez faire approach to being a lead writer and planner. His approach to his job was not unique to the job for he took the same laissez faire approach to his entire life, except for anything involving his wallet which he squeezed tightly and rarely showed in public. He had this uncanny ability to disappear from a restaurant or bar just before the check showed up… leaving the rest of us tribal schmucks to foot his share of the bill. It was like he had this anti-check invisible shield which prevented him and a check from appearing in the same room at the same time. He could have been a character in an H. G. Wells novel… at least as far as disappearing before paying a check was concerned.

I stopped at the key cabinet in the secretary's cubicle, got the keys to Lurch's desk and file cabinet and walked over to Lurch's cubicle. The Cardinal was already there, sitting on Lurch's desk reading a magazine that Lurch had left there. It was one of those poetry magazines, this one a quarterly published by the local state university.

As I entered the cubicle, the Cardinal asked me, "You ever read any of Lurch's poetry?"

I said "Never. I knew he wrote poetry but I never read any of it."

"Well you ought to. Here's one he wrote about making his wife scream during sex. It's titled, 'Missy's Many Songs of Love' and it's a blow by blow verse description of him screwing the shit out of his wife and the different sounds she makes for each of his techniques sex-u-al. It's very personal to say the least. It'll give you a hard-on and some of it even rimes. Listen to these lines '… and I love those little staccato piggy squeals as I massage her with my tongue. Her buttocks stiffen and she shivers as she baths me with her come.' Here's another part. Apparently Lurch is hung like a horse."

"Enough! That's more information than I need to know about Mr. Richard Tadd. Look, I'm here to get his project file to review. I want to see outlines and drafts of all those pseudo TNLs he's supposed to be writing and review the committed dates."

The Cardinal looked up from the poetry periodical and asked, "Where's Tadd? Why isn't he here with us?"

"He's been arrested."

"Arrested? What for?"

"Assaulting the evil Buddy of Buddy's Auto Repair Shop fame."

"Over that old Mercedes? I told him to junk the damn thing. It isn't worth the two grand it'd cost to fix. I also told him that Buddy was a scam artist and related to most of the police force and at least one judge, but apparently Buddy gave him the lowest estimate. Why are you so concerned about his TNLs and dates? The project isn't shipping until next year."

"You tell me that Lurch is having his junker fixed by a scam artist related to half the police force and at least one judge. He's been arrested for supposed assault on said scam artist by a policeman who's probably the scam artist's cousin, and you ask me why I'm concerned about Tadd's work and his professional judgment? I just got his progress report and he's erased all the dates... all the source material dates, all the review dates, all the production dates..."

every fuckin' date. Where the hell were you? You're the lead writer. In the future, you're going to wipe his ass after he shits… that's how close you're going to work with that bastard."

The Cardinal was indignant: "Hey, this is the Cardinal you're talking to. Last I saw, all those dates were in there. I never gave him permission to change anything. For cryin' out loud, I'm not a baby sitter. I plan his work, I don't actually do it. I never gave him the OK to change anything."

"Well guess what? He did and you should have known. He's a junior writer and you're his lead. You're going to baby sit that bastard to be sure he doesn't screw up. He's writing 13 pseudo TNLs for 5 different labs, six if you include us. If he fails, I fail, and if I fail, you can be damn sure you'll fail."

"What's gotten into you? This is very un-bear like. This isn't related to that Screw Magazine business?"

Why'd the Cardinal refer to your behavior as 'un-bear' like? Shouldn't he have said 'un-flashlight' like?

Maybe because he's not a fuckin' idiot like you!

The Cardinal was sharp and knew how KTI management worked. He monitored all the rumors and was considered the official rumor monger for our organization. If anyone so much as whispered a rumor in a closet to himself, the Cardinal knew about it. He even started strategically invented rumors when necessary to protect the organization, for rumor played an important, if not officially recognized, part in management's decision making. After all, reality is what people think it is. No?

Right, Bobbo, remember that Irr Irr Irv memo business?

Dick knew where Lurch kept his work files. I unlocked the file cabinet and he retrieved the files from the top file drawer. There were all the outlines and a complete progress report with all the dates. The Cardinal smiled at me coyly and said, "Looks like Lurch just sent you a back level draft of his schedule. In fact, he sent you a blank form." He smiled and left the cubicle.

My curiosity peaked by the Cardinal's earlier remarks, I opened the poetry periodical and took a peek at Tadd's poem describing his having sex with his wife. There was a suggestively lurid pen and ink drawing on the facing page of what appeared to be a bushy headed Tadd with his head stuffed between what I supposed were his wife's legs. I closed the periodical and shoved it under some papers strewn about his desk and since I had the key to his desk, I considered unlocking his desk drawers and seeing what else he had hidden there. Then I had second thoughts. There's just some stuff I didn't want to know and, to be truthful, I feared what I might find. Sometimes ignorance is bliss and sometimes it's a strategy. I wasn't sure which this was but I really didn't care. I took Tadd's progress report with the completed schedule along with all the pseudo TNL outlines and headed back to my cubicle secure in the knowledge that my small world and the larger world of KTI were safe from the bastard at least for the afternoon.

Do you really think that reality is what people think it is? Didn't some English philosopher kick a rock and say, "Thus I refute you!"

135

For once I agree with you. There is a reality and it may not be the one that everyone else agrees on, rock or no rock. People can be blind to what stares them in the face. Just because they can't or won't see it, doesn't mean it doesn't exist! As to Mr. Richard Tadd, he existed all right, but what I saw was a really squirrelly dude who looked screwy enough to be one of those god damn pre-Morlock Judas Goats, but too fuckin' insane to Judas anyone but himself.

Fashionable Anarchy Reigns in Creepdom's Softball World

I had just begun reviewing Lurch's actual progress and work when my phone rang saving me from this most odious of tasks. It was the Flake: "Hey Bear, dance your ass over to my cube. The shirts are finally in for the softball team… all 57 varieties. I need help sorting through them to make sure we got what we ordered. With the first game being tonight and all, we gotta get these shirts in the hands of our idiot creeps before that stupid go-home bell rings." This order verification process was going to be a pain in the ass. More complicated than sorting through project reports and schedules… more complicated than you could ever imagine… but still, much preferred to slogging through Tadd's shit.

We'd ordered shirts, perhaps jerseys is a better term, for the departmental softball team. We competed in one of the local KTI recreational softball leagues… the "B-league modified fast pitch"… translated "no windmill "… and not only did the guys (and one gal) on the team order jerseys, but so did just about everyone else in Pubs as well.

At first, I thought that the ordering process would be a snap since virtually all the creeps and creepettes agreed to red jerseys, white collars with white block letters and numbers with only one exception… there was always at least one exception. Unfortunately, that agreement was the high point of the process. Then the tribe reverted to character and the ordering process became an organizational nightmare, as was the case in most of what we tried to do as a function, for we were, in truth, a non-functioning function socially speaking. The much feared pubs anarchy yet again reared its disorganized and very ugly head. It wasn't Kansas, Dorothy; it was Creepdom… where all our pee-yellow brick roads always led us to the Oz of anarchy.

First, the team could not agree on an official team name for the front on the jersey. Ought to be a simple choice, right? After all, the name of our organization was 'Publications' or 'Pubs' for short. Either would suffice, right? There wasn't much difference, right? Choose one and go with it, right? Well, in Creepdom, not right!

Some wanted the abbreviated "PUBS" to be our official name since, as technical writers their reasoning went, we should value succinctness. Others felt that our official name should be "PUBLICATIONS" since, as technical writers, we should value completeness. The first group advocating 'succinctness' also argued that since we had to pay by the letter, succinctness also cost less as was usually the case. The second group valuing 'completeness' argued that since the first ten letters of the name were part of the base cost of a jersey, the word "PUBLICATIONS" was not actually eight more letters from a cost standpoint, but only two. Thus at 15 cents an additional letter, 'completeness' only added an additional 30 cents to the cost of each jersey, hardly a heavy economic burden to bear in order to make such an important statement regarding our profession. And there were two "special orders": one for a light blue jersey with dark blue lettering for our secretary Phyllis Kopke, who claimed she didn't look very good in red and who became "the Lady in Blue" ever after; and one for a red jersey with the name "Norma Jean's Dream Machine" on the front of the jersey… this one for our own Magic Mike who was obsessed with Marilyn Monroe.

To resolve this vexatious nomenclature impasse, the Flake and I convened a series of negotiations between the two competing ideologies. Each ideology elected two representatives to negotiate for their position. No one represented our Lady in Blue or Norma Jean's Dream Machine. Even after a long series of these negotiations, ideological intransigence ruled and neither side would bend. At one point, the debate became so heated that the confrontation became physical. The lead representative for succinctness, Georgia Longstreet, all six-foot, 200 pounds of her, whom we dubbed Georgie Girl and who also happened to be the only female actually on the softball team (our shortstop and best hitter)… well Georgie Girl attacked Stubby McNeill, the lead representative for completeness (and our second baseman and lead-off hitter). Georgie Girl grabbed ol' Stubby by his tie, lifted him off the ground and threatened to strangle him. From his raised position due to being held off the ground by the tie, Stubby looked like he was about to bite a chunk out of Georgie Girl's left breast and not for erotic pleasure or nutritional sustenance. The Flake and I quickly stepped in and separated the two before either could put his or her battle plan into full effect. We had to move the two ideological camps to separate cubicles and continue the negotiations via teleconferencing.

The negotiations continued for three days, always over lunch.

Things were getting pretty nasty. Writers working on the same project but of different team-name ideologies refused to communicate with each other. There was even one instance of sabotage where one writer shuffled the punch card deck of another writer and destroyed a week's worth of work. The Lady in Blue and Norma Jean's Dream Machine were being officially shunned by both groups as ideologically ignorant miscreants unconcerned with the standing of our organization in particular and of the technical writing profession in general both within and without the hallowed halls of KTI. And most important, our precious luncheon routines were being disrupted.

The solution was simple but economically unacceptable to both ideologies. We could let the proponents of each ideology use their preferred team name, but there was a catch. If we did so, we'd lose the group rate for the base cost of each jersey, raising the cost of each jersey by five bucks. Each ideology would go along with this solution provided the other ideology paid for the difference since that other side was obviously wrong and was thus responsible for the additional expense. The Flake and I ended the controversy by agreeing to pay the additional $235, which, unbeknownst to all concerned, we'd pilfer from the end-of-season party fund. So in the end and unbeknownst to all concerned, both sides, along with the Lady in Blue and Norma Jean's Dream Machine, paid for the additional base cost of each jersey, which seemed pretty fair to me, ideology aside. So in the end, we allowed each tribal member to choose the name for the team he or she wanted on the front of his or her jersey.

Then we had to deal with the back of the jerseys which had the individual's chosen name and his or her chosen number. Our checking ordeal continued. It took forever. There were seven

139

'69's, 13 '1's, one '666', several '13's, one '796666' (which was apparently someone's KTI man number), one '?', one 802,701 (my number) and sundry others, most seemingly chosen at random. The names on the back of the jersey above the numbers were pretty much the tribal nom de plumes although our second baseman Stubby McNeill had 'NOYFB' above his number (the above mentioned '?') which we all knew meant 'none of your fucking business'. I chose 'Time Traveler' and not either of my nom de plumes.

So you didn't choose 'Dancing Bear' and you didn't choose 'Flashlight Bobb', right? Perhaps you could be a bit more forthcoming and tell us why you chose 'Time Traveler'... sounds awfully familiar.

Look, you intrusive asshole, it's my journal and my life... and I'm writing it for me. If you must know, I chose that name because I was tired of being called Flashlight Bobb. How would you feel if you were called Flashlight Bobb?

All the jerseys checked out except for the one ordered by Phyllis Kopke who claimed she did not look good in red. She had ordered a light blue jersey with dark blue lettering and her jersey turned out to be a see-through material with ironic black lettering spelling out 'Lady Blue'... the size?... a daunting triple X. She had stated on the order form 'no number' and so to top her order off, below her chosen name were the words 'no number'. Our Lady in Blue took the jersey to the ladies room and changed into it. She returned to the Flake's cube wearing said jersey as a very short dress with a black belt at the waist. She was thrilled with the look and accepted the jersey as delivered. We were thrilled too... she looked good enough to eat… given the skimpy black bra and lace panty combination she was wearing beneath her shear jersey-dress. Our Lady in Blue would be the belle of Creepdom's soft ball team when she attended the games this season and, I might add, the celebrations at the Bridge Circle after what unfortunately turned out to be her last season, her fate being a whole other story yet to be told.

Good enough to eat? Her last? Why not tell your version of the rest of her story now? Hiding something?

I'm not hiding anything. I'm being something you aren't… discrete! I'll tell the rest of her story and its terrible implications when the time's right. There's no rush. I'm not going anywhere any time soon and whatever happens happens. If I don't get to tell the rest of the story… if my time runs out… so be it.

It took all afternoon to check out the jerseys and deliver them. The 'go-home' bell buzzed just as we delivered the last one.

Odyssean Softball, Pubs-Creep Style

Let hands speak for me!

~~This journal interloper is starting to get on my nerves. No matter what I do to hide the damn thing or keep it securely in my possession, I wake up the next day, open my journal to review my latest journal entry… you know, mull over what I wrote… and there's the interloper's fuckin' comments, written in a neat script… sometimes the bastard even writes between the lines. Maybe I~~

141

~~should stop double spacing my entries and at least squeeze him off the page… and if I stop skipping every other page, he won't have any place else to write. Starting today, that's what I'll do… I'll put 'operation squeeze' into effect and force him to leave me alone.~~

God damn you!

With all the jersey's delivered so that all, or at least most, of Creepdom would be sartorially splendid for our season's opening softball game under the lights, I said to the Flake, "Time for our pregame meal!"

We drove to the 7-11 across the railroad tracks from the KTI Rec Club's softball field #7 and bought a six pack of Budweiser and a large bag of Wise potato chips. I parked the Auschwitz on Wheels next to the railroad tracks across from the softball field so that we'd be off company property. Old man Holmes, a teetotaler 'til the day he died, frowned on the consumption of alcohol anywhere and particularly on his company's property, thus setting the policy forever after for KTI… except for the plants and labs in places like Germany where our German brethren and sistren were allowed to 'slack their thirst' as the Germans put it with vending machine beer. Since we did not happen to be in any of those labs at the moment, we were forced to the wrong side of the tracks in the ol' U-S of A for our pre-game meal of Wise potato chips and Bud to make our pre-game preparations complete.

We popped a couple of cans of Bud, gobbled a fistful of chips and chugged the first beer of our pre-game meal. We liked to toss down at least three cans before the first pitch. Took the edge off. We ate the chips believing that if we were to sweat during the game, the extra salt would come in handy. The whole salt thing was a precaution. Better safe than sorry. Besides, it made the beer taste even better.

I took a long slug from my second beer and asked Flake, "Who we playin' tonight?"

The Flake, who always matched me slug for slug, took his required slug from his second Bud and said, "I think it's those green shirt assholes from maintenance." The maintenance department at KTI wore standard issue green shirts and pants, all of the bastards, and clever creatures that they were, they chose to wear green jerseys on the softball field. Apparently variety is not the spice of plant maintenance life.

I stared across the tracks and asked, "That meatball Vinnie goin' to pitch for them?"

The Flake sipped at his Bud and said, "Yup. Rumor has it a fully recovered and conscious Vinnie will be on the mound tonight."

Thinking about those green shirts and their asshole pitcher gave me agita, "I hate those arrogant bastards. Every year they go undefeated and win the fuckin' softball trophy... except for last year. Sure they won the trophy again, but we put one fuckin' blemish on their record... only team to do so... last game of the year... sweet... made up for the first time we played them... if it weren't for the mercy rule, we'd probably still be playin' that first game chasing softballs all over Holmes's little softball acre... God, that was embarrassing."

I took a long gulp of Bud to settle my stomach and continued my tirade, "And why the hell wouldn't the bastards be the perennial champions. The greenies get to recruit all the best hometown athletes what with KTI wanting to fill the plant with as many locals as possible. Good for community relations, I'm told… and damn few locals with college degrees. Hell they can't even qualify as techs in manufacturing. That requires an associate's degree or at least a stint in the military, so off to maintenance it is."

The Flake frowned, "I'm a local and I have a college degree from Harvard."

I smiled, "And you, my ivy-league scum, are the exception that proves the rule."

That meatball, AKA Vinnie the Guinea, was some piece of work. Last year when Vinnie was pitching against us that final game of the season, the batter, who happened to be Georgie Girl, yelled "Throw me another meatball"… meaning of course a fat pitch to hit. She was our clean-up hitter and had already hit a bases loaded double. We were beating those green-shirted bastards by a run at the time. They had already slaughtered us once and were expecting more of the same. Hell, they'd already won the Holmes trophy, named after our esteemed founder William J. Holmes Senior. The Holmes trophy was awarded to the winners of each athletic league regardless of the sport. And winning was a big deal locally and they'd already done it... many times. Their pictures would be on the sports page of the local rag. They'd attend the Holmes Trophy Dinner and be entertained by some famous sports figure after what I am told was a great dinner of surf and turf. I heard that Y. A. Tittle, ol' Yelberton Abraham himself, the great New York Giant Hall of Fame quarterback, spoke last year.

Ol' Vinnie was unused to Georgie Girl's rude treatment of

his famous fastball earlier in the game and was hotter than a firecracker. I saw the whole thing unfold from first base. In his rage, he must have thought that Georgie Girl was referring to his person and not his pitching. Thus in his addled guinea mind, he interpreted Georgie Girl's use of the word "meatball" to be an ethnic slur hurled at him… and by a girl no less, a girl who had already given his fastball such rude treatment. In uncontrolled rage, he charged the batter's box. Georgie Girl… she bats left handed… stepped out of the batter's box, swung at the charging meatball's ankles with her bat, knocking his feet out from under him. He tumbled headfirst into home plate, all 250 very odd Italian-American pounds of the fat guinea bastard, landing with a thud on his fat head. She yelled, "Yer out!" and sure enough, he was… out cold. Because of the incident, the umpire, fearing an all-out brawl, declared the game complete after an incomplete fourth inning and we walked away with a game shortened 3-2 victory, the only loss those maintenance bastards had suffered in living memory.

The Flake pondered for a bit and said, "Ya know, we should have each batter yell 'throw me a meatball' in the first inning. Get that guinea bastard off his game quick."

I finished my second can of Bud and said, "I don't think that's such a good idea. We should wait until we need it… like when they get ahead and we're not hitting Vinnie."

The Flake finished off his second can, "What are the chances of us hitting Vinnie? We got lucky last year. An error, a hit batter, a scratch single, and Georgie Girl's now famous double. Hell, we hadn't scored off the bastard in three years. We gotta rattle his cage before he gets us under that greasy thumb of his. After last year, there's a chance he won't take the bait regardless of when we taunt him, particularly if they're way ahead. But my money's still on that guinea temper of his."

"I see your point. I stand corrected. Get that fuckin' Vinnie off his game before he has a game. How do you think Vinnie's goin' to react if Stubby leads off with 'throw me a meatball' before the first pitch?"

The Flake threw his now dead soldier down the railroad tracks and said, "Who the hell knows?"

The field lights were on and the two rival teams had started gathering around the back stop. Both umpires were standing behind home plate in what appeared to be a rather serious tête-à-tête.

I whispered to the Flake, "There's that fuckin' Vinnie the guinea. I'd like to shove a bat up his fat guinea ass. That'd change that fuckin' arrogant expression on his fuckin' face."

The Flake grabbed his third Bud, tossed me mine and tried to calm me down, "Easy big fella. Drink this. It's too early to get indignant. We haven't even finished our pre-game meal." He chugged his entire third can of Bud as did I, me chugging in high dudgeon, the Flake less so. We threw the dead soldiers onto the railroad tracks, dropped trow and took a leak behind the Auschwitz on Wheels. I strapped on my knee brace, pulled on a pair of sweat pants and my precious team jersey, donned my spikes and was ready for action. The Flake did the same without the cumbersome knee brace. We proceeded across the tracks, our metaphoric Rubicon, and onto KTI territory having completed our relaxing pre-game meal and the other preparations necessary for battle.

The stands behind both first base and third base were full by now, mostly our tribe, and our tribe of fans looked quite fashionable, if not somewhat idiosyncratic, in their new softball jerseys. Maintenance was the home team so we were first up. The green shirts looked pretty grim as they took the field. Looked like they had revenge on their minds for the rather ignominious game-shortened loss we had pinned on them in the last game of last season. It was the first loss they'd suffered in at least three years… and particularly for such as them, that's beyond living memory.

Stubby was up first. As planned, he yelled "Throw me a meatball" before the first pitch and Vinnie hit him with a fastball. Stubby limped to first base. Our own Norma Jean's Dream Machine stepped into the batter's box and yelled "Throw me another meatball" and Vinnie did, hitting the Dream Machine on the left shoulder. We had the bastard rattled. The umpire called time out and walked toward the pitching mound. He warned Vinnie to stop hitting batters. Vinnie yelled, "Make them stop yelling the word 'meatball'. It's unsportsman-like."

The umpire, being a lawyer from our legal department, took a freedom of speech approach to the problem and yelled back, "It's their right to yell whatever they want. They aren't yelling 'fire' in a crowded room."

Vinnie looked a bit puzzled and yelled back, "This ain't no room. It's a god-damn softball field. And they ain't yellin' 'fire'. They're yellin' 'meatball!'"

The umpire ignored Vinnie, turned and walked back to the plate. He took his position behind the catcher and yelled "Play ball!"

Oxbow Lake The 2nd

I got into the batter's box and yelled, "Throw me one of your meatballs, you turkey." Vinnie threw me a brush back pitch. The umpire took off his mask and yelled to Vinnie, "Hit one more batter, and you're out of here! Any more funny business and I'll forfeit the game. Play ball."

Vinnie threw me one of his fastballs which I slammed into short left field. He was obviously off his game. The short fielder played it cleanly and forced Stubby out at third. The plan was working. The table was set for Georgie Girl, our clean-up hitter. Men on first and second, one out.

Georgie Girl entered the left-handed batter's box and blew Vinnie a kiss. She swung the bat a few times and yelled "Throw me a fat pitch." She pointed the bat at him and mouthed the words, "You guinea meatball bastard." I saw the whole thing from first base. The umpire behind home plate didn't see it and neither did the umpire behind second base. However, Vinnie did. To this day, I'm not sure that Vinnie knew exactly what words Georgie Girl mouthed, but he obviously believed them to be of the very grievous insulting variety, so he charged Georgie Girl. His catcher, realizing that if Vinnie reached home plate, they'd more than likely forfeit the game, charged Vinnie and tackled him about halfway to home plate. Vinnie, in his rage, grabbed his catcher by the back of his neck as they scuffled on the ground. He took a wild roundhouse swing at the catcher with his pitching hand, hit his catcher's mask full force with a vicious right hook and screamed in pain.

Georgie Girl, realizing that the ball was in play, nonchalantly nodded at me, motioning for me to start around the base paths. I walked towards second and whispered to the Dream Machine, "Walk to third and then home. I'll follow you." The green shirts

were busy separating Vinnie and his catcher, as the Dream
Machine and I slowly walked around the bases and scored,
unbeknownst to all but Georgie Girl and the home plate umpire.

The green shirts, all eight of them, finally got Vinnie and their
catcher separated and pulled them to their feet. Vinnie stood on
the mound screaming in pain. His pitching hand was as big as a
watermelon. The home plate umpire yelled, "Play ball!"

The catcher turned back toward home plate and yelled, "Where are
the god damn base runners?" The umpire yelled back, "They both
scored. The ball was in play when you tackled Vinnie. Score's two
zip. You're the zip. Play ball!"

Now the catcher went nuts, throwing down his mask and charging
the umpire. He shoved the umpire against the backstop, knocking
him to the ground. The Pubs Creeps rushed to the umpire's aid and
surrounded him to protect him from the now furious catcher. The
umpire scrambled to his feet and yelled, "Game over. Green Shirts
forfeit!"

Pandemonium now ruled the world of green shirts. Vinnie yelled
something at the catcher who charged back to the mound. The
target of green shirted ire had shifted from the men in blue to other
men dressed in green. As the green shirts pushed each other around
the infield and screamed obscenities at each other, we walked the
umpires over to their cars and they drove off. The green shirts now
stood around the mound in stunned disbelief. The tribe exited the
field and drove over to the Bridge Circle Bar and Grill to celebrate
their hard fought victory. Later, when the green shirts protested
the forfeit, their protest was denied and they began the season
with a loss. They also lost Vinnie, their star pitcher, for the rest of

the season as well since he had broken his pitching hand in three places. They won the god damn Holme's softball trophy again anyway and got to listen to some retired second string catcher from the Milwaukee Braves, a guy named Bob Uecker, after a fine dinner of surf and turf, the bastards.

I'll bet you'd like to write about how Larry the Lobster felt as the water boiled... not to mention the way those beef cows felt just before that sledge hammer nailed them between the eyes.

No comment! I talked to Doc and he says it ain't him writin' in my journal... like I believe the queer bastard. Says I gotta keep writin' the same way as before if I ever hope to get the hell out of here. Fuck!

The Bridge to Elysium

Ah yes, the Bridge Circle Bar and Grill… my clandestine observation post, home away from home and watering hole for the tribe. I liked everything about the dump, particularly its location. It sat on a hill above the traffic circle for the 199 bypass to the Kingston-Rhinecliff Bridge overlooking the KTI facility. That traffic circle to the bridge is where the 'Bridge Circle' part of its name came from.

It was a converted old two-story frame house with blue-gray wooden shingles and white trim. There was even a trellis, sans vines and flowers, surrounding what had once been a side entrance to the house but was now the front and main entrance to the bar and grill. What made the location strategically special to me was that from the Bridge's parking lot you could see the KTI facility with its many buildings and parking lots off in the distance across 9W. Many a night I'd slip out to that parking lot and using my German binoculars that I kept in my van, the small kind, I'd observe the goings on at the KTI facility keeping a sharp eye for anything out of the ordinary.

Now we're getting somewhere. What did you consider out of the ordinary?

None of your fuckin' business!

The bottom floor of the Bridge was the bar and grill. An enclosed front porch served as a banquet room. Unfortunately the dump no longer exists, having disappeared many moons ago... after a suspicious bankruptcy... replaced by a spanking new, modern, glass KTI Credit Union building. Don't believe that bull shit that the more things change the more they remain the same. You can go tell the proverbial Joe that it ain't so! The Bridge Circle is long gone, never to return.

Time never goes backward even if you can. If it seems like it is, you're being fooled... or worse, fooling yourself. It's a kind of temporal optical illusion, for time only goes one way... sometimes fast, sometimes slow, but only forward at least as far as I can tell. However, no matter how times goes... and it only goes one way... granted sometimes fast and sometimes slow ala Albert E, but an individual... someone with the right technology could travel through time... both forward and backward... hell, maybe even a whole bunch of individuals (maybe species would be a better word here) could if they had the right technology and here I was employed by a corporation that called itself Kronos Technologies

151

International… what better place for that technology to exist… maybe the "I" should stand for "Intertemporal".

Hold on Bobbo! Back to the Bridge Circle… Benny, the owner, was an old, fat, balding bastard who drank copious amounts of his private stock of scotch and the more he drank, the more he shared his bar's other liquors, gratis, with all his friends and everyone was his friend by that time of night. If you needed cash and didn't have much of a bank balance, you waited until around nine when Benny would cash a pre-dated check, any check, which as it turned out was something like an interest free loan floated by that local financial institution known to its clientele as Benny the Bank.

To recoup the losses Benny the Bank suffered because of his alcohol fueled generosity and his associated banking proclivities, he rented the second floor to one of the bar maids, Sally, known to the Bridge's regulars as Long Tall Sally. As her name would suggest, Sally was tall, maybe five foot ten and rather thin… a typical slightly over-the-hill bleach-blonde… and, as Little Richard sang… she was built for speed. In spite of her thin build, she sported two huge firm jugs. She was decent looking early in the evening, but her beauty must have been of the time-release variety, for as the evening wore on, she mysteriously became more and more beautiful until around midnight she was stunningly so. I have seen this transformation many times myself.

She supplemented her income by acts of carnal consumption… that is by giving off-shift blow jobs in her rented second-floor apartment, which was really more like a garret, and being built for speed, her genetics had given her a distinct productivity advantage over any potential competition... which presently there wasn't much of. She limited her services to those of the fallatial variety because, as she put it, "No services below the waist (meaning her waist). I'm saving myself for marriage." By all accounts, her plan for her personal marital savings account was obviously of the very long range variety and one that must have begun decades earlier with a series overdraws, for she had as yet not accrued much of an account balance since.

The setup was ideal for all the customers… the Bridge provided food and drink to sustain the body and some semi full-service entertainment to sustain the soul or at least the libido portion of the soul… Hell, the establishment even provided financing for all the costs. Have ol' Sally serve you pizza and beer during happy hour, which, due to Benny's generosity, lasted well into the night. Put the bill on a tab. Then when Sally's shift ended, follow Miss Long Tall Sally up those steps for some of her personal service, for a man lives not by beer and pizza alone… even when spiced with a depth charge or three… and then put those personal services on another tab. Run the tab downstairs with Benny and the one upstairs with Sally… all within a stone's throw of the KTI facility, which, strangely enough, had its own credit union to service its employees and its own credit division to service its customers and its own way of fucking its employees. Why, there were services of all kinds all over the god damn place. But unlike the services provided by Benny and Sally, KTI fucked you and the horse you rode in on below the waist, above the waist, wherever the hell they saw fit to waste you… whether you wanted it or not… and without Vaseline.

Irony of ironies, looking back on the situation… you know, looking at it from a big picture point of view… Benny the Bank goes bankrupt and is forced to sell that sacred institution known as The Bridge Circle Bar and Grill. The Bridge Circle is bought by the KTI Credit Union, torn down and replaced with a building which houses the KTI Credit Union apparatchik, while, rumor has it, it is slowly going bankrupt. At least that's what the Flake told me the last time he visited the place. Maybe the site is haunted or something. But what aroused my suspicions was the fact that Benny went bankrupt shortly after what happened at the lab. That's when my life got turned upside down and why I'm here writing this stupid journal.

Look, asshole, your life's been upside down since the day you were born. You're just a natural shitty-end-of-the-stick kind of guy. God has done you no favors. And now you're suspicious? Talk about having no self-awareness...

Self-awareness? You talk about self-awareness? By the time you're self-aware, your liver will be pate and the rest of you barbeque whoever the fuck you are!

Back to Long Tall Sallie who as far as I know did not go bankrupt. When upstairs for servicing in her rented garret, you could observe the goings on about the KTI facility from a large half-circular window which faced the ol' bom-bor fac-tor-ee while Sally was polishing your knob. For some reason, the sight of KTI at such times inspired both the gobblee… as in Sal's customer, and the gobbler… as in Sal herself, making those services that much more pleasurable for both the gobblee and, I suspect, the gobblor. May have had something to do with the taste of forbidden fruit or maybe the exhilaration of rebellion. Who knows? All I know is that the sight of those brightly lit KTI parking lots turned ol' Sal into a man-eating tiger and turbo-charged the whole experience.

What are you implying? Say it outright. Admit it.

154

Listen, stop writing these comments. You're ruining everything. What I admit is that you're an asshole.

The Bridge's menu, Sally aside, claimed that the place was a restaurant in spite of the use of the term 'grill' in the establishment's title. In actuality, its restaurant menu, when restricted to the edible and drinkable, was pretty much a pizza, beer and shots kind of place. Even the mixed drinks were iffy, depending on who was behind the bar and the time of night. I have to admit that the pizza was pretty good, not in Frank's league, but still pretty good. The rest of the menu… not so good. I had ordered a well-done hamburger there once… well-done to be on the safe side… and the damn thing could have walked to my table on its own. I pretty much decided never to do that again. From that day on, I stuck with the pizza, which had to be served hot.

The place was the local hangout for the dregs of KTI society and the tribe qualified. We were more than regulars… we more like semi-permanent residents, for within the confines of that sacred hall, we celebrated something every night. Sometimes it was an athletic victory (rarely) like tonight… sometimes an athletic loss (often), occasionally a promotion (rarely) and sometimes a demotion (too often) as well as firings (at least one a year) along with transfers, retirements, birthdays, deaths, marriages, births, adoptions, divorces and just about any other reason we could conjure up. We even celebrated the arrival of a litter of seven puppies in the Stubby McNeil household last October. Ol' Stubby had to take out a major loan from Benny the Bank to meet the demands of his fellow, very enthusiastic celebrants.

The tribe had dribbled in from the softball game and through dint of numbers gained possession of the banquet room. I stood next to the Flake at the bar to order pitchers of beer for our huddled masses. I asked, "How about a depth charge… you know, something to kick off the evening properly?" The Flake gave me a thumbs-up and I yelled to Sally, "Two depth charges and 10 pitchers of beer. Put it on the tab." Sally slid two mugs of cold beer down the bar to us and several moments later, two shot glasses of very cheap whiskey slid in behind the mugs of beer. The whiskey was so cheap you could see the impurities floating on the whiskey's surface, but who gave a shit. We dropped the full shot glasses into our mugs of beer and watched them settle down and into the mugs, clinking as they hit bottom.

We picked up the mugs, smashed them together and chugged the beer. As the beer drained from the mugs, the shot glasses, still full of whiskey, dipped onto their sides and slid toward the mugs' lip, slowly releasing the whiskey, which we drank. When the now empty shot glasses reached our mouths, we lipped those shot glasses and slammed the mugs onto the bar. By now the entire bar was watching us. We faced each other and spit the shot glasses high into the air toward each other. Flake's shot glass went high into the air over my head. I reciprocated and spit my shot glass high over his head. I caught the Flake's shot glass behind my back and then slammed it on the bar. The Flake did the same with my shot glass. The bar broke out in applause. Sally came over to retrieve the mugs and shot glasses. I blew her a kiss and she said, "Anything you break, you pay for, Flashlight Bobb. That's quite a trick for the likes of you two. You know, you're almost as good as a couple of trained seals I saw down at the Bronx Zoo, but they're even better. They do their tricks without hands." I thought to myself "Ol' Sal, you could do your tricks without hands too. In fact, you often do." She flashed one of those big, toothy shit-eaten grins of hers and strutted back to the beer taps to finish pouring the ten pitchers of beer we'd ordered.

When Sally finished pouring the pitchers of beer, we set up a relay of sorts to transport the containers of the precious liquid back into the banquet room. There was a commotion at the table to the left of the banquet room's doorway impeding the progress of our relay system. Fortunately after the delivery of the first five pitchers. One of Benny's most prized patrons, Jay McGonagall, from Product Test, was really pissed about something. The Product Test guys were much like the pubs guys, necessary evils despised by both engineers and programmers. The difference between us and them was literacy. We had it and they didn't, not that it mattered much. From what I could gather, Jay's wife had kicked him out, for he kept yelling, "That fuckin' Snow Queen. Kick me out! No fuckin' way. She'd freeze the heart of Jesus Christ... the bitch!" I was pretty sure my conclusion was correct since he always referred to his wife as the Snow Queen, drunk or sober.

In his rage, Jay picked up a chair by the back and raised it above his head. He wobbled a bit and had to shuffle his feet to steady himself, for he was about to smash the chair against the floor when Benny intervened, "Put the chair down, Jay. That chair costs 25 bucks."

Jay gently put the chair down and pulled out his wallet. He counted out two twenties and a ten and handed the fifty dollars to Benny, saying, "I'll take two. This one", as he pointed to the chair he'd just put down, "and that one" as he pointed to a second chair in which sat this other guy from Programming. From the way Jay pointed, I got the distinct impression that Jay knew the other guy and did not like him very much. It was apparent that the enraged Jay was going to punish someone, anyone... and there before him was someone who fit the bill…. someone he already disliked… disliked enough to become a substitute for his own lovely Snow Queen and thus an excellent recipient of his misplaced ire.

From what I could see, the feeling was mutual, for the programming guy in the other chair yelled about as coherently as his condition would allow, "No fuckin' way. This my chair" and he pulled out his wallet and handed Benny three tens and said in a very determined voice, "Keep change. I'm taking chair home as souvenir."

A large crowd gathered around the two combatants, for it looked as if some arcane rule of the Bridge's sacred code of honor had been broken. Someone would have to pay dearly for so violating this little known unwritten section of said unwritten sacred code. Benny, fearing that many more chairs would be broken and most of them unpaid for, stepped between the two combatants and held up his hands palms out, "This will be settled in the traditional way… rocks, paper, scissors. Each of you know the rules. Two out of three. May the best man win!"

'Rocks, paper, scissors' is that old bar game. Two guys face off and on a set count each combatant throws out his hand, a fist representing a rock, an open palm representing a sheet of paper and two open fingers representing scissors. The rock breaks scissors, the paper covers rock and the scissors cuts paper. Ties, throw again. I've played the stupid game at the Bridge a million times but never in a contest of honor. I played for beer or the occasional depth charge.

Benny looked behind the two combatants and realized that each hero had a group of avid, boisterous and very drunk camp followers. Being experienced in situations such as this, he defused the potential disaster by yelling, "After the contest, beers on the house!" taking the minds of these rival camps off the impending contest and focused on the free beer that would be available after the contest, changing their motivation from seeing their chosen hero victorious to seeing the contest over. Sometimes Benny could be brilliant, unfortunately for him, usually at his own expense and thus ultimately bringing into question his said brilliance.

The Titanic Clash of Heroes

This writing down what happened in my life is getting complicated. It's taken me eight days to write what happened in just one, including what I write about today… and I haven't really gone through much of that thinking about it bullshit yet. You know, that introspection stuff. How can that be? For me to write an autobiography, it would take me eight times as long as I lived. I'd spend most of my life writing about writing about my life. Hell, I'd be dead before I could finish writing the damn thing. Go figure. Another one of those time conundrums. At this rate, I'll never get out of here.

Anyways, back to Jay and that programming guy as they faced each other in their epic battle of honor. Both warriors were grim-faced, determined although somewhat bleary eyed. The crowd surrounded the two combatants. Supporters from each camp gathered around their respective heroes, some standing on nearby tables to better witness the impending titanic clash. The luscious Molly Mau-Mau stood in all her glory on the table not far from the Flake and me and behind the programming guy, having apparently sworn allegiance to her professional compatriot, the aforementioned programming guy. She raised her arms in the air and pumped her fists violently revealing both her ardent support for her champion and the back of her panties, which read ironically, 'Last Tuesday'. She screamed, "Smoke the mother-fucker!" in support of her programming hero.

Benny raised his arms for silence and the crowd quieted. He yelled, "One, two, three, throw!" Both hero combatants viciously threw their fists forward. You could see the muscles of each combatant's forearm strain under the effort. Benny yelled, "Two rocks, throw again!" The crowd screamed its support for whomever they happened to be supporting at the time. Benny raised his arms for silence a second time and repeated the count.

The two hero combatants steadied themselves and upon Benny's command to throw, they shot their hands forth a second time. Again the crowd went wild as Benny yelled "Two papers! Throw again!" The tension grew, approaching the breaking point. Benny raised his arms for silence a third time and started the count. The sweat poured down the faces of the hero combatants as the tension for the next throw mounted, the physical effort of battle obviously sapping their strength. The contest was not only one of strength and cunning but also of endurance. Benny yelled "One!" Both combatants held their ground, although more unsteadily this time. Benny yelled "Two!" and both heroes wobbled a bit but held as steady as they could under the strain of the battle and their present physical condition. Benny yelled, "Three!" The crowd held its collective breath. Benny yelled "Throw!" The programming guy wobbled, and as he threw out what was to be yet another hideous blow at his hated foe, his forward momentum brought him to his knees. He collapsed and fell prostrate upon the hardwood floor with a sickening thud. Jay wobbled as well but managed to maintain his balance and threw out his hand… this time a scissors. Benny waved his hands above his head and yelled, "Contest over! Jay wins on a TKO! The contest is over. The contested chair is his." Benny faced the now defeated programming guy as two of his supporters pulled the thoroughly spent and defeated champion to his feet. Benny smiled and stuffed two of the three ten dollar bills that the programming guy had paid for his souvenir chair into the fallen hero's shirt pocket.

Jay raised his arms and shouted, "Fuck the Snow Queen!" as he danced his victory dance in a tight circle about the chair that had in part initiated the great clash of heroes. The crowd screamed its delight. Then Jay picked up the chair by its back, raised it above his head and with an almost super-human effort, brought it down against the hardwood floor with an ear shattering bang, smashing it to pieces. As the chair shattered, the crowd shouted in joy. Holding the remnants of the chair, the victorious champion raised what was left of his prize above his head and brought it down against the hardwood floor smashing it a second time, sending wooden shards about the room. He raised the back support of the chair, for that was all that was left, above his head and yelled, "Death to the chair!" The crowd started chanting "Death to the chair! Death to the chair! Death to the chair!"

Terror spread across Benny's face, for he apparently feared that many more chairs, this time unpaid-for chairs, would join their recently slaughtered brother in a massacre of biblical proportions. In defense of his realm, Benny yelled "Beer on the house!" The chanting ceased and silence reigned for a moment as the crowd, now drunk with victory, paused to absorb the meaning of Benny's words. Then someone yelled, "Free fuckin' beer!" The crowd, valuing the consumption of free alcohol over the slaughtering of chairs, came to its senses and rushed the bar. The two supporters of the programming guy dropped their support and joined the rushing crowd. Gravity had its way with their defeated champion and he again slumped to the floor.

In Achillian haughtiness, Jay stepped over the fallen hero, grabbed his prized second chair and pulled it over his now prostrate foe. He stood admiring his recently won battle prize without apparently realizing that he had paid for it. With great gravity he yelled, "This prize is too valuable to destroy. From this day forward, this chair shall be known as 'Jay's Chair… Beware' and only he… meaning me… who won this prize in glorious combat shall be allowed to sit in it. Anyone else who sits in this chair will get the shit kicked out of him. Ask that fuckin' programming guy."

The Mau-Mau jumped to the floor and stepped over the programming guy now slumped unconscious below her, for she had apparently taken a second vow of allegiance, this one silently. She ran to Jay, and yelled, "You destroyed that mother fucker!" as she grabbed him giving him a long tongue sucking kiss and shrinking Long Tall Sally's potential customer base by one at least for that evening.

Later in the week, Jay spray painted his battle-won prize an emerald green and screwed a brass plate to the chair's back. The brass tag formally proclaimed "Jay's Chair Beware" and below that proclamation, the date of his hard fought victory. His epic battle became known as the "Battle of Beware Chair" and a part of Bridge Circle legend… a great oral tale handed down from KTI drinking generation to KTI drinking generation. For several years the emerald green Beware Chair sat in a place of honor alongside the bar. When Jay visited the Bridge Circle, as he often did back then, he used the Beware Chair when not standing at the bar. Two years later KTI fired him for poor attendance as he apparently spent too much time in the Beware Chair. I heard that after he got fired, he moved to middle America's Elysium, Toledo, Ohio, opening a bagel shop there, I think. But the Beware Chair stayed and the legend grew as each new generation of KTI drinkers were initiated into the folk lore of the Bridge Circle. Unfortunately, the Legend of the Beware Chair is now the fading memory of a few, yet another victim of Benny the Bank's going belly up during his tragic but suspicious financial collapse, the forfeiture to end all forfeitures in that now all but forgotten legendary realm known as the Bridge Circle Bar and Grill... inexorable time again having its way with me yet again.

I stood next to the Flake and watched the two hero combatants go at it. When the fallen hero collapsed to the floor and Benny declared Jay's TKO victory, I nudged the Flake with my elbow and said, "Two fuckin' forfeit victories in one night! Fate must be on some kind of victory through forfeiture kick."

The Flake and me continued our beer pitcher relay until all ten pitchers had been delivered to our tribe. By the time we delivered the last pitcher, it was time to get another ten. The fierce fire of our softball victory, intensified by the thrill of Jay's hand-to-hand epic victory, was going to take a lot of beer to extinguish. By the time we had delivered enough beer to do so, it was close to 12:00 midnight. The Flake and me sat at the banquet table discussing how we'd handle the expected protest by the green shirt assholes when the juke box blared away with Little Richard's familiar oldie but goody:

Well, long tall Sally she's

Oxbow Lake The 2nd

built for speed, she got

everything that Uncle James need

Oh baby,

ye-e-e-eh baby,

woo-o-o-oh baby,

havin' me some fun tonight.

I said to the Flake, "There's Little Richard announcing that our own Long Tall Sally will be accepting dances shortly. Sally's put out her squeegee list." I have no idea why she called her dance card a "squeegee list" but she did. She limited her dance card to seven dances and her dance card, or "squeegee list" as she called it, was usually full. Maybe Uncle James wasn't gettin' any tonight, but seven others were.

The Flake drained his glass and slammed it down on the table, "Why the hell does Sally limit her squeegee list to seven?"

I drained my glass and slammed it down on the table, "Someone said she claims that more than seven makes her jaw sore. Ruins the quality of the experience. It's her way of maintaining a high-quality service. It's a quality control thing, but seven's a pretty good number. At ten bucks a pop that's 70 bucks a night and if she works six days a week, that's a tax free 420 bucks. Not bad. And she doesn't need to take a week off every month if she doesn't feel like it. Even if she does, she clears at least over 1,600 bucks a month… tax free."

The Flake smiled, "And by limiting the supply, she maintains a high demand for her services. She's a real entrepreneur."

I had my suspicions about Long Tall Sally. She was an entrepreneur all right but she was also a carnivorous creature if you think about. She consumed flesh or at least the essence of human flesh… like it was an appetizer. She knew her business and she did it well… all the more reason to suspect her. She could have been a plant, one of those Judas goats. I'm still suspicious of her even after all these years. I just couldn't figure out her angle. I knew she had one. I just couldn't figure it out. Night after night, seven customers climbed up those steps and seven customers usually climbed down those steps, the descent being a bit unsteady sometimes. Every now and then some guy would disappear… not climb down those steps… which made me very suspicious. But I'd see the bastard the next night at the bar slaking his thirst as they say in Germany, apparently no less the wear for the experience.

How come you never mentioned any of this to the Flake or one of the other assholes you hang with in your tribe?

For the same reason I'm not going to discuss it with you.

I poured another brewski for both of us and said, "Yeah, ol' Sal's got her business process down pat except for that tab thing. I'll bet half the assholes in this place owe Sal at least ten bucks. If she'd decrease her intake of alcohol during the evening, she'd increase her cash flow at night. But she does have that quality thing down pretty good!"

The Flake smiled, "She sure do, brother. She sure do."

I asked, "How much you owe her?"

"Thirty bucks, give or take. She took me off the tab last week until I pay up, so she does keep track. Even after a drink or three, she still knows what's up and until I come up with 30 bucks, I'm joinin' Uncle James. Neither one of us is goin' to be on that squeegee list anytime soon. Maybe I should float a check with Benny the Bank to pay Sally? Is that some form of kiting?"

"How much you owe Benny?"

"I think one fifty."

"It's not exactly kiting but it sure ain't friendly."

"Benny ain't exactly a friend. He's more like an acquaintance."

"Well then I guess it's OK."

Chilled by a Philosophic Draft

I was rummaging through that box of stuff that the Flake brought me way back when he cleaned out my cube… when I first got slammed into this fuckin' dungeon… the stuff I'd squirreled away if I ever needed evidence. Well it turns out, I couldn't use any of it... at least back then. Never got the chance. Rummaging through the stuff now, I thought I might come across something that'd trigger my memory. I needed something to write about in this fuckin' journal to keep that queer Doc off my back, preferably something around the time that I was dealing with the Richard Tadd imbroglio… you know for the sake of continuity and to show that my marbles hadn't gone free range.

Rummaging through those papers was like an archeological dig.
The stuff that occurred around the same time clustered around the
same depth within the box. I must have filed stuff chronologically
and when Flake dumped the files into the box, he musta just
grabbed and dumped keeping the files pretty much in the same
order in which I'd filed them. I dug down and found a copy of
Screw Magazine... probably the Tadd's. Never did give it back to
him. I opened it to the centerfold and sure enough, there was that
signature by Twyla Twatly... it was Tadd's copy all right. That's
about where I found that report I wrote about my investigation of
Tadd's Screw Magazine travesty... the one I taped in this journal.
Was about as I had remembered it.

I knew I was at the right depth. As I flipped through some of the
official looking documents... stuff I was probably not supposed to
keep but did... screw the rules... I came across a copy of a draft
deferment application for one Randolph Andrew Sedgwick the
3rd... ol' Randy Andy. That old application brought back detailed
memories all right... of something that occurred during Tadd's
involuntary incarceration as a guest of Ulster County after that
fight he had with his personal mechanic, the evil Buddy. Ol' Randy
Andy is... or was... a hero of mine. He gamed the system and
actually got away with it... something neither that idiot Tadd nor I
could ever pull off.

I remember when the whole Sedgwick affair went down. It's like
a movie playing in my head. I vividly remember staggering into
KTI after a long night and early morning at the Bridge Circle. I
entered my cube balancing a cup of that life saving java in my
unsteady hand... hoping for some peace and quiet. This was just
before the coffee started smelling like shit and I stopped drinking
it. But at that time I was still drinking... in fact, I was living on the

stuff… black and very sweet! My head was killing me with one of those depth charge headaches and my balls itched like hell and badly needed scratching. Those depth charge headaches are killers. Instead of desperately needed privacy and quiet so that I could wash down a handful of aspirins with a gallon or two of black sweet java and give those itchy balls of mine a good scratching… thank you very much Long Tall Sally… I got startled out of my fuckin' mind, spilling that hot very sweet and black elixir all over my right hand… splashing some of it on the individual who startled me and into whom I almost bumped. There, standing just inside my cube and leaning against the wall was none other than our own unperturbed Randy Andy. He was cool as a cucumber, as he always was, reading. He was always reading.

Ol' Randy Andy paid no attention to the drops of hot coffee that had inadvertently splashed onto the pant legs of his neatly pressed tan chinos. The scene unfolded in my head now in slow-motion. There he stood… thin and straight as a very straight arrow… flat head covered with bright red hair… with a cowlick standing tall in the middle of that flat head… made him look kind of like a human candle. I thought "Yup, that's Randy Andy, a libertarian from his toes all the way up to that red cowlick… our own Philosopher King Extraordinaire… known to the outside world, which apparently included his parents, as Mr. Randolph Andrew Sedgwick the 3rd but referred to by the tribe as 'Randy Andy'". I'm getting ahead of myself. That real randyness stuff didn't become an actual part of his life until after his divorce several years later. Hell, he wasn't even married yet. I got the rest of the story from the Flake several years later… or was it last year?

Anyways, when the tribe first nom de plumed him "Randy Andy", they did so with a great deal of irony in mind, thinking of him as a human candle that never got lit… that is, someone who had no erotic fire… a cold overly rational fish… cerebral to the max. Like I said, he was a straight arrow's straight arrow. However, the tribe's mindful irony turned into mindless prescience several years later when, as the Flake tells it, Mr. Randolph Andrew Sedgwick the 3rd transmogrified himself into a randy, wick dipping fool… his actual wick turning out to be a bit lower on his personage… and he apparently lit that wick often. Again, according to the Flake, his wicking required female tag teams in order to sate his wick dipping obsession… and he only sated his obsession with black prostitutes, all of whom also happened to be addicted to several different kinds of both uncontrolled controlled legal substances and uncontrolled illegal substances, the apparent favorite of the mix being heroine… The icing on Randy's wick dipping cake… according to rumor as relayed to me by the Flake… one of those black prostitutes actually lived with him from time to time eventually giving birth to a bastard mulatto son that caused him great legal and financial consternation (but apparently none of the social or psychological variety) years later. Hearing this news, I was shocked that he didn't end up with some dreaded STD. Hell, maybe he did for all I know. But like I said, that all occurred after they stuffed me in here and after his divorce which didn't occur until after his marriage which hadn't happened yet… so as to keep the record as straight as I can and so as not to get the cart too far ahead of the horse, I'll rewind to the events of the time of the Tadd imbroglio which also happened to be the year that the cold wind of the military draft chilled many and almost froze our Randy Andy solid up in the icy tundra of Canada.

The reserved Mr. Randolph Andrew Sedgwick the 3rd peered down at me through his Mr. Peeper's glasses as he stood calmly just inside my cube, leaning against my cubicle wall reading. He was always

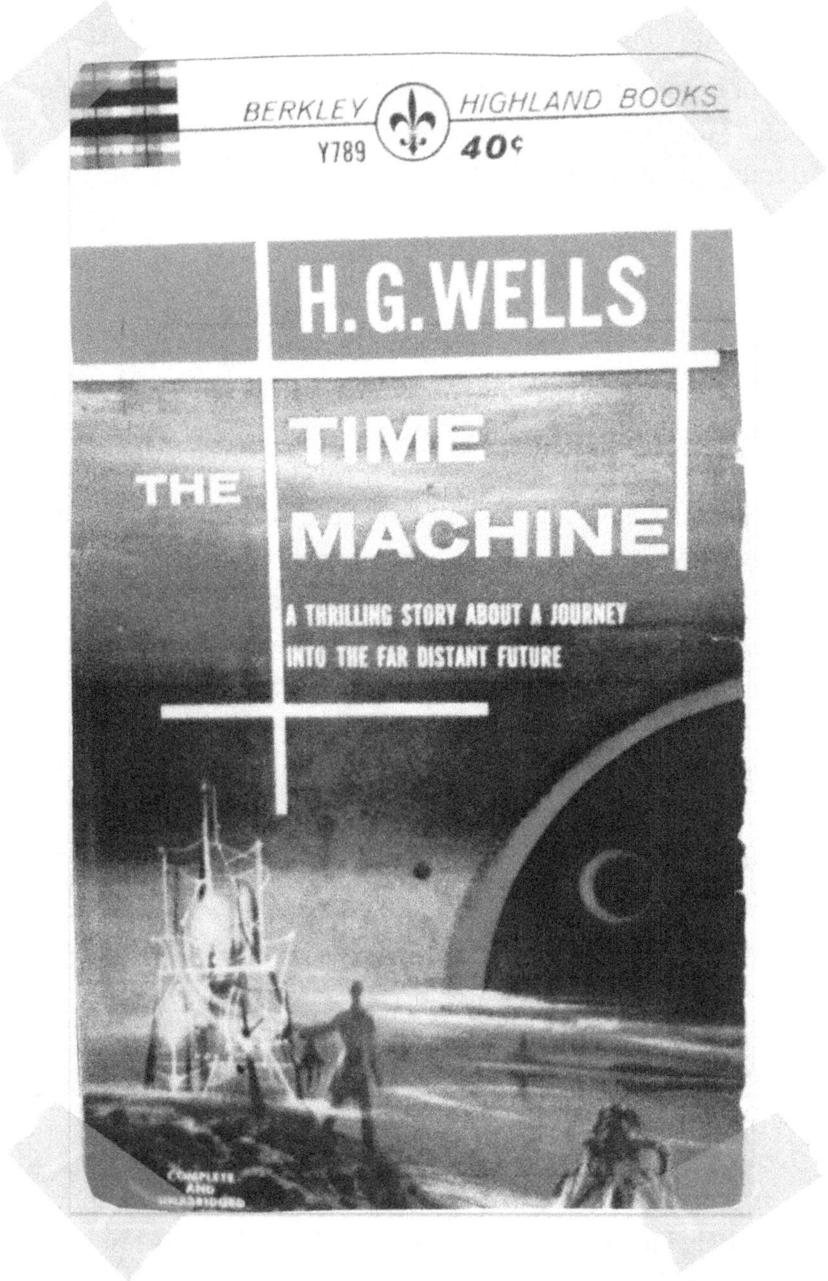
BERKLEY HIGHLAND BOOKS
Y789
40¢
H.G. WELLS
THE TIME MACHINE
A THRILLING STORY ABOUT A JOURNEY
INTO THE FAR DISTANT FUTURE

reading… in this case reading one of my copies of The Time Machine. He looked down at me and said rather casually in that monotone of his, "I need another deferment. My year for the last one is up next month."

He schlumped into my guest chair as I slumped into mine. I can't schlump because of my back. Schlumping is a postural form of body relaxation that involves reclining in a chair. If Randy Andy didn't invent it, he surely perfected it. To schlump, one must push back into a chair and slide onto what is close to the small of one's back. With Randy's classic schlump, we were now eye-to-eye even though he was considerably taller than was I when standing erect.

Without a word, I unlocked my desk and pulled out the randy one's personnel jacket, opened it and determined that he had already been granted three deferments. Then I called Lady Blue and asked her to bring me the departmental deferment folder which had all the corporate rules, procedures and forms.

Sedgwick continued thumbing through my copy of The Time Machine as I spoke with Lady Blue on the phone. When I hung up, he pushed the copy he was reading toward me, cover first, and said, "You have seven copies in your bookcase if I count right. You an H. G. Wells fan, a book collector or both?"

He caught me off guard. "Your count is close but not exact. I have an eighth copy in my desk along with a copy of the magazine where the first installment of the story was published. I don't collect books but I do collect copies of Well's The Time Machine. The copy you're reading, I bought way back in 5th grade. I've kept it all these years."

"Interesting. If you don't mind me asking, what's the attraction?"

Normally I don't discuss H. G. Wells with anyone, but this morning, but with our own philosopher king and dedicated libertarian, I felt the urge. Maybe I was still a little drunk from the night before. I really don't remember exactly how drunk I was. Anyway, I do remember deeming him worthy of such a discussion, for he too had a principle upon which he based his life. I lowered my voice and said, "He's more than a writer of science fiction. He's more than a social commentator. He's more than a philosopher. He's a prophet... a writer of prophecy."

"Why so many copies. They're all the same, aren't they?"

"You'd think so, but I've got a number of copies and there are differences... some of them significant. I compare them word for word to find those differences. To date, I've found 37. I'm going through a detailed analysis and assessment of the differences to determine which ones are significant and then an exegesis to determine their meaning. Most of them appear to be typographical errors, but like I said, there are some very significant differences. I even have a first edition of the novel's publication in America, which I consider one step away from a sacred text. If I could only get a copy of his original manuscript which I consider THE sacred text!"

"Sacred text?"

I pulled closer to him and whispered, "Yes, a sacred text. You see H. G. Wells was more than a writer of science fiction, as you may have thought. Like I said, he was a prophet. He saw the future. He was a modern day biblical prophet. The Time Machine is like The

Book of Revelation. The Prophet Wells warns us of the coming Apocalypse, and how one man, symbolically named Time Traveler, can prevent it. Wells warns us, but we pay little heed. Hell, instead of heeding his warning, we turn his apocalyptic prophecy into a god damn movie... and a god damn B movie at that. And he's not the first. There are many others in the past and not just those of the Bible. God has tried to speak to us many times and we have pretty much ignored him. Wells is the latest in a long line of creative artists who have sought to warn us going back to Homer and beyond. The creative artist sees through the veil we call reality... not always clearly... catches glimpses of God's warning. Wells warns us that technology and institutions like KTI destroy that creativity and thus our ability to receive God's warning. Computers are Satan's work. Well's Morlocks are Satan's soldiers."

Randy's brow furrowed as he said, "As an individual, Wells was an ardent collectivist. He fought to pave the road to serfdom."

"I really don't care about his politics. I care about his prophecies. Does anyone care about how good a carpenter Christ was?"

"OK, for now let's accept your premise. What were his prophecies as presented in The Time Machine?"

I thought to myself "Finally, someone I can trust... someone who will take Well's revelations seriously. I don't feel like some Cassandra wandering around the beaches of Troy screaming 'the wolves are coming, the wolves are coming, and they're going to eat you alive' to a world gone deaf and knowing that there was a good chance that Ajax the Lesser was going to be great enough to rape the shit out of me."

Big boy, aren't you mixing your metaphors. Cassandra was a woman and you're not. As to those prophecies you've discovered, ask yourself this: Why am I the only one who's discovered them? After all, millions, literally millions, of people have read The Time Machine in just about every language imaginable and none of them seem to have discovered that Mr. H. G. "I'd like to fuck your wife" Wells ever prophesized anything other than his own ostracism and eventual demise.

I don't know why I've been chosen. I just know that I have. There was only one Moses and now there's me.

I looked over at Randy and said to him, "You've read The Time Machine, right?" He shook his head 'yes' and did NOT look at me like I was nuttier than a fruit cake… which happened the last time I spoke to someone about Wells' prophecies and that was several years ago when I was a high school teacher. Word got around pretty quickly amongst those uneducated retards in the teachers' room and they treated me like I was an order of fries short of a Happy Meal thanks to that bastard Mr. Thomas fuckin' Wolfe. That's when I learned to keep my mouth shut, but Mr. Randolph Andrew Sedgwick the 3rd was different. I felt I could trust him for he was a serious man of letters and ideas. "You know the basic plot line… humanity evolved into two species… the Eloi and the Morlocks… the Morlocks running the industries below ground and feeding the Eloi who live above ground. The Morlocks raised Eloi like a herd of beef cows and harvested them periodically for food. Well suppose there are Morlocks?"

The expression on his face remained unchanged and he said, "So you're interpreting his prophecies literally and not metaphorically." I knew I could trust him! "That's an interesting point. At first I thought that Wells was being metaphoric and his point was that technology would destroy humanity as we knew it through Darwinian evolution, but then… "

The Lady in Blue knocked on the door and entered with the deferment folder. She handed it to me, turned and walked out. She was wearing a mini skirt and looked good enough to eat… which as it turns out… another time. Anyway, the spell was broken and the randy man and I were back to the business of his particular future and not that of Lady Blue, not that of me and certainly not that of all humanity.

I looked down at Randy's personnel jacket again and read the detailed information concerning his draft status and deferment applications. The Vietnam War was raging at the time and many unwilling participants got swept up in it because of the draft. Deferments were worth millions, particularly to corporations like KTI. The United States government had ruled, in its infinite wisdom, that the computer industry was essential to the war effort and thus its male engineers and programmers of draft age, sons of the most likely voters, were eligible for deferments if KTI management supported the prospective draftee's request for said deferment. This ability to obtain deferments was literally worth gold to KTI because the ability to obtain deferments made employment with them very popular. Much of the best young talent who under normal circumstances wouldn't work for a large faceless corporation accepted KTI's institutional employment offers in hopes of avoiding the Mekong Delta.

Hell, we'd just hired another a kid… this one from Massachusetts, another one of those ivy scum... Brown this time… a kid named William Skrimshander. Remember him well. We snuck his offer in just before the hiring freeze. I did one of his three interviews. Mr. Skrimshander made it patently obvious why he chose a career at KTI. My buddy and fellow manager, Crazy Al, who handles all the recruiting, said Mr. Skrimshander set a land-speed record with his acceptance… and his application for a draft deferment. When Al called him with the offer, Skrimshander yelled "I accept" before Al could even give him such minor details like salary, terms of employment and starting date. The next words out of Skrimshander's mouth… "I want to apply for a draft deferment." So much for another dedicated employee.

The catch with all these deferments (there's always a catch): they were for one year and could only be renewed twice. I guess the Feds figured that if a programmer or engineer couldn't finish a project and train a replacement in 3 years, he deserved to be sent to the Mekong Delta. By manipulating the tangled web that was the KTI bureaucracy, the Polish Prince, bless his blackened little heart, managed to get our charges classified as programmers and thus pubs creeps also qualified for deferments. It wasn't all altruism on his part, for the deferments, at least in the short run, meant he didn't need to be constantly recruiting and training replacements. Turns out, I didn't need a deferment because of a bum knee with the added advantage of a wife whose name I can't remember and several nameless kids. I could do most of the physical stuff but only when I wore a heavy knee brace and even with the brace, my knee went out every now and then on its own, so I was home free. The marriage and kids were a bonus at least as far as my draft status was concerned. Others such as Randy Andy weren't as lucky for they had no debilitating physical impairments to disqualify them from a vacation in the Mekong Delta and killing gooks… or worse, being killed by them.

I looked over at Mr. Randolph Andrew Sedgwick the 3rd and said, "Doesn't look good. You've already been granted three deferments and KTI is very reluctant to support a fourth. They do occasionally, but it's rare, usually in cases where the government believes the project that the supplicant is working on has direct national security or military application. And that ain't you."

He looked at me with that expressionless face of his, "The draft is a form of slavery. No government has the right to use legal force to take away my freedom of choice, my personal liberty."

He didn't seem worried about that Mekong Delta vacation. For him it was all about principle. I wanted to help him, but there was little I could do. "Look, I'll process your request. That's the best I can do. I don't decide. All those decisions are made by corporate, but you have to go through our local personnel rep. Without the reps support, chances are pretty slim that corporate would even consider granting the deferment. Our personnel rep now is William Whitmore and he's a prick and hates pubs. You're just lucky he wasn't our rep when you applied for the first 3 deferments. If I were you, I'd develop a plan B or head for Canada." He handed me his application for a fourth deferment which he had filled out as I rambled on and left my office as nonchalantly as if he had stopped by for a chat about the weather.

I approved his deferment request and forwarded it to that prick Wet Willie. Three weeks later, I was notified that Sedgwick's request had been denied. I called him into my office and informed him. He sat across from me and took the news with his usual aplomb. I asked, "Have a Plan B?"

He said, with all the enthusiasm of a man having a casual conversation about the price of vending machine peanuts, "I've packed my car with all that I'll need and if I can't get a deferment, I'm driving to Canada the minute I receive my draft notice. I've got a thousand dollars in traveler's checks to cover my initial expenses. After I'm there, my sister will wire me what I need."

"What are the chances of you getting drafted in your district?"

"Excellent. My district is in Long Island and most of the draft eligible men there have college and employment deferments. It's pretty much a once you're available, you're drafted. In a month, I'll receive my notice."

"Have a plan B that doesn't involve fleeing to Canada?"

"I might. I need a couple of days' vacation... the rest of the week."

"Anything I should do to cover your project?"

"No. They're still debating what to name the thing. It doesn't ship for 18 months."

"OK. Let me know if I can do anything to help." And with that he disappeared for the rest of the week. I sat back, scratched my balls and thanked god for two things: 1) I wasn't Randy Andy and 2) Randy Andy wasn't Lurch. Beginning the day with Richard Tadd slouched in my cube would have turned my horrendous hangover into a paralyzing stroke. I wandered over to Lurch's cube and... surprise, surprise... no Lurch. My guess... he was still enjoying the hospitality of Ulster County, gratis.

No comments from Mr. Busy Body?

Chilled by an Actual Draft

When the following Monday rolled around, there was the Randy Andy at his desk, as nonplussed as ever. I asked, "How'd plan B go?"

A faint smile appeared on his face, which for him was like a glorious howl of joy, and he said, "Quite well. Can't get into particulars." And so I said quietly, "Super" and headed back to my cubicle, wondering what Randy Andy had managed to arrange. Later that afternoon I found out. It appeared that his plan B had a very good chance of either getting him rejected by his draft board or sent to jail with the unwanted side-effect of getting him fired by KTI in either case.

As I wondered what Sedgwick had done for plan B, our secretary Phyllis Kopke, the now ill-fated and notorious Lady in Blue, ran into my office, huffing and puffing, waving a handful of papers in the air. She stood for a moment to catch her breath and then whispered, "Randy's girl found these copies in the self-serve copier out in the hall." (The Randy's girl comment is a whole other story that I'll get to in a minute.) She then carefully placed the documents on my desk, said, "You're not going to believe this" and strutted out.

There were two copies of the documents which our Randy Andy

179

had apparently left in the self-serve copier… one set which I kept… the documents in my archeological box of the deeds past that I referred to in yesterday's journal entry. (I'm not sure why I kept the damn documents other than I'm a suspicious pack rat. Anyway, I kept one of the sets of documents.) They appeared to be official documents of some sort. The first was a letter to Sedgwick's draft board. I looked down at the signature first. It was from Dr. Alan R. Beebe, a psychiatrist whose offices were in Philadelphia according to the letter head. I thought "OK, what does the shrink have to say about our Randy Andy?" As I read, the hair on the back of my neck stood at attention, and I quote verbatim:

"After my recent full and complete physical and psychological evaluation of Mr. Randolph Andrew Sedgwick the 3rd, I must inform you that Mr. Sedgwick remains a drug addicted sociopath prone to violent outbursts and who is also a compulsive liar incapable of accepting or following directions. Additionally, he suffers from nocturnal enuresis, commonly called involuntary nightly bed wetting. His prognosis is not good and I doubt that even after years of treatment, he would be fit for service in any organization, including and particularly the United States military."

The letter went on and on with more reasons why its subject was pretty much incapable being, well… human, stopping just short of declaring Sedgwick a serial killer in waiting. The other documents were summary reports of evaluations and treatments over the last five years. I thought to myself, "If personnel ever gets a hold of this, Sedgwick will be out on his ass ASAP, for if these documents were true, he lied on his job application and could actually be considered dangerous. And if they weren't true, he was still a liar, just of a different sort and kicked out the door ASAP."

Like our recent new hire William Skrimshander, Sedgwick had
made it pretty clear why he accepted KTI's employment offer
by applying for a draft deferment. Unlike Skrimshander, our
Randy Andy waited until after his first week on the job. Many
professional new hires applied for deferments, but unlike our draft
eligible pubs creeps, those others usually waited for a month or so
before doing so to at least give the appearance of actually wanting
a career at KTI. Apparently our guys didn't give a good god damn
about appearances. I called Sedgwick and asked him to come to
my office. He appeared, slid into my guest chair and assumed his
patented schlump about as casually as one could be and still remain
even quasi upright.

I pushed one set of the found documents across the table to him,
having already squirreled away the other set. "I think these are
yours."

He stared down at the first document and said, "Yes, they're mine.
Where you get them? The copier? I was in a rush and must have
left a set of the copies in the machine. I was in a hurry."

"Well someone found them in the copier. Randy, what the fuck
was going through your head? One of the secretaries found them in
the copier and gave them to Phyllis, who gave them to me. Right,
they're yours. The question is what exactly are they?"

"They're my get out of jail free card."

"I'm not so sure about that. These documents may very well be
your get INTO jail free card. And if personnel sees them, you'll be
kicked out of here and quite possibly all the way to Leavenworth.
How the hell did you get them?"

"I called a friend of mine from high school who just got declared 4F and asked him how he did it. He told me about this psych in Philadelphia, who would write a letter declaring you unfit for service for a thousand dollars… and worth every penny. I'm taking a chance here since I had to use the traveler's checks I had for my escape to Canada, but I'd rather get my 4F and stay here. It's a risk I'm willing to take."

"Well one of the risks you're also taking is that the secretary who found them will go to personnel and rat you out. If that happens, I can't cover this up. It'd be you or me and you'd be toast. Guess who found them."

"No idea."

"How about your girl… you know, the nominal Randy's girl."

"She's not my girl. It's a joke."

"I know it and you know it and she probably knows it, but maybe… just maybe… she doesn't think it's all that funny. And then there's this business that you've been under treatment for five fuckin' years."

Now there's a show of courage. When the going gets tough, the tough get going and in your case going for the exits. There's a reason he got away with his little game and you didn't get away with yours. It's got to do with fate. He's fated to be lucky and you're fated to be an asshole.

So you're back. Enjoy your little vacation? Look, I've got other fish to fry, more important fish. I like Randy, but I can't jeopardize my mission. There's too much at stake. Fuck fate... fuck luck! And fuck you!

Randy did not look overly concerned. Rather he looked pensive: "That five years business… yeah, I know. The psych says it's the only way to prove that my health and psychological illnesses are long term and most likely not curable."

"But you just met with the asshole last week. Right?"

"Right. He post dated the reports and faked up a treatment log and an appointment record. He knows what he's doing. He's gotten hundreds guys declared 4F."

"Well someone might notice that he's the asshole that's signing hundreds of these letters and all for the same reason. If he gets found out, you're going to Leavenworth."

"Look, it's a chance I'm willing to take to secure my freedom. Besides, it's only the second letter he's sent to my district. The bureaucracy is so screwed up and so overwhelmed with paperwork that there's virtually no cross-checking and coordination between all the draft boards. And if the Feds get close, he plans an office fire that'll destroy all his supposed records."

"All this is on his say-so. You OK with that."

"Sure am. And I don't think that Alexis will squeal on me"… Alexis being the previously mentioned Randy's girl.

183

Oxbow Lake The 2nd

Ah, Alexis! Alexis is… or was… a raven haired, olive skinned beauty. When the tribe dubbed Sedgwick THE 'Randy Andy' in what they thought to be great irony, the coffee clotch question arose immediately thereafter as to exactly who Andy was now desiring and planning to be randy with… the unstated assumption being that there were many others previously. Fate intervened and presented the tribe with Randy Andy's next victim of randyhood… kind of a random randyness, for Alexis happened to strut by… she was very good looking… had an ass that wouldn't quit… and she became the object of the randy one's supposed next randyness for all present with the exception of Randy himself. All in good semi-clean tribal fun.

The question often addressed to our Randy Andy during many of our coffee cloches thereafter: "How's it going with your girl?" And his "girl" thus became "Randy's girl" even though she didn't know he existed and he seemed to not care if she did. But like virtually all tribal jokes, it grew and took on a life of its own.

The tribe invented a rival for our Randy Andy… someone attempting to steal Randy's girl and that someone was a writer who worked as a reporter for the Lab's internal organ, one Sean O'Shaunessy... and Sean became "that demon Irish lover" who was attempting to capture the heart of Randy's girl presumably to get access to the rest of her body. Someone would say to Randy, "That demon Irish lover was seen in close proximity to your girl's cubicle this morning. He had that look in his eye… the look of a demon Irish lover and he's moving in on your girl." Questions arose as to what Randy Andy should do to counter the attack of that Demon Irish Lover. Advice was given: "Listen Randy, you've got to take out that demon Irish lover and you've got to do it in such a way as to leave no finger prints."

The Flake formulated a complex plan for him, "This is what you gotta do... buy that demon Irish asshole coffee... try to do it every day... bring him the damn stuff, but before you give that demon Irish bastard the cup, dump some salt peter into it. After a couple of doses, the demon Irish lover won't be much of a demon. He'll lose that fire, go limp if you know what I mean, and your girl will lose interest in him. She'll be yours for the taking." The plan actually sounded pretty good.

Why am I not surprised? Of course the plan would sound good to you.

Fuck you!

At first Randy would attempt to explain in fine rational discourse that Alexis was not his girl, but the more he did so the more Alexis became his girl. Finally, he gave up and accepted his role in the joke which eventually pretty much killed the joke. In classic irony, the demon Irish lover did in fact end up dating Randy's girl which breathed new life back into the joke, for now the tribe could concentrate its advice on how to seek revenge... all in good semi-clean fun.

Eventually, Alexis found out about the joke and went along with it, which, come to think of it, may have been why she dated that demon Irish lover in the first place, but like I said, the joke died of its own weight. The joke now sprang back to life in a most unfunny manner, for the question now was... is?... will Randy's former girl get him fired and send him to Leavenworth? Well, the long and short of it is she did not! I think she just wasn't interested enough to bother. I'm pretty sure it had nothing to do with protecting Randy. She just couldn't care less. Anyway, he gets away with his gaming of the system and Tadd and I do not. The difference: he stays out of the army and keeps his job at KTI, Tad spends time in the Ulster County slammer and me, I'm in a slammer of a different sort and humanity remains at daily risk ever since.

The Gooper Brings Back Bad Memories

Friday, the Polish Prince calls a status meeting of his management team. There are five of us… four first lines, one of them being me, and a real jabroni, Mr. Karl Kendricks, a former first-line manager in Pubs who upon returning from a foreign assignment reports to Igor because he originally comes from Pubs and they don't know what else to do with him… the deformed penny returns! Kendricks is like an unwanted minister without portfolio, the trick being to keep that portfolio empty. All of which follows one of the basic tenets of KTI management: some managers suck and virtually all former managers suck the biggone, Kendricks being the poster child for former manager biggone-ness.

I announce that I am positive that Sedgwick will be declared 4F. My three peers smile approvingly for we will not have to recruit and train another writer… programmer-writer anal-ist for those in the know… and we're already one up with the hiring of Skrimshander. Crazy Al, the manager responsible for our recruiting program, is ecstatic. The Admiral, the first-line responsible for our training program, is just as ecstatic as Crazy Al in his naval discipline sort of way. Rip Van Sam, our production manager, is fading into dream land, his head popping forward every now and then as he attempts to remain upright. He's the least concerned since he has nothing to do with the hiring and training of writers. Then that fuckin' Karl Kendricks opens that mouth of his and spits out, "How can you be sure? Why are you so sure? Shouldn't we put a backup plan in place just in case?"

Fuckin' Kendricks, AKA the Gooper, holds a special place in my blackened and hardened little heart. He is a despicably strange duck whose looks do not belie his despicability. From a distance, he looks awkwardly tall and quite thin... which he is. When he shambles closer, you notice that his head is misshapen... his forehead is squished in on one side so that it bubbles out on the other... like the finger of God has pushed in the one side causing the bubble on the other. He wears glasses which he manages to cleverly balance on his crooked nose in such a way so as to accentuate his misshapen head. When he speaks, he speaks out of the left side of his mouth, and when he speaks excitedly, he slobbers a bit. I learn quickly to stand or sit to his right, my left, when speaking with the left-sputtering asshole. He always wears the same shiny brown suit that doesn't quite fit and as he walks toward you, you notice that he walks at an angle tilting towards the bubble side of his head.

All this makes him look... well... quite distinctive, but as strange as it might seem, none of these physical oddities is his most distinguishing feature. His most distinguishing feature is his neck. It is extremely long and thin. It extends out of his collar at an odd angle and appears to have the ability to telescope his head outward beyond his body. This neck is the source of his nom de plume, which no one intentionally uses in front of him for obvious reasons. The tribe, including me, is convinced he could use his neck to telescope his head ahead of his body at will much like that old-time comic book character Plastic Man. This ability to telescope his head is known as the goop. I don't remember why, but that's what this unique ability is called, and since Mr. Karl

Oxbow Lake The 2nd

Kendricks is the source and performer of the goop, he becomes known as the Gooper. There is the half goop, the full goop, the under the desk goop. I believe that his under the desk goop is particularly useful when, as a first-line manager, he counsels Maggie, the only female writer in his department at the time. Then there's the corner goop which enabled him to see around corners before actually reaching them. The Gooper was a master of all of them.

When I first see the Gooper, I think "Can God be that cruel?" but after I know him a little better, I change my thought to "The bastard deserved it!" His outside is a mere reflection of his inside, and given my relationship with him, I don't give a good shit which came first.

We have a history. When I first meet him, I don't know any of this gooping business. In fact when first I meet the bastard, none of this gooping business has been recognized and identified for there is no tribe to recognize and identify it. At the time, Mr. Kendricks is interviewing me for a job at KTI. I am still married to what-cha-ma-call-it, and with two kids no less, and I need a job badly. Somehow I manage to get this interview with a KTI recruiter at Albany State or whatever it's called now, even though I have graduated several years earlier and technically am not eligible for job interviews. A kind secretary in the placement office prepares an interview package for me anyway.

How I get the interview is a tale unto itself. All the slots for interviews with the KTI recruiter are taken, but the interviews are to be held on a Saturday morning beginning at 8:00 AM. Given the drinking propensities of college students, particularly graduating seniors on Friday nights, I know that at least one of the prospective interviewees will wake up with a crippling hangover and will not show up for the scheduled interview, so I show up at the placement office at 7:30 AM with my interview package in hand and patiently await the inevitable. Bingo… I hit the interview jackpot… the first interviewee calls and cancels. I am the first to be interviewed by the KTI recruiter that day. I do well enough in that initial interview to get invited to take the Programmer Aptitude Test and I do well enough on that infernal test to get invited down to Kingston for an interview.

Suffering from the 'I need this fuckin' job' pre-interview jitters, I am unable to sleep the night before and get up at 4:00 AM. I sit around drinking coffee before driving down the Thruway to Kingston. I am already exhausted when I arrive. A personnel rep meets me at the personnel entrance, which I have difficulty finding and escorts me through a labyrinth of attached buildings and hallways to the Pubs area. The personnel rep and I stand at the doorway to manager Kendricks' office. I can picture it like it is yesterday. You know, that movie in my head business. I still have the letter inviting me for the interview. It's probably at the bottom of my archeological box of memories. The personnel rep introduces me and the all-powerful Mr. Karl Kendricks who slowly looks up, says nothing and with an annoyed wave of his left arm motions for me to enter his cubicle and sit down in his guest chair on the opposite side of his desk, which I do. When I turn to thank the personnel rep, he is gone… disappeared.

There I am sitting opposite this very odd looking man who stares down at a document on his desk and then up at me and then down at the document again. He does this several times and clears his ears, nose and throat each time with a rather jarring "Hrrrrahggg". He's yet to say a word. He blows his nose into a tissue he holds

189

in one hand and then puts the used tissue on the side of his desk in front of me and next to a cup of that dreadful vending machine coffee. He pulls open one of his desk drawers and pulls out a pack of saltine crackers which he opens and puts next to his snot-filled tissue… the one in which he's just blown his nose… and that cup of dreadful vending machine coffee. I think to myself, "Boy could I use a cup of that dreadful vending machine coffee." None is offered so I sit there and keep my mouth shut. The Gooper continues reading and without looking up, grabs a saltine cracker and munches on it spraying crumbs about his desk as he does so. Then he takes a sip of that dreadful machine coffee cup.

I think to myself, "Who the fuck is this idiot? He makes Quasimodo look like a well-mannered character played by Robert Redford." Keep in mind the Gooper has yet to speak to me. After several more minutes he looks up and says, "You know, Mr. Bobb, you did not do all that well on the P-A-T. Your score is marginal."

I am stunned by these, his first words to me, and say, "Mr. Kendricks, marginal? I think I do quite well, particularly given the circumstances. The only day the P-A-T is given in the Albany area, we get over three feet of snow. The half hour drive to the KTI branch office where the test is being given takes me over three hours. I arrived half an hour after the test begins and am told that I can take the test but I will not be given any additional time. The test monitor says he is noting this on my test sheet. Given the circumstances, I think I do very well."

That fuckin' Gooper-to-be looks up at me and says, "I see the note, but it's irrelevant. Your score is your score. There are no extenuating circumstances. Personally, with this score I do not think that you can pass our programming school and you have to pass programming school to become a programmer-writer analyst. Your employment is provisional and if you fail, you'll be terminated." That word terminated gives me the heebie geebies. He picks up his soiled tissue and blows his nose into it again and returns the now very soiled snot-filled tissue to its place on his desk and before me. He reflexively grabs another saltine cracker and commences to spray more crumbs about his desk.

I think to myself, "Maybe I should rearrange that fuckin' face of his. I'd be doin' the bastard a favor." True, doing so will pretty much end my career at KTI before it begins… but after what that fuckin' gooper says, it looks like I never have a career there anyway. It is the thought of spending time in the local jail for assault that keeps my temper in check. I take a deep breath and say, "I don't understand. If I'm not qualified for the job, why am I invited down here for an interview?"

He smiles his crooked smile and says, "We are considering you for another position… that of Editorial Assistant. You'll work with the programmer-writer analysts. You can take Vol Ed courses in the evening right here in the Lab to prepare for programming school. They're free. After a year… eighteen months at most… providing you do well in the courses… we'll send you to programming school, and since you're already an employee, your employment would not be provisional. I suggest that you take introductory programming courses and calculus. I see from your transcript that you don't have much math. All this depending of course, if we decide to make you the offer."

I need the job real bad, having already submitted my resignation… effective the end of the school year… from my job teaching idiot junior high retards how to sit at a desk and not punch each other.

191

I mean real idiots. They are called seven-threes… the kids the Special Ed teacher won't take because they are too big and too disruptive for her to handle. One year of this is enough for me so I resign, effective June. I need this job real bad.

That is the interview. That fuckin' Gooper calls the personnel rep who comes down to Kendrick's cubicle and escorts me out of the building. Not a goodbye, not a "we'll be in contact in x days or weeks"… nothing. Kendricks just pulls another folder from a pile of them on his desk and buries that crooked nose of his in it. I sit there waiting to be kicked out of the damn place positive that I am never to hear from the bastards again. I think to myself "This is the most efficient, employee friendly corporation in the world?" That fuckin' place is about as friendly as a Nazi SS detention camp.

I should have known what they are up to even back then. The evidence is there before me writ large. All I have to do is read it… but I am illiterate so to speak. And the Gooper…. that deformed Judas goat bastard… he even looks like a cannibal.

Say it. Go on, say it.

Shut the fuck up, you interfering bastard!

Low Expectations Rewarded

I hear nothing from the much vaunted and caring Kronos Technologies International just as I expect, and I think that while I need a job to support my family, not getting one at KTI has its distinct advantages. Then one day upon returning home from a long day of preventing seven-threes from beating the shit out of each other, I find a telegram slipped under the front door of our crummy little apartment on Washington Ave. What a dump. Anyway, I open the telegram and to my surprise, it is from KTI. It says, rather cryptically, "Please call KTI recruiter James Day at" … and it gives a number… a number not in my area code. I think to myself, "Those fuckin' bastards want me to spend my money to make a long distance call to them so that they can tell me that they're not offering me a job because I did so poorly on that god damn programming test… that I was a cry-baby to even mention extenuating circumstances. After all, there are never extenuating circumstances at KTI. Sorry, Mr. Ward Bobb the 3rd, but you're not smart enough to work at KTI and your unacceptably low score on the test proves it. Well fuck them!"

I sit in the kitchen drinking beer and mulling over that telegram. The wife and kids aren't home yet. After the seventh beer, I think that it's worth the price of a long distance call to give those bastards a piece of my mind, so I dial KTI recruiter Mr. James Day.

"Hello, this is James Day. KTI recruiting."

"Mr. Day. This is Ward Bobb."

Before I can begin yelling obscenities into the phone, he says, "I'm so glad you called. We've been trying to contact you for several weeks. You're a hard man to get a hold of. We'd like to make you an offer."

I am stunned and say, "What'd you say?"

"Mr. Bobb, we'd like to make you an offer."

Oxbow Lake The 2nd

I am unable to reply.

"Mr. Bobb, are you still there?"

"Yes."

"Well there is a slight problem. Your requested salary…"
I ask for a bump of a thousand bucks over my salary as a teacher
which is $5,200. The wife… what's her name… is a secretary
at the time and makes a base salary of $5,800 as a temp, plus
overtime. So I ask for a salary of $6,200 on my application to KTI.
I do a quick calculation in my head and figure that if KTI offers me
the same salary I'm earning now, I'll still come out ahead since the
benefits at KTI are non-contributory while those at the school are.
All that hatred of KTI fads into the deep recesses of my mind.

Mr. Day continues, "It's too low."

I am stunned again, "Too low?"

"Yes, our base salary is $6,800 for the position of Editorial
Assistant. It's a level 18 ."

I have no idea what that Level 18 business means, but $6,800 is
a damn good salary. More than I've ever made. I stutter into the
phone, "I'll take it!"

"That's super, Mr. Bobb. Mr. Kendrick asks that you begin the first
Monday after the July 4th weekend. I'll send you more information
about our moving and living program and a contact at KTI so that
you can make all the arrangements. I'll mail out a formal offer with
all the details tomorrow. Congratulations."

He hangs up before I can reply. I slump back into my kitchen chair trying to make sense of what has just happened. I admit that I am relieved and happy to have the job in spite of all my already blind hatred of KTI. The money is good… very good… I am desperate and the problem of supporting the family is now solved. What's her name can stay at home and with the kiddies and I can work. The money is tight without her working, but we can squeak by since there are no child care expenses. Still, a quiet whisper from those deep recesses of my mind says, "But the place is full of assholes and now you'll be one of them. You're going to hate working for KTI asshole number one, Mr. Karl Kendrick." And I have this very bad feeling about the place.

Telephonically Stepping in Shit

Things move fast after that phone call from Mr. James Day, that KTI recruiter. The wife and I buy a raised ranch across the river from Kingston in a place called Red Hook… one of the few financial coups of my life. Talk about steppin' in shit. We look at a dreadful slab house north of Kingston. It is one of the few houses in our price range. The place is a mess. I'd rather live in a refrigerator box under a bridge than live in that dump. Looks like we are going to remain renters.

Then the realtor shows us this house on the other side of the river, the one I finally buy. Love the place. What isn't there to love about it… new raised ranch with four bedrooms on a cul-de-sac, great school district, easy commute to KTI. The problem: it is way out of my price range. I tell the realtor, "No way. Too expensive." That evening the builder calls me… he has a strange accent… kind of sounded French… he drops the price… a lot. I have no down payment to speak of and I know I won't qualify for a mortgage for that house, even after the bastard dropped the price, so I give the asshole an emphatic 'no' to the deal. A couple of days later this builder calls and drops the price again. I still don't have the down payment and I still can't qualify for the mortgage, and so I give him another emphatic 'no'. The whole thing starts to sound fishy. Then he calls and drops the price a third time and says, I can hear him say, "Mr. Bobb, I am dropping the price ten percent below the house's appraised value. Use the difference as a down payment. I'll arrange for a mortgage from a local bank. It's up to you." Another unexpected and stunning phone call… this one not from KTI, at least on the surface.

The whole thing sounds even fishier to me now so I am reluctant to jump at the offer. It just looks too good to be true. I tell him I am thinking about it. What's her name works as a temp for an Albany law firm and she asks one of the junior partners to look into the builder… find out if he is a crook. The lawyer makes some phone calls and finds out that the builder is apparently legit and the whole thing is pretty much on the up and up. Turns out this builder is a Belgian citizen and his American wife is divorcing him and freezing all his business assets, most of which are in land and buildings. He is leaving the country and can only take cash with him, so he is selling off as much as he can… which is why he keeps dropping the asking price for the house. He is now down to twelve-five and even makes arrangements for a mortgage in order to get at least some cash out of his investment in the house. He needs to turn his hard assets into liquid cash… very badly and very quickly.

Before I can call him back, he calls me. He says, in what I now know is a Belgian accent, "Mr. Bobb, I am willing to also pay the closing costs and first year's taxes. To own that house, all you need to do is show up at the Saugerties Savings Bank next Wednesday at 10:00 AM on Friday to sign a couple of documents. It's yes or no. You are a fool not to. Stop all the hard-nosed negotiating. You win." I mumble "yes" and hang up. There is Saugerties poking its friendly little nose into my business for the first time but definitely not the last. Now I think that all my roads lead not to Rome but to Saugerties of all places, known as the arm-pit by the rest of the Ulster County… a combination of New Jersey and Iowa on a much smaller scale.

That Belgian bastard apparently thinks all that no-ing I am doing is a hard-nosed negotiating tactic. Shit, I'm negotiating diddly. I have no money to speak of. Truth is, I have nothing to negotiate with and don't know how to even if I do. He thinks I'm gaming him, probably because that's what he does. Hell, I am too naïve to game anyone about anything. Anyway, I buy the house and sign all the official documents the second week of June. I pay bubkes, zero, zilch at the closing. In fact, I pay nothing up front for the house. Later I am told that paying nothing to purchase a house is unheard of. Like I say, I step in shit… and goat shit at that, according to my Jewish friends.

KTI pays movers to move us into my gift house. We don't have to do a thing. Movers show up at our apartment in Albany, pack everything and move us. They put everything where we want in the new house and all we have to do is point. Easiest move I ever make and I make a bunch of them… before and since. Hell, they even wash the dishes before they put them away.

We are all moved in two weeks ahead of schedule, so I call that KTI recruiter, Mr. James Day, and tell him that I buy a house, move in and am ready for work. I can report for work two weeks early. He says something that seems rather strange to me, "Mr. Kendricks is very specific and says that he wants you to report the first workday after the July 4th weekend and not a day before. Use the time to get settled in and learn about the area. Congratulations again" and he hangs up. I think "Well who knows why the great KTI wants me to wait two weeks?" KTI is as KTI does!

Later, I find out why. The cheap prick. If I begin work before July 4th, I qualify for two full weeks of paid vacation. After… just one. The prick was saving KTI one week's paid vacation for a lowly editorial assistant… namely yours truly. That extra week of paid vacation would probably have broken poor KTI's financial back. What a prick!

Since we have two weeks to settle in as Mr. James Day puts it, what's her name and I do all that settling in stuff. The electricity is already turned on and so I concentrate on getting the telephone service installed. Turns out to be an adventure of sorts since the phone company is a small locally owned outfit. I drive into town to the Red Hook Telephone office. It is a small, neat house, a residential house… even has a white picket fence out front. I knock on the front door and enter. It feels like I'm walking onto a set for a 1930s detective movie. There against the far wall is one of those old fashioned switch boards. An old woman with blue hair pulled back in a bun sits at the switch board. She has huge earphones wrapped around her head. Protruding from the earphones is one of those old-fashioned not so micro microphones… more like one of those old fashioned speaking tubes. She is speaking into the damn thing and pushing in one of those manual switch board connections into that huge switch board.

She looks at me and points to a room off what I guess is the living room and there is Mabel, the person who handles the business operations. I am pretty sure it is Mabel since there was a big sign on her desk that says 'Mabel's Desk'. If it isn't Mabel sitting behind that desk, it is at least her desk. Turns out it is Mabel. She looks like the blue-haired telephone operator's twin sister. As it turns out, she is one-third of the operation… handles old business, new business, scheduling of maintenance and installation, billing, complaints and just about everything else that connects to the business end of the phone service that the Red Hook Telephone Company provides. Her putative twin sister handles phone operations, so between them, it appears they are two thirds of the staff.

Mabel waves for me to sit down, which I do and asks, "How may I help you?"

"I want to get phone service installed."

"Address?"

I give her the address and she pulls out this huge loose-leaf binder from behind her, plops it on her desk and pages through it. After several minutes of study, she says, "We have two party lines available for that address. A three-party line and a five-party line."

I am stumped. "What's a party line?"

"It's a line with three to five parties using the same line."

Then from deep in my memory I recall that when I am real young, I think my mother and father have a party line, but that is many decades ago. I don't know what it means other than my father complains about this lady who is always hoggin' up the line.

I can hear dear old Dad complaining, so I ask, "Do you have any lines without other parties?"

"You mean private lines, correct? There are several that run out to that development but they are all taken. We only have these two party line openings."

I am stunned. I do not know that this kind of service even exists anymore but I am obviously wrong.

Mabel smiles at me and says, "I suggest that you take the three-party opening. It's an extra two dollars a month, but there are two fewer customers on that line which increases your chances of getting access to the phone service. If someone else is on the line, you can't use it until they hang up."

"How do I know they're on the line?"

"When you pick up the phone, you can hear them talking so you just hang up. Our policy is that no one should listen to someone else's phone conversations. It's common courtesy, but if I am you, I'd be careful what I say on the phone. It's better to assume that someone's listening even though they're not supposed to. You know how people are."

This whole party-line business floors me. I didn't expected to have to make this kind of decision and say, "I'd like to think about it."

Mabel slams the huge loose-leaf binder closed, smiles and says, "I wouldn't wait too long if I am you. We only have two openings in that development and when they're taken, that's it for phone service until we run more lines out that way and we have no plans to do that."

"You mean it's now or possibly never for phone service?"

"Yup."

I make one of those trap decisions on the spot, "I am taking the opening on the three-party line."

She pulls a contract from her file drawer and has me sign it. I ask, "When can the telephone be installed?"

Mabel looks down at a sheet on her desk and says, the first Monday after the July 4th weekend and writes my name and address on what I guess is the installation schedule.

I am again stunned. I think to myself, "Have I moved into some kind of time warp?" I say, "Maim, that's over two weeks from today. We just moved in and we need to make all kinds of arrangements. Is there any way you can get the phone installed sooner?"

"No, unfortunately. Gino's on vacation."

"Who's Gino?"

"Gino does all the maintenance and installation work and like I said he's on vacation"… Gino apparently being the final third of the Red Hook Telephone Company staff.

Oxbow Lake The 2nd

"Don't you have any back-up for Gino?"

"No. Mr. Bobb, we aren't Bell. I suggest that you make arrangements with one of your neighbors to use their phone in the mean time. It's done all the time." So there I am... required to beg for the use of someone else's telephone for the next two weeks... most likely another party-line at that... while Gino enjoys his vacation.

I accept my phoneless fate and asked, "Can you please put me on the waiting list for a private line?"

"Sure can. You'll be number 23 out that way on the list, but I warn you, someone's got to die for another private line to become available and as far as I know all the private lines are pretty healthy. J. R. Johnson is in his seventies but he's as healthy as one of his horses."

"You mean I have to hope one person who possess a private line dies and is joined in the afterlife by 22 others in order for me to get a private line?"

"I wouldn't say it that way, but that's about it."

I put my technological tail between my legs and walk out of the house-slash-office for the Red Hook Telephone Company expecting my world to turn black and white. I am about to work for one of the most technologically advanced computer corporations in the world and I must wait two weeks for Gino to return from vacation to install three-party telephone service in my home.

And that three-party telephone service? It'd be easier than hell to ease-drop, as in spy, on me with such a system. I think to myself "There's something very wrong with this picture!"

Did I Imagine the Whole Thing?

We tour the local grade school which is just up the road and across the street from a large corn field, speak with the principal, wander around the village and do most of the settling-in things that we need to do. I decide to show the little woman and kiddies where I'll be earning our daily bread, so I drive over the Kingston-Rhinecliff Bridge to the KTI site.

You haven't really written much about the family... you know, and I quote, the so-called "little woman and kiddies". What's up with that? Surely they play an important role in this little drama of yours. Whatever happened to your little brood?

None of your fuckin' business. It's a touchy subject. Some things are just a little too personal to write about... particularly when there's voyeurs and snitches reading your stuff. No way Jose will I be getting into specifics about that part of my life like I say below.

I know that I haven't said much about the wife and kiddies... at least any specifics. It's a painful subject just now. Maybe later. Anyway the roads around the ol' bom-bor factoree are jammed with cars. I stupidly choose to reconnoiter at quitting time on the last day before the July 4th weekend. It is like a NASCAR race as the KTI faithful race to escape their captivity for a long weekend of freedom. The wife is impressed with the size of the place. She says something like, "This place is huge. There's buildings all over the place. Which building will you work in?"

I am getting nervous. Cars are zooming all around me. They know where they are going and where they want to be and I don't. I answer her question a bit petulantly if memory serves me, "I have no damn idea. It's a labyrinth in there. I'm pretty sure it's toward the back."

She says something like "How will you find it?"

I remember thinking that I should get the hell out of traffic and say, even more petulantly, "On Monday, I report to personnel first. I guess they'll show me. We gotta get the hell out of this traffic before we get creamed." I spot this place, a Price Chopper super market… at least I think it's a Price Chopper… across the street from the south end of the KTI site, make a sharp right into the super market's parking lot and park in front of the store. I sit there for a moment catching my breath. It looks like it'll be a while before the traffic thins and slows down.

The little woman says, "We might as well do some shopping. We need groceries," so into the Price Chopper we traipse. We wander around the aisles filling our shopping cart with all kinds of goodies. The place is huge. You can fit Red Hook's entire business district into the building. We turn down the aisle for drugs and medical supplies and… I vividly remember this like it is a scene from a movie… there stands Mr. Karl Kendrick, the future Gooper himself, stuffing a shopping basket with various hemorrhoidal products. Fuckin' hemorrhoidal products. The bastard is in Preparation H heaven. I yell to him, "Mr. Kendrick" as I trot up to him. He looks at me furtively as I approach, "Remember me, Ward Bobb. I report to work on Monday. I'll be working for you."

He looks at me like he doesn't know me from Adam… better yet, like I have some kind of air-borne anal plague… and says, "You don't work for me," and hustles off to the express check-out counter leaving me standing amongst the hemorrhoid products dumbfounded. The little woman catches up to me with the kiddies in tow and says something like, "Who's that?"

"It's my manager… at least I think it's him… the manager I'll be working for, Mr. Kendricks, but the bastard looks at me like I'm hemorrhoid Mary spreading a rare form of hemorrhoid fever which could make his present condition fatal… like it's the first time he's seen me… and mutters 'You don't work for me' and runs off to avoid me. Shit, he's the asshole who interviews me and he's the asshole I'm told I'll be working for."

Dire thoughts arise within me muddling my mind with fright. Here I am in a dip shit city, buying a house I can't afford in the dip shit town… all based on the assumption that Mr. Karl Kendricks hires me to work at the world famous Kronos Technologies International… an apparently erroneous assumption.

In a panic, I run to the pay phones at the front of the super market. I shuffle through the pages of my pocket organizer, find the number for Mr. James Day, the personnel recruiter who makes me the job offer, frantically jam a bunch of coins into the pay phone until I get a dial tone and dial his number. An answering machine picks up and says that Mr. Day is unavailable at this time and to leave a short message. I hang up. He is obviously out for the long weekend and it is fruitless to leave a message since I report to personnel early Monday morning… most likely long before Mr. James Day could return a phone call to my still phoneless home in Red Hook. It is going to be a long weekend.

I spend that weekend… a long and torturous long weekend at that… biting my finger nails to the bone. In my finger-nail biting frenzy, I imagine that this hemorrhoidal asshole Kendricks and his personnel sidekick, James Day, are in cahoots with that crooked Belgian developer to sell houses and use a phony job offer at KTI to get schmucks like me to buy houses and qualify for mortgages. The mind can be a labyrinthine device generating fear, self-deception and self-destruction and mine is working overtime generating copious amounts of all three. I sit in the kitchen of a house I am sure I now can't afford and which I am also sure is soon to be foreclosed, drinking beer as my fevered mind constructs a complex conspiracy involving banks and lawyers and developers, with those two KTI assholes in the middle of this complex plot. Maybe this Belgian guy isn't having his assets seized by an angry wife. I learn later how this would feel, but back then I am pretty naïve about such things. I even come to admire the effectiveness of their plot and performance… of how they even fooled our volunteer lawyer… unless of course the lawyer is in on the plot too. Like I say, the mind is wondrously creative when constructing its own little reality even when that creativity is destroying its host.

Now you're cooking! Take the next step, turd brain!

Sometimes you must comb through your experiences and carefully separate the real from the imagined. That's one of the reasons for this entire journal writing exercise. However, I begin the process long before I touch pen to journal as is obvious from my later journal entries. Reality can play tricks on you and can be manipulated. The trick is to know which events are real and which are created or imagined and if events are created... who creates them and why? If they are imagined, what sparks the imagined events and what creates the spark... a spark, which... if not doused... causes a conflagration. Things are never like what they seem, as my dear interloper, you'll find out, my little mutton chop.

Into that Good Night?

I don't sleep at all Sunday night into Monday morning. I can't eat anything for breakfast, in fact for the long holiday weekend I fear-fast, maintaining a liquid-only diet, the liquid being primarily Budweiser. I even cut myself shaving as I prepare for what I hope would be my first glorious day on the job at KTI but fearing it would not. I must show up at the KTI personnel lobby at 8:00 AM for orientation. I get there at 7:30 and the parking lot is already pretty full. The offer letter is jammed into my jacket pocket... a letter I am convinced is a forgery... my wallet is stuffed in my back pocket with my identification and no folding money... two quarters jingle in my front pocket for the bridge toll for the drive back to my about-to-be-foreclosed house and that's it. I think I am early but like I say the personnel lobby is already packed when I arrive... packed with what I suspect are a bunch of new hires for the much vaunted Kronos International Technologies. Looks like they all have legitimate offers although I think that Operation Schmuck could be snaring several other unsuspecting souls... as it has yours truly... sitting about the lobby and who are about to be notified that their job offers are cruel jokes and then sent back into that cold, cruel non-KTI world to face another fate.

Oxbow Lake The 2nd

I introduce myself to the receptionist who checks a roster, finds my name, which she checks off, gives me a temporary badge and tells me to have a seat. Endorphins fill my formerly nightmare conjuring brain. I am euphoric! Not only am I on the list, there's a badge for me… true it's a badge but it's a badge with my name hand-written on it. I inspect the badge and something doesn't seem quite right… I realize I'm not totally in the clear, for glaring back at me are the words 'TEMPORARY' formally printed in large bold letters above my hand-printed name. I nervously survey the group who anxiously sit about the lobby and they all have temporary badges too. I am pretty sure I am OK… unless Operation Schmuck is a lot bigger than I suspect.

I take a seat as instructed and survey the group. The place is packed. I count 62 apparent new hires, 63 if I include me. It is a pretty motley group with a surprising number of women. I am pretty sure that many of these new hires are not engineers or programmers. A young and very nervous young woman sits across from me. She is wearing a short skirt which has ridden up her thighs and in her nervousness… she has splayed her thighs showing a fine camel-toed pink panty covered bush. I am so thankful for her nervous carelessness. Takes my mind off all that I contemplate the previous four Budweiser-filled days… and she is pretty good looking to boot. She notices me noticing her and slaps her thighs together with a look of embarrassed disgust.

The clock continues to tick ever so slowly, now in that Einsteinian manner of how time is slowly relative, particularly when sitting on a hot stove as I am. Finally this pocket-protected, white-socked, high-watered guy makes a dramatic entrance and ushers us into a large nearby conference room that isn't quite large enough for all the apparent new hires. Some of us must stand in the back as there aren't enough chairs. Mr. Pocket Protector is a squirrely looking dude who speaks very fast and with great enthusiasm. While this isn't the greatest day in my life quite yet, it is obviously his. He informs us that KTI has the highest average IQ of any corporation in the world and how proud we must be to join such an intelligent organization. How anyone can determine this is beyond me, but I go with it… going with the flow. I look around me and think that from what I can see that world-leading average corporate IQ is about to take a hit of a couple of points today and if another corporation is breathing down KTI's neck in this average IQ race, KTI can easily fall into second place.

He introduces some guy dressed to the nines who speaks about benefits, very little of which I can hear. He shows what I later learned is a "foil" in KTI-ese using an overhead projector to display a KTI check stub on a large screen in the front of the conference room. He explains each of the fields and what they mean. He spends a great deal of time with a box labeled "meal/shoe" and how it is an indication of how much KTI cares about its employees, i.e. us. In fact, big brother cares so much that he gives his beloved employees, i.e. us, a meal allowance if we work any overtime (apparently the "meal" part of the meal/shoe box) and even pays for one pair of steel-toed shoes a year (apparently the "shoe" part of the meal-shoe box)… the amount of the reimbursements appearing in that precious aforementioned "meal/shoe" box. Then he qualifies the whole thing by saying that this benefit is only for "non-exempt" employees upon approval by your manager.

This meal/shoe business brings me great consternation. First, the speaker is very enthusiastic about this "meal/shoe" business… so enthusiastic that he speaks quite loudly. Thus it is one of the few parts of his presentation I am able to hear. Second, I am troubled by my need for steel-toed shoes. I wonder why the hell an editorial assistant such as me would need steel-toed shoes. What kind of editing am I doing here? Cement manuscripts edited with hammer and chisel? And then this business of being non-exempt. I have no idea what that means or if I am one of them, so it is unclear to me if KTI actually cares about me. If I am exempt, am I exempt from KTI caring about me as evidenced by that precious meal-shoe business? If I miss handle one of those cement manuscripts while editing it with that hammer and chisel and drop the damn thing on my foot, would said foot be crushed because I am not allowed to be reimbursed for steel-toed shoes using that meal-shoe box, being exempt and all?

Then things get even more confusing. Some safety guy shows us a movie about not walking between railroad cars so as not to get inadvertently squashed and how a yellow warning light should flash before my eyes if I ever contemplate doing so. This throws me for an even greater loop. To my knowledge, I never contemplate walking between railroad cars at KTI. Would my work at KTI require me to walk over railroad tracks in steel-toed shoes, if I am in fact allowed to buy them, lugging cement manuscripts for editing with hammer and chisel? For Christ's sake, what kind of job is this editorial assistant position? Wearing steel-toed shoes while walking along railroad tracks beside trains and seeing yellow flashing lights? What the fuck!

Then we are taken on a tour of the plant. Mr. white-sox high-water pocket-protector waxes eloquent about the place. He is so excited that I think he is going to cream his pants. He rattles on about how the place isn't a factory but a "manufacturing facility" as he puts it and how the sainted Mr. P. T. Holmes Senior, the beloved founder of KTI, loves his employees so much that he gives the corporation his first begotten son, Mr. P. T. Holmes Junior, who now runs the place, and how the old man cares so much more about us that he even has wooden floors put down in this great "manufacturing facility" so that his employees, whom he loves so much, won't hurt their feet as they march around in their "meal/shoe" steel-toed shoes while avoiding marching between railroad cars. Seems to me that the sainted Mr. P. T. Holmes Senior and his beloved and sacrificed son are more concerned about their employees' feet than what those feet are connected to... particularly at the very top, i.e., its employees' brains in spite of KTI's great pride in having the very highest average corporate IQ. After all this steel-toed, avoiding being squashed between railroad cars business, I begin to seriously question my going with the flow in regards to this highest average corporate IQ claim. However they calculate this average IQ business, I am pretty sure that KTI somehow jerrys the numbers. The whole thing is a big ol' shit-filled crock designed to make the assholes around me feel good... me not being one of them... from the very fuckin' get-go!

We wander back to the personnel reception lobby and Mr. white-sox high-water pocket-protector tells us with great enthusiasm that our managers pick us up shortly and take us to a wonderful lunch on KTI and how great the cafeteria is. This news thrills me for I am starving to death having had nothing to eat for the better part of four days while drinking many six packs of Bud, sometimes two at a time... and since I have no money in my wallet to buy anything to eat.

Managers show up, introduce themselves to their new employees and lead them away for what I imagined is a delicious and filling lunch at that great cafeteria... on the part of an all-caring meal/

211

shoe, don't step between railroad cars… K-T-I. Inexorable time marches on and the mass of new hires thin until I am the only one left. The clock ticks unmercifully on… tick tock… tick tock… and it is a KTI manufactured clock high on the wall over the receptionist's desk. A quarter to one, I stagger up to the receptionist, now faint with hunger, and ask, "Are you sure I'm on that list of new hires?" Thoughts of Operation Schmuck again creep into my thoughts. Doubts return.

She gives me a puzzled look (she is either not a part of the conspiracy or a very good actress) and says, "Of course you're on the list? What in heaven's name would lead you to believe you aren't?"

I think, "Perhaps the plan to have me become so faint from hunger that I drive off the bridge and into the Hudson River on a futile attempt to return to my soon to be foreclosed home", but I hide my fears from the receptionist. After all, you never know. I say with relative calm, "Well, everyone else is picked up by their managers and taken to lunch and I am not."
She looks down at the new hire roster and says, "I'll check and find out why."

I stumble back to my seat and collapse into my chair, now even more faint from hunger and stress. My brain goes into conspiracy overdrive. I think: "She says 'why'. Does she mean why is my name on the list in the first place?"

She makes several calls and yells over to me that someone is coming down to pick me up for lunch and so I wait some more. At one thirty, I am still sitting there, so I stagger up to the receptionist yet again and again as... this time even more weakly, "Are you sure

I'm on that list?"

She answers a bit petulantly, "Please have a seat. I'm sure your manager is going to pick you up shortly. Mr. Bobb, this is KTI and not some local Mom and Pop."

I think to myself "I'd settle for a Mom and Pop grocery store, one where I have credit, instead this KTI institution that starves its employees" and beat an unsteady retreat back to my seat.

Finally this dumpy looking older guy pokes his head through the door leading to that much vaunted "manufacturing facility". He looks around the lobby apparently trying to puzzle through the profound problem of who in the room is the new employee. It really shouldn't have been all that profound a problem. Shit, there is only me and a female receptionist in the damn place so how much thinking should be required from a manager in the corporation that claims to have the highest average corporate IQ in the world. Even a member of the corporation with the second highest average corporate IQ in the world should be able to easily solve the problem at hand. I think to myself, "Please Lord, not him", but I guess the inscrutable one has other plans for yours truly on this day. After several minutes of profound thought, this dumpy looking older guy with a grey complexion shuffles over to me and says rather abruptly, "I'm Delton Meriwether, your manager. Follow me." He keeps his head down and never looks me in the eye. No handshake, no greeting, no nothing.

He shuffles back to the door to that much vaunted "manufacturing facility" and I stumble after him and into the mysterious world of KTI, where body squashing trains run amuck, steel-toed shoes are required to protect one's toes from falling cement manuscripts

213

and God knows what else. He keeps a fast pace and says nothing. When I catch up to him, I ask "Aren't I working for Mr. Kendricks?"

Without slowing his shuffling pace or looking at me, he says, "There's been a reorganization. You're not working for Mr. Kendricks. You're working for me." End of explanation.

My stomach grumbles and I asked, "Are we having a late lunch?"

Without turning to look at me or slow his pace, he says, "The cafeteria closed at one thirty. We just missed it. You'll be skipping lunch."

This news does not please me. We walk along those wonderfully considerate wooden floors that are so good for my feet... even when said feet aren't covered with KTI meal/shoe steel-toed footwear. Right... left... right... left... I march on behind the shuffling Mr. Delton Meriwether as he leads me down grey-walled hallways, all of which looked alike, through a series of turns, even having me retrace my steps at one point. It feels like he's trying to confuse me so that I am unable to find my way back. A feeling overwhelms me... I am following a Morlockian-like creature into a well lit heart of darkness. Gives me the heebie-jeebies, for I do not want to be an Eloian entre. I want to eat lunch, not be lunch! Where is Mr. H. G. Wells and his time machine when you need him? Faint from hunger and worried about being unable to find my way back to my car, I cowboy on. If a sack of bread crumbs magically appears in my hands, I'll have a tough choice to make. Eat or mark my escape route. Eating probably wins out. Maybe I am an Eloi.

So the truth comes out. Right? You are what you eat, what you don't eat and what eats you, my walking entre of a friend.

Like I said earlier or at least implied, you've got to peel back that onion of perceived reality one fold at a time to get to reality's core. It's not an easy thing to do, but you can't shy away from where the peeling takes you as frightening and seemingly unlikely as that might be. My world is becoming much more complex than I had ever imagined. Is some force peeling reality back on itself to confuse and confound little ol' me?

Are there Morlocks at KTI?

My journey continues as this shuffling Morlockian-like creature who is apparently my manager leads me down the mysterious grey-walled labyrinth towards what I think is the publications area, but instead of turning right at the large sign saying "Publications," we continues another fifty feet or so to a cement wall. A creepy feeling spreads through me, not quite outright fear but close. I yell ahead to the creature, "Did we miss the turn to the publications area?"

The Morlockian-like creature turns quickly and I almost stumble into him. A creepy grin spreads across his face as he stares at me like I'm dinner and says "No"… no further explanation… just a straight monotone "No". For the first time, I am face to face with him and I am overcome with the stench of rotting flesh. If he's human, he suffers from what has to be close to a terminal case of halitosis. I think "Do these KTI creatures feed on the flesh of Editorial Assistants?" My stomach is growling as I stumble along,

215

but in that instant, I lose my appetite. My mind wanders on, "Too bad I'm not the victim of Operation Schmuck. At least that would only consume me financially... at least initially."

Looking back, that's when those god damn nightmares start again. Every night I am overcome with this feeling that I am being consumed. I fight to stay awake so that those fuckin' creatures can't grab me and barbeque me or do whatever they do to prepare their meals. Rationally, I know it's only a nightmare, but it sure doesn't feel like a nightmare. It seems all too real.

The Morlockian creature turns to his left, pulls open a heavy steel door and shuffles in. I grab the edge of the door so it won't smack me as I follow the creature reluctantly through that steel door. The place is like a cave. No windows. Dim overhead lights. There is a row of five... maybe six of what I shortly learn are called "cubicles" on each side of this center aisle. At the end of the aisle is another heavy steel door like the one I just pass through. This one with a huge yellow symbol on it. I immediately think, "What the fuck's behind that steel door?" I know one thing... if that Morlock tries to force me to walk through that second steel door, he'll need a bunch of his friends to do it.

I am led to one of the cubicles in the middle of the row on the left side of the aisle and Mr. Delton Meriwether, my Morlockian leader, says, "This is your cubicle." Without any further explanation he shuffles off and out that first heavy steel door we just enter. I stand there for a long minute staring into what is apparently now my "cubicle" thinking, "Is this the holding tank for the Eloi?" I feel like a god damn entree.

The silence is broken by a yell from across the aisle, "You a KTI guy?" Scares the shit out of me. I turn and for the first time notice that most of the other cubicles appear to be occupied. I wonder if this cave isn't a Morlockian meat locker. The voice from the cubicle across the aisle comes from a long, skinny balding young man. Obviously not a Morlock. He sits in his chair with his feet up on the desk leaning back with his hands clasped behind his neck. If this is a Morlockian meat locker, this guy doesn't seem to care… leading me to believe it isn't. The young man continues, "You look like shit, my man. I'm Bernstein." He repeats the question in his clipped Brooklyn accent, "You a KTI guy?"

I slowly turn and shake my head 'yes'. Bernstein scrambles to his feet and bounces into the aisle thrusting out his hand which I tentatively grasp and he vigorously shakes. He looks down at me and says, "Let me treat you to a cup of rotten KTI vending machine coffee. (That was my first cup of that dreadful stuff.) There is this rumor another KTI guy is showin' up today. Appears you're it."

I just stare at him. He grabs my arm and leads me back out that imposing steel door, down the main aisle passing the sign declaring "Publications". He points toward the sign and says, "That's where the regular KTI guys sit. I'm a subcontractor. Everyone in that god damn cave where we sit is a sub… everyone but you. What'd you do to get banned? Flunk out of programming school? You're sittin' in the Dance Hall."

I mumble a two word response, which is a question, "Dance Hall?"

Without skipping a beat, this Bernstein guy continues, "Yeah, the Dance Hall. Usually that's where they shove the guys who flunk programming school. They're the ones about to suffer what those management screws call, and I quote, 'a management initiated separation'. In other words, the poor bastards are being fired. You look like a condemned man. You about to be fired?"

I shake my head 'no' as we turn into an alcove off the main aisle and say again, "Dance Hall?"

"Yeah, the Dance Hall. That's what the screws in Sing Sing call the execution chamber where ol' Sparkie fries the bad boys. I think the name comes from when they used to hang them. You know, dance at the end of a rope. Anyway, your cube is the publications Dance Hall. Like I say, it's where the management screws bring the guys they're firing. That's why we call it the Dance Hall. It's kind of a KTI execution chamber… away from the regulars, very private… except for us and we don't count. In the Dance Hall the poor bastards are formally told they're being canned. Rumor has it, they sign a bunch of papers and get a separation check if they're good little incompetent boys. But it's not only boys. Last week they fire a girl. She cries like a baby. Anyway, like I say, rumor has it they get a check and then disappear out the door."

I just look at him bleary eyed and ask, "Which door? That other steel door at the end of the aisle… the one with the big yellow symbol? Do the managers march them through that steel door at the other end of the aisle?" I can't get those fuckin' Morlocks out of my head and if I'm a Morlock, that's what I'd do. I wonder how they serve those Eloi. Fried extra crispy? Mr. Morlock, sir, will you have fries with that?

He ignores my question and ushers me into an alcove off the main aisle. There stands a huge Xerox copier, and three vending machines: one for various blends of coffee and tea… it even dispenses soup… one for cold soft drinks and one for candy, pretzels and the like. Bernstein babbles on, "When a guy's about to be canned, they don't want the poor bastard killing the morale of the other poor regular KTI bastards... depressing the little darlings... so they bring him and sometimes a her to the Dance Hall. We're just subs. We don't have morale, so it's OK to stick those condemned bastards with us. Sometimes it takes days to can the poor assholes. And they don't even give the poor bastard a last meal. It is not a pleasant sight, but you get used to it."

I ask again, "What happens to them after they're fired? Do the managers march them through that steel door at the end of the aisle?"

Bernstein answers my question this time, "No, they usually march the poor bastards out the other steel door to the main aisle. I'm really not sure what happens next since they never come back, but I think they just march them to the nearest exit and take their badge." His explanation does not bring me relief... rather it gives me more food for fearful thought.

He shoves several coins into the vending machine for coffee and tea and says, "Choose your poison. I got a box of donuts back in my cube if want something to dunk in your coffee."
I stand before the vending machine and say, "I don't think KTI fires anybody or lays anybody off."

Bernstein laughs and says, "Don't believe that bullshit you hear or read in the newspapers. They fire people all the time. They don't bother to lay anybody off. They just fire them. There's never a mass firing or layoff. Just an endless series of ones and twos. Push some buttons and choose your poison. What's your name anyway?"

219

"Ward Bobb, I think." He laughs at my response only I'm not joking.

I choose my poison and we walk back to Bernstein's cube and he offers me a donut from a large box of them. I take one from the box and he says, "Take two… hell take three. What we don't eat, I throw out." I greedily take a second, thank him and walk back to what becomes my own personal Dance Hall.

Funny thing about coffee. I used to love the smell of coffee and the taste… even that vending machine swill tastes pretty good. Now I can't stand the stuff. Sometimes I can but mostly I can't. The taste makes me sick to my stomach. Even the smell of the stuff makes me queasy.

There on my desk is a pile of manuals and on top of the manuals is an envelope with my name written on the envelope. I open the envelope and try to read the note it contains. The hand writing makes a doctor's prescription script look like a calligrapher's triumph in clarity. I puzzle over the note for a while. I finally yell over to Bernstein for help interpreting the note.
Bernstein walks over to my own personal Dance Hall and I give him the note to read. He says, "It's that asshole Merewether's hieroglyphics. He scribbles so that no one will notice he can't spell. I think it says you have an appointment at Security to get a permanent badge tomorrow at 10:00 and you're to read all these manuals." There are five thick manuals in the stack.

The Morlocks are coming, the Morlocks are coming!

I have difficulty getting this Morlock thing out of my head and not without at least two big reasons. Doc says that my perception is a little off kilter… at least that's what that idiot says during our last session, being polite and all. He calls it a prodome kind of thing, whatever the hell that is and he's upped the meds. But that fuckin' place gives me the willies for a reason. Doc says my Morlock obsession is a metaphor going wild. What's he know? I have my doubts about him and HIS perception of reality… and maybe his true identity. He has ME writing this god damn journal to myself to figure all this out. Well maybe he ought to be writing his own journal, the fuckin' idiot. He's got a lot of figuring out to do himself. And those god damn meds… he's stupid if he thinks I'm swallowing that stuff. Makes me goofy. Can't concentrate. Won't be able to defend myself and complete my mission. All I do is tongue the stuff and spit it out later and then act goofy. It's so easy to fool these idiots. No wonder they can't see what's going on.

Anyway, I go to work every day that first week. I walk past the sign proclaiming the Publications area, pull open that steel door to the left of that cement wall and walk into that creepy cave. I sit in my Dance Hall cube sipping my cup of dreadful vending machine coffee… which tastes worse by the hour… and stare at that steel door at the other end of the aisle… the one with the huge yellow symbol. Every day, I wonder what the hell's going on behind that fuckin' door but am afraid to ask. Besides, who would I ask, one of the fuckin' Morlocks? Same routine every day. When the caffeine kicks in… I still like the taste of coffee back then, even that vending machine stuff… I start to read those stupid manuals. They are about this text processing system I am to use. Talk about tough sledding… after a morning of reading that shit, I want to slit my wrists. What doesn't bore me puzzles the shit out of me. Thank god for Bernstein and his subcontract compatriots.

My second day on the job, Bernstein walks me down to the security office where they take a mug shot of me and issue me an "official" employee badge. I get the distinct impression that these security guys only smile at traffic accidents, a fender-bender brings a grin and only a really horrendous accident, preferably one with a fatality or two, brings a true smile. I wonder what these KTI Gestapo do with the bodies.

If it isn't for Bernstein, I'm still wandering those stupid halls looking for the place. The picture on my badge makes the photo on my driver's license look like a work of art. I think that the bastards might even tattoo my so-called man-number on my arm… you know, like the Nazis do to the god damn Jews. Later my 'man-number' becomes an 'employee-number' when the stupid corporation realizes that they also hired human creatures without testicles. Must have come as a real revelation. My guess, KTI appoints a task force to investigate the situation and after several years of consultation with highly paid medical specialists decide that they hire a number of employees who, in fact as well as theory, do not have testicles. Thus the name of the number issued to each employee should be changed. I bet that it takes a second task force another year to come up with a new name for the stupid number. Hell, my first day on the job, I could tell them that some of those new hires don't have testicles. Some of them had beautiful bushy camel toes between their legs.

Anyway, my stupid Morlockian manager doesn't show up for the rest of the week. I have a lot of questions about that text processing program and this sub guy, Rich, Bernstein's subcontract buddy and roommate… they split the rent for a small house in Lake Katrine… knows a little about the program and answers my questions as best he can. He tells me that the program is shit and a retarded cockroach can write a better one. This does not fill me with confidence.

One morning, I think it it's that Friday, I'm sitting there sipping my morning dose of that dreadful caffeine-filled liquid that KTI termed rather loosely coffee, and the steel door from the main aisle slams open. I hear it. Don't see it. I turn and over my cubical partition I see these two giant yellow creatures slowly clomp down the aisle toward the Dance Hall. There is a narrow slit in the face covering where the eyes usually are… a narrow slit. Might be made of some kind of transparent natural eye covering like snakes have. I can't tell what's behind it. I about piss my pants. I think that the Morlocks make a comeback and are out to harvest their crop of Eloi, me being a new member of the crop. Scares the fuckin' shit out of me. The phone rings as those two yellow creatures approach my own personal Dance Hall of a cube. I hold my breath. I think that my heart will burst it is pounding so hard. The phone continues to ring but I don't dare move to answer it.

The creatures are speaking to one another but I can't make out what they're saying. Sounds to these ears like a series of grunts and whistles. I think that they are probably communicating in a foreign language I don't understand… some kind of Morlockian babble. I hold my breath as they approach. One of the creatures turns as he pulls even with the doorway to my cube and pauses for a moment. It turns its head toward me. Two large piercing yellow eyes stare at me. It looks like the pupils are dilated. Absolutely frightening.

Oxbow Lake The 2nd

The first great yellow creature then turns and continues forward and his equally large and yellow companion follows him. I sit there frozen, not moving a muscle. If I don't move, I think, perhaps they can't see me. My phone continues to ring and I exhale and draw in another breath which I hold, praying to God Almighty that the Morlocks don't notice my ringing phone. They continue shuffling down the aisle passing my cube, pull open that other steel door with the large yellow symbol and disappear behind it as it slowly slams shut behind them.

I exhale and start breathing again in short labored staccato breaths. I have difficulty catching my breath. I reached down, pick up the phone's hand set and answer the call. I whisper a breathless "Who's calling?"

The party on the other end of the line indignantly replies, "Mr. Bobb, that is no way to answer the phone. It's poor business practice. You should have said, 'Mr. Ward Bobb, Publications.' I know you're a new employee, and may be unaccustomed to standard business practices and general courtesy, particularly those we follow here at KTI. So TODAY we'll let it slide." It was my manager Delmont whatever. I get the distinct impression that if I make the same mistake tomorrow, I'll be sent down to those security goons for an unforgettable lesson in phone courtesy.

His admonitions about proper business practice and courtesy, particularly those practiced at KTI, give me enough time to catch my breath. I mumble a breathless "Sorry".

He continues, "Please exit your cubical immediately into the main aisle" and hangs up.

None of the other phones in the other cubicles ring. I yell over to Bernstein, "That call… from my manager… says to leave the area immediately. Sounds like those two yellow creatures are up to something. I think you guys should get the hell out of here too."

Bernstein yells to the other subs and they gather rather slowly in the aisle and casually walk toward the steel door through which those Morlockian creatures first enter. I am already at the door frantically pushing it open. Bernstein yells to me, "Ease up, cowboy or you'll pull a muscle."

I look back and see Sub Rich in the aisle leaning against his cube wall. He yells between guffaws, "Hell, if that cowboy don't ease up, he'll pull them all." I think he says something else but I am already out the door and can't make out what it is.

The group gathers outside the steel door as casually as if they are taking one of their regular coffee breaks… which as it turns out they apparently are. Bernstein says to the group of five or six subcontractors, "Coffee on the Twitch." That's when I am first introduced to this nom de plume business. Sub Rich has a facial tick. His left eye blinks as his left cheek twitches whenever he speaks. I take notice for the first time. Sure enough, if you watch his face for a couple of minutes, he twitches away. Thus he is dubbed 'Rich the Twitch' by his subcontract buddies. Maybe it's a Brooklyn thing. Anyway, Rich the Twitch yells "Coffee on me!" and the group casually saunters to the coffee machine down the main aisle.

I stand there, not moving one of those potentially pulled muscles. Bernstein yells to me, "Cummon, you schmuck. Like it or not, you're an honorary subcontractor. You look like you could use a cup. What the hell's wrong? You're covered with sweat. You look like shit. Did you see a ghost or somethin'?"

I gather my thoughts. None of these characters seem the slightest bit concerned with those Morlockian creatures that shuffle down our aisle. Maybe they're in on it. I think that maybe Morlocks use trained Eloi as Judas goats to get the poor other bastard Eloi to follow them to the slaughter. I keep my mouth shut about the Morlocks... remembering what happened in that room full of idiots, the teacher's lounge... and follow the group of subs to the coffee machine where Rich the Twitch keeps shoving coins into the coffee machine until everyone has a cup of the dreadful stuff in their hands. The group saunters back to the steel door and stands before it sipping their dreadful swill and chattering away.

I ask Bernstein, "What the hell just happened?"

He sips his swill and says, "Dunno. Maybe a chemical spill. I think there's a chem lab back there. It's happens every now and then. Nobody knows for sure."

I think to myself, "He thinks there may be a chem lab back there? What the fuck!" I ask, "How come you guys aren't warned to leave?"

He sips some more of his swill and replies, "We're subcontractors. Lowest of the low."
I think to myself, "And maybe Judas goats."

He looks down at his watch and proclaims, "Damn, it's almost noon! Lunch anyone? Jerry's in town."

Lunch with Judas Goats?

I take the last sip of my swill and dump the empty cup into the trash as I mull over the Morlockian events of the morning and the possibility that I am surrounded by Judas goats. Apparently only I am bothered by what transpires. Bernstein turns to me and says, "Want to join us for lunch. We go to this restaurant every Friday, the Bowery Dugout. It's a neat place. Upstairs it's a fancy kind of restaurant. The dugout part is the cellar where they serve lunch. They specialize in sea food and deli sandwiches. Great deli sandwiches like you get in the city and it's reasonable. Wouldn't call it cheap, but it's reasonable. And downright cheap if someone else picks up the tab."

I stand there for a moment trying to calculate whether I have enough money to cover a lunch, my calculations slowed by my preoccupation with the morning's frightening events. Before I get very far into my preoccupied calculations, Bernstein grabs my arm and tugs me down the main aisle toward the exit on our side of the building. "Cummon, it'll be fun. Besides you look like you could use the break. The honor's ours. You'll be the first KTI regular to break bread with us. Don't worry about the tab. Like I said, PSA is picking up the tab today. For you, it's free."

I mumble a rather puzzled, "PSA?"

"Yeah, Programming Science Associates. The company all us subs work for. They have this huge contract with KTI. Once a month our boss Squirrely Jerry drives up to Kingston from the city and takes us to lunch at the Dugout. Today is the day. He likes to keep tabs on what's going on. Hell, since you're regular KTI, he might buy you two lunches and all the beer you can drink. He'll try to pump you for info. Just give him a line of bullshit about how KTI can't find qualified people to hire. He'll come in his pants."

I think to myself, "Chem lab my ass. As to the Judas goats, what are the chances that all these bastards are Judas goats?" Makes no sense then or now… now being on a conceptual basis only of course, just to keep the record straight. There are too many of them. I've never heard of a Judas flock. But then again maybe one of the subs is the real thing and uses the others for cover, the others thus being inadvertent Judas goats in a manner of speaking… conceptually, of course. Anyway, I think that it can't hurt to go to lunch since as long as we are in public there is little chance that I'll be the lunch. Besides, the lunch I'll eat is free. Some guy Bernstein calls Squirrely Jerry is picking up the tab.

The dugout part of the Bowery Dugout is pretty neat. It's the cellar of the place like Bernstein said but it's been pretty much fixed up to look like a grotto kind of thing. The brick walls are painted and covered with New Yorker style cartoon scenes. Looks like the kitchen is in the other half of the cellar. Like I say, it's a neat place. At first the place gives me the willies but after a couple of beers ala Squirrely Jerry, the place settles into OK land.

When we get there… Bernstein drives his new lime green convertible Mustang, a Shelby with more power than all the horses in North America… he slowly glides his precious Mustang to a gentle stop in the Dugout's parking lot to await the others. Another sub, someone Bernstein calls Software Suzie, is driving another car with a bunch of other subs. Later I find out that Software Suzie is a genius at debugging software systems… a kind of idiot savant since she pretty much handles the rest of life rather poorly. Well Bernstein parks that new Shelby of his on the far side of an almost empty parking lot. I ask him, "Why the hell you parking way over here?" He smiles at me and says "Watch, my man. Eyes on the road."

I watch the road rather causally. Moments later, brakes screech as a white sedan makes a sharp right from the road into the parking lot and cuts off another car traveling in the opposite direction. The white sedan almost gets creamed. Horns blast, expletives are yelled and middle fingers flashed out of car windows as the white sedan speeds into the parking lot. There's a portico over the entrance to the Dugout supported by two posts. The white sedan screeches to a halt knocking into one of the supporting posts so that it's now at an angle. The post doesn't fall, but the portico leans toward the post that's hit. Bernstein smiles and says "Two for two! Second time in two months."

Rich the Twitch jumps out of the front passenger seat of the white sedan, casually walks over to the post that Software Suzie creamed and with the flat of his foot, kicks it a bunch of times. With each kick, the portico moves several degrees up as the post moves toward perpendicular until with one final kick, the portico jerks pretty much back to level. Another women oozes out of the back seat and the rear of the car rises with a groan as she pushes herself to her feet. She is huge. I ask, "Who's the big momma?" Bernstein says, "Jumbo Jean… Jean Burdick."

"How come I haven't seen her before? A blind man couldn't miss her."

"Well, her cube's a couple down from you. She arrives early and once she squeezes into her chair, she doesn't move around much for obvious reasons. She always brings her lunch and pretty much stays in her cube until quitting time. She doesn't leave until she's sure the parking lot is clear. We usually bring her coffee two or three times a day. She must have the bladder of an elephant… which by the way she probably outweighs. She comes to lunch when Squirrely Jerry's in town."

"God, she must weigh 300 pounds."

"Three hundred and twenty seven pounds to be precise… as of Monday."

"How the hell do you know that?"

"Every Monday morning, she announces her weight when one of us brings her coffee. She's very proud of the poundage that she carries beneath that tent she calls a dress. You're new so she'll tell you all about it at lunch. She always brags to new guys."

I think to myself "There's enough protein and fat there to feed some fortunate extended Morlockian family for an entire Hudson Valley winter and then some." Software Suzie and Rich the Twitch casually strolled into the Dugout and Jumbo Jean waddles in after them. Bernstein and I jump out of the Mustang and follow.

Squirrely Jerry is already there sitting at a long table awaiting the arrival of PSA's meal tickets, my subcontract friends. His minions pin an appropriate nom de plume on the bastard… and that's several years before the advent of the golden era of the nom de plume… for he is in fact a squirrely looking dude… skinny, nervous and jerky. He speaks fast and has to stop from time-to-time to catch his breath. At the time, I think that he won't rise to the level of a snack in that other situation.

Bernstein introduces me as the new automated text processing guru at KTI and Jerry jumps to his feet and greets me like I was a combination of the Pope and the King of Prussia. He grabs my hand, clutches it with what I suspect is all his might and shakes it so vigorously that I fear I'll lose my hand at the wrist. He ends the attack with "I'm so glad you can join us, Mr. Bobb. Lunch is on us."

I sit across from Jumbo Jean who actually occupies two chairs, both of which groaned as she lowered herself into a seated position. I order a pastrami on rye, which comes with cold slaw and potato salad. We all order more beer and after a couple of brews, everyone is quite jovial. Jumbo Jean lives up to her nom de plume and orders two meals… two full meals. She is obviously in training. I am still chomping on the first half of my pastrami on rye as the jumbo one digs into meal two. Like I say, she is obviously deep into her weight training program… a very unique weight training program, I might add.

She looks over at me cackling away and asks… more like demands, "How much do you think I weigh?"

I am taken aback by the question and think that this is one of those trap questions that lead to trouble regardless what I answer. I mumble, "I haven't the foggiest."

She presses on, "Go on… take a guess!"

The rest of table, except for Squirrely Jerry, presses me to make a guess. The band of merry subs has obviously been through this ritual before and seems to enjoy it thoroughly. Finally I relent and say, "Two hundred a fifty pounds." From my little conversation with Bernstein, I know she weighs at least 327 pounds before lunch and probably well into the 330s by now… particularly after she consumes her first entre… but I think it best not to give an answer indicating that her weight is the topic of a previous discussion. Besides, I don't want to take the wind out of that sail of a tent she wears.

A jovial laugh shakes that huge body of hers and tears well in her eyes. Finally she says, "Wrong… wrong… wrong and, you guessed it… wrong again! You are so wrong that you are unworthy of knowing my last known exact weight." She laughs some more, shaking the floor under my feet. The rest of table smiles and remains silent for they know that there is more to come and it does. "In Saudi Arabia I am considered quite beautiful. One of the Saudi princes proposed marriage to me a number of times. He is quite smitten by yours truly. I am working as a systems analyst at the time for British Petroleum. You know, beauty is a very relative concept."

I think to myself, "And you're getting more and more beautiful for that Saudi prince with every mouth full. In order to consummate the marriage, that Saudi prince would have to have a couple of his eunuchs roll you in flour and he'd have the pleasure of searching for the wet spot, the one below your neck." However, I'm not a Saudi prince and my relative concept of female beauty is obviously quite different from that of a Saudi prince. The moving picture in my head of a naked Jumbo Jean being rolled in flour by two burly eunuchs to create a carnal wet spot and then an ardent Saudi prince groping about that humungous reservoir of adipose tissue searching for that wet spot… that wet spot of carnal love… the image rolling about my imagination is killing my appetite. Morlocks would drool at the image. Finally, Squirrely Jerry breaks up the ritual inquisition and says, "Bernstein, what's up at KTI."

Thank God.

"Looks like they're going to move us into the Pubs area and restructure one of the rows of cubicles where we sit now. They're setting up a key punch and typing pool. I think that there'll be 12 to 15 girls in the pool. They're putting another seven tech writing positions out to bid. You should hear from KTI contracts sometime next week."

Jerry looks at me and back at Bernstein and then back at me again. Bernstein points at me and says, "Ward Bobb here is OK. He's more one of us then one of them." He turns to me and says, "You'll be moved over to aisle eight next to ol' Delmont next Friday. The actual move will be over the weekend. Good luck, good buddy. We won't be far away. We'll be clustered over on aisle ten."

I am stunned and ask, "How the hell do you know all of this? I haven't been told a thing." Now I realize how lucky I am to be moved away from that hell hole that Bernstein thinks might be a chem lab. Out of sight, out of mind.

Interesting turn of phrase... out of mind... Freudian slip anyone?

He smiles, "I buy Jan, Bill's secretary, coffee and shoot the shit with her. The writers treat her like a typing service, in other words like shit. The blueprint for the moves is on her table and the memo confirming the request for bid, in her typewriter. It weren't no James Bond action."

Rich finishes off his beer, wipes the suds from his lips with his sleeve and says, "Look, Jerry, we don't have any work now. I sit around all day reading stupid manuals. By the end of the day, I'm contemplating putting a bullet in my head. What the hell are another seven subcontractors going to do? Someone's going to eventually catch on and cancel the contract and then we'll all be out of work."

Squirrely Jerry smiles. "Look, they have a budget and they have to spend it or they'll lose it. The management in Pubs has gone through all the budgetary justifications and they sure aren't going to go back to their management and say they were wrong with their projections. Besides, KTI is expanding so quickly that they can't keep track of anything. They're investing millions in their new main frames. The place is our cash cow."

Bernstein looks down at his watch and says, "Look, Jerry, we got to get back to that cash cow so you can keep milking her. It's one o'clock. We should have left 15 minutes ago."

We all rise and Squirrely Jerry vigorously shakes my hand a second time, "Glad to meet you." He hands me a business card and says, "Give me a call anytime. Hope to see you at our next luncheon."

Since Jumbo Jean isn't riding with us (for attempting to do so would violate one of those laws of physics about objects being unable to occupy the same space at the same time), we reach Bernstein's Mustang before the others get out of the building. We jump into Bernstein's mustang and Bernstein just sits there. I ask, "Aren't you taking off? Don't we have to get back to the lab." He smiles and says, "Watch Suzie and the road."

By now Software Suzie's sedan, leaning heavily to the left rear, starts up and rolls to the exit to the main road. Bernstein pulls up several car lengths behind her and to her left. I can see Suzie lean forward and check the traffic to her right. The way is clear. No oncoming traffic. She turns to check for traffic to her left and by the time that way is clear, more traffic appears on her right. She takes off anyway and into the path of the new oncoming traffic. There is this loud screeching of tires, the shouting of many colorful expletives and the waving of middle fingers as Suzie turns left onto the road and speeds away.

I yell, "For Christ's sake, what the fuck is wrong with that woman. Doesn't she notice that more traffic is coming from her right."

Bernstein smiles and says, "She drives like she writes programs. She checks right and sets the clear bit. Now she checks left. In programming, the bit stays set, there's no need to recheck it once your program has control. So in her mind the right traffic bit has been set and her only concern is the traffic bit to the left. Once that's set, she's free to go. What makes her a great programmer makes her a very bad driver. But get this, she's never had an accident."

Looking back now, like I'm supposed to do, I can see how moving away from that so called chem lab takes the pressure off and makes me less aware of the danger. The threat appears to disappear... at least from my mind and we are safe to live our lives with a false sense of safety. It is as if the Morlocks go into hibernation... at least that's how I feel at the time. Don't get me wrong. I'm pretty sure now that that isn't the case, but it does get one wondering. Explains the lag time between... incidents.

Another Moving Experience

Well, just as Bernstein says, I move out of my dungeon Dance Hall and into a cube in the Pubs area close… very close… to my manager Delton Meriwether… in fact so close that I can smell his halitosis… if it is halitosis. Let there be light and please dear God, some fresh air! For reasons never given, Bernstein and the other subs stay put… at least for the time being.

My move to my new cubicle takes the form of organizational and managerial insanity… an accusation I do not make lightly given my present circumstance. I land in a row of seven cubes all in a row. Ol' Delmont has the lead cube… the one at the head of the aisle. The other cubes are all occupied except for the last one at the far end of the row… the seventh cube, the one farthest from ol' Delmont. Apparently ol' Delmont must want me in the cube next to his what with my dangerous lack of good business practice and courtesy and obvious need to be carefully watched, monitored, corrected and trained to follow KTI business practices when using the telephone. So no way is he moving me into that last cube. God knows what I'll do what with my poor phone courtesy. Who knows? I may inadvertently destroy KTI with my lack of telephone business civility.

So how does ol' Del arrange the move to get me in the cube next to his… a plan conjured up by a manager apparently in good standing at KTI, the renowned international corporation with the highest average IQ in the world? Well he has all the occupants of the first five cubes move back one and thus freeing up the one next to his for yours truly. The ding bat requires six moves so that I can be moved into the cubicle adjacent to his. How fuckin' stupid can you get? What's with these assholes with programmer training? I conclude that programming is in fact not a form of intelligence but rather a form of low cunning... a conclusion that creates within me a great fear of attending programmer training. It's interesting that even KTI does not call it programmer education. It's a form of training as in training a dog... which could easily be construed as an insult to dogs given the parties being trained.

The months roll by and I settle into my new professional life as a newly minted editorial assistant. I am surprised to learn that there are two other editorial assistants: Joseph Popovich and Butler C. Davenport, something ol' Del has neglected to mention to me and both of whom also report to ol' Delmont. Joe is a young, short, skinny dude who never stops moving, apparently suffering from an untreated OCD condition now in adult overdrive. He talks in a high pitched screech and so fast that his sentences became single words. Butler C. Davenport is a heavy set older man who is as slow as Joe is fast, except at quitting time when the Butt Man moves with the grace and speed of another Joe... Joe DiMaggio as he patrolled center field in Yankee Stadium before Marilyn Monroe slowed him down some. The Butt Man's exit at the end of the day... provided he isn't milking the overtime budget... is a wonder to behold... the very example of universal grace and speed... in a Three Stooges kind of way... the Butt Man being big enough and talented enough to play all three roles.

Ol' Delton tells me to work with Joe Popovich to learn the procedures and the process and to pick his brain to learn how to be an editorial assistant. I understand this to mean that I am something like apprenticed to Joe, so follow him around I do. Popovich flits into a writer's cube, picks up a computer listing which is a software manual marked up with changes, and flits out. He flits over to his cube and marks up the changes the writer is

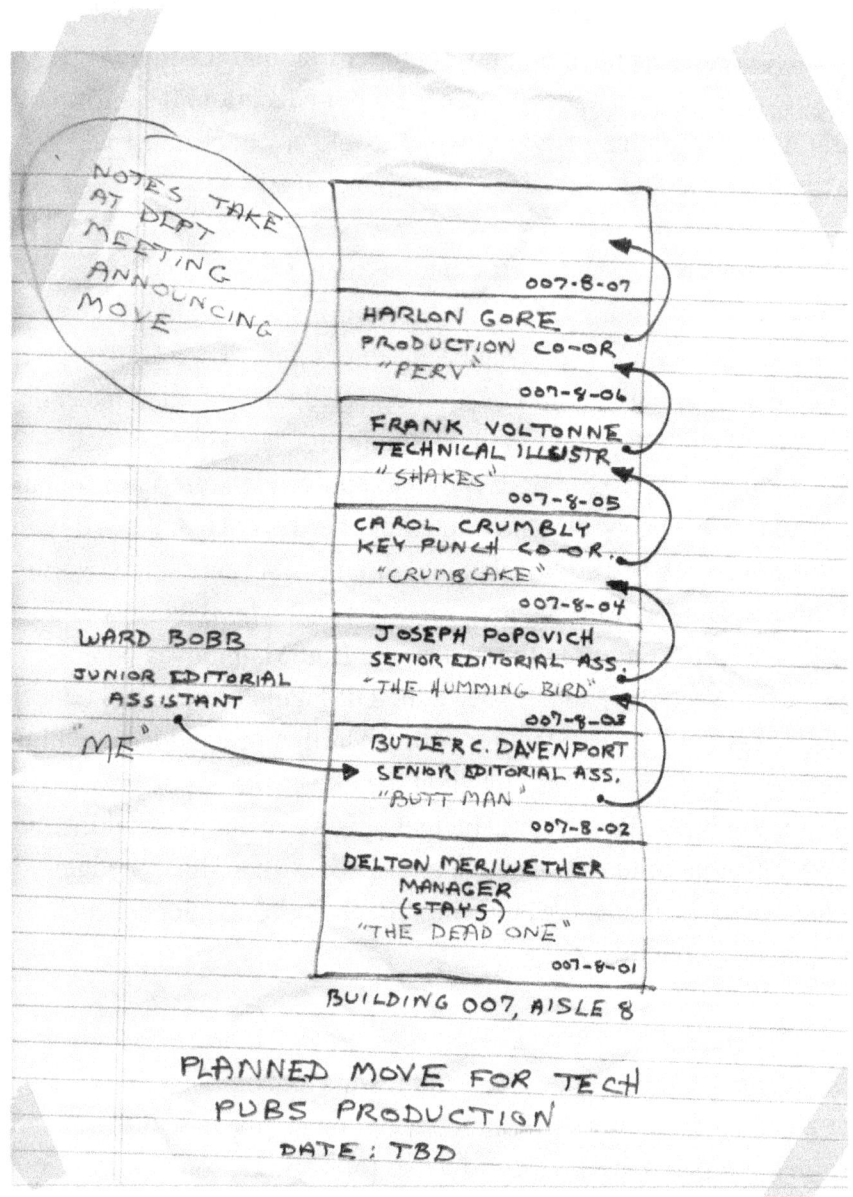

NOTES TAKE AT DEPT MEETING ANNOUNCING MOVE

007-8-07
HARLON GORE
PRODUCTION CO-OR
"PERV"

007-8-06
FRANK VOLTONNE
TECHNICAL ILLUSTR
"SHAKES"

007-8-05
CAROL CRUMBLY
KEY PUNCH CO-OR
"CRUMBCAKE"

007-8-04
JOSEPH POPOVICH
SENIOR EDITORIAL ASS.
"THE HUMMING BIRD"

WARD BOBB
JUNIOR EDITORIAL
ASSISTANT

"ME"

007-8-03
BUTLER C. DAVENPORT
SENIOR EDITORIAL ASS.
"BUTT MAN"

007-8-02
DELTON MERIWETHER
MANAGER
(STAYS)
"THE DEAD ONE"

007-8-01
BUILDING 007, AISLE 8

PLANNED MOVE FOR TECH
PUBS PRODUCTION
DATE: TBD

making with the appropriate text processing commands so that the computer formats the changes properly, albeit poorly. Then he flits over to the infamous Harlan Gore and drops off the listing. Here the process gets a bit murky since everything beyond Harlan is shrouded in fog. Eventually I learn that Harlan schedules the necessary key punch work, which is sometimes done in house and sometimes sent out to a subcontractor. Then the job is run on a mainframe computer in the comp center to update the listing, i.e., the manual, with the key-punch changes.

When Joe turns the job into Harlan, Harlan gives Joe a date when the work is completed and we can pick up the updated listing in the comp center for a final check before returning it to the writer. If the listing isn't correct, Joe makes the necessary changes on the listing and resubmits it to Harlan and the process begins anew. As far as I can tell, most work is submitted on a Friday and returned on the following Monday, most of the key punch work and the computer runs being done over the weekend. Harlan takes most Fridays and Mondays off… apparently he has a ton of vacation days since he's been there forever… making his steps in the process rather shaky.

When Joe submits the job to Harlan, he flits back to the writer with a form that has the due date for the completion of the work and informs the writer as to when he (or occasionally she) can expect to get the job back. When the listing must be run through the process a second or third time because of errors, Popovich informs the writer that the schedule is changed and that it'd be another week before the updated listing is available. I still remember every baby step in that stupid process.

When the job must be resubmitted, this blame game begins, for something stinks in Denmark. and the origin of that stink, an actual person, must be identified and receive the prerequisite blame for said stink. Perhaps the writer hasn't marked the changes clearly... perhaps the editorial assistant hasn't coded it properly... perhaps the coordinator, the inimitable Harlan Gore, hasn't managed the work flow properly. When this happens to one of Popovich's jobs, the Popovich flits about the lab covering all his bases making sure he isn't blamed for the delay. Joe plays this blame game consummately. Back then, the Polish Prince is a writer in the group and has to deal with Popovich, setting up a very interesting competition in this game of blame.

I remember the first time I meet James. Joe flits into James's office and says that his updated listing isn't available as scheduled. James yells, "Why the fuck not." Ol' Popovich flits about James's cube, refusing to sit down and spurts out one word or at least what sounded like one word, "Don't-know-I'll-check-with-Harlan" and flits out. I can't keep up with him and decide to await his return standing outside James's cube. What seems mere seconds later, back flits the Popovich, "Key-punch-says-your-inserts-were-incorrectly-marked."

James yells, "How the hell would a key punch operator know where I want text inserted?" Out flits the Popovich and in what seems again mere seconds, back he appears: "Harlan-says-it-is-a-processing-problem." James yells "What the fuck's a processing problem? I have a bunch of programmers that need that updated listing to submit to Product Test." Out flits Popovich again. I stay out of James's cube so as not to get hit by any verbal shrapnel.

I hear James cussing to himself, "That fucking humming bird." Bingo, with a little nudge from yours truly, the age of the nom de plume is born. On that day, Joe Popovich becomes, and I quote... the humming bird.

Eating Huge Chunks of Blame Pie in Absentia

Joe Popovich is a come-to-Jesus meeting fool… in spite of his Jewishness. Every time the slightest bump occurs in the work process, he doesn't act to smooth out that bump. No siree… he schedules a meeting about the bump… a meeting to prove he is blameless, i.e., he is not the source of the stink. He even schedules a meeting when there is no bump. Hell, he schedules meetings about holding meetings. He meets with managers, he meets with programmers, he meets with writers. He meets with Harlan (on days other than Friday and Monday). He apparently even schedules meetings with himself. If a scheduled completion date for work is missed, he meets with all of them at once. Since I am an insignificant piss ant and thus unworthy of credit or blame… particularly blame, I am pretty much out of the blame loop for now, being recently apprenticed to Joe and all. I am just a naïve, foreign observer at these gatherings… a mere fly on the wall beholding what I can behold… soaking in Joe's wisdom. Everyone else is always balls to the wall right up to their professional scrotums if they have one. This meeting mania is not unique to the Popovich as I later learn. It is the way of KTI's world.

Missing that schedule for James's manual causes Joe to schedule one of these mega meetings, for missing this particular schedule is apparently particularly egregious… a very big deal indeed… for reasons I do not understand at the time. Later I learn that a draft of this particular manual is required for a major programming checkpoint in the programming development process… something they called Product Test Entry where that Jay McGonagall character, later of Beware Chair fame, spends his time when not

241

at the Bridge Circle and before he got fired and opened that bagel shop in Toledo, Ohio… at least I think it's Toledo.

Even though Popovich calls the meeting, James and his manager cede control through some arcane rule of the KTI development process since it is James's manual that has gone AWOL and James's manual going AWOL apparently being a very big deal. Thus James's manager at the time, the Gooper, chairs the meeting and we are technically on James's turf even though both James and the Popovich are from Publications. Of course, James is there, Harlan is not… it being a Monday… but Harlan's manager ol' Delmont is… as is Joe Popovich (the recently dubbed Humming Bird) and myself, both of us working for ol' Delmont as well. Across the table sits the manager of the programming group Irr Irr Irv Silverberg… he stutters. Irr Irr Irv later becomes famous to some, infamous to others, throughout KTI for creating the now famous organizational principle, 'the memo is reality'. He brings his programmer Freddie Schwartz, AKA the Snowflake, with him. Freddie earns the nick name, which becomes his own personal nom de plume, early last winter… his first full year in the Hudson Valley. If one snow flake falls, Freddie hightails it home, declaring the rest of the day his own personal snow day. He is from Miami and is not only unfamiliar with the concept of snow but actually fears it in reality as well. He must be pretty good at his job as far as anyone can tell, for his fear of snow and his snow-driven absences are at least tolerated by his Attila the Hun reincarnation of a manager, Irr Irr Irv. And Irr Irr Irv would have run over his beloved ancient and ailing grandmother to get his next promotion… as would, as it turns out, virtually all dedicated KTI managers, so the Snowflake must have been a damn good programmer or Irr Irr Irv would have squashed him like a bug in a monomaniacal KTI nanosecond!

Even as a lowly apprenticed editorial assistant, it is obvious to me that programmers are a totally different breed... perhaps even a different species... a kind of genetic aberration... Freddie being typical of this aberrant subspecies. Touted as having a very high IQ, the Snowflake obviously makes a much heralded contribution to KTI's putative #1 ranking in the corporate average IQ contest, but still he is your typical programmer... that is his programming is done intestinally and not intellectually since he has his head up his ass most of the time.

As you can see, Mr. Ward Bobb, I conclude that programming is not an intellectual endeavor but rather some genetically inherited form of animal cunning... IQ be damned! Those who possess this animal cunning would slowly be weeded out of the genetic pool had it not been for this quirk in technology's so called march forward to what we call the computer. In the 19th century the most hardy of these genetic aberrations who survive to adulthood would be Bartleby the Scrivener clones, working in the back rooms of law offices barely eking out an existence copying legal documents... provided of course it isn't snowing. Evolution's survival of the fittest would weed them out of the genetic pool of the human race by now if not for the invention of that infernal device, the computer... which unfortunately changes the criteria for survival... a kind of evolutionary glitch which may alter humanity's evolution forever... something which H. G. Wells foresaw and prophesized. But the prophet foretells a future hundreds of thousands of years in the future in a kind of time warp. As it turns out, time warped a lot faster than the prophet prophesized and the distant future turns out to be a mere 70 years.

The question I have: are these genetic dweebs precursors to the

243

Oxbow Lake The 2nd

Morlocks or the Eloi? Your average programmer like Freddie Snowflake doesn't have the balls necessary to be an in-charge Morlock but he is on the wrong side of technology to be an Eloi. I think on it for a while and then it strikes me, for there is Irr Irr Irv, a programming manager. While Freddie doesn't have what it takes to be a fully functioning in-charge kind of Morlock, Irr Irr Irv does. He is a full-fledged master Morlock in-waiting. And to make matters worse, now there are a bunch of women programmer dweebs thanks to all that feminism and equal opportunity crap so that there is now a breeding pool of females for the male dweebs and their masters to breed with to produce even more of the dweeb bastards and in-charge monsters. How ironic, women get jobs as programmers so that they can have professions and not be condemned to cook and breed and what's their role in humanity's evolution: to be breeding partners for the destruction of humanity as we know it. It is apparent to me now that these aberrations are the ancestors of the vile creatures we call Morlocks… hell, maybe they are these vile creatures. They just don't look like Wells describes or I expect.

Maybe these Morlocks evolve into a different species… even though they still looked like us… and then into different subspecies like different kinds of ants… you know, worker ants, soldier ants, flying breeder male ants and the egg laying queen ant… although I think that given where humans have already evolved what with any female being able to breed, there isn't a single queen. They're all God damn queens.

Like I say, maybe the Morlocks evolve in a separate species… there's that word 'evolve' again… and into two different subspecies: the Irr Irr Irvus Dominus Morlockius and the Snowflakeus Subservius Morlockius… for Irr Irr Irv is a programmer but I doubt that he is ever an intestinal programmer, for he doesn't walk around with his head up his ass bumping into things. He walks around shoving other peoples' heads up their asses. Not having their heads up their asses is what makes members of this subspecies, the Irr Irr Irvus Dominus Morlockius, so dangerous and why I fear them... at first naively from a career standpoint when I first begin to think about them and now from a survival standpoint.

And as I work at KTI, I come to the realization that Irr Irr Irv is not a rare genetic aberration at KTI. He is your typical run of the mill programming manager. Later when I become a programmer writer analyst... the programmer half of the title giving me the heebie geebies... I must work with this other programming manager and he is way up the management chain... Mr. Nick Kingsley or 'Choppers' as he became known. I remember vividly my first meeting with ol' Choppers... on his ground... a most frightening experience. He sits behind this huge desk covered with listings. As I enter, he yells, "You Ward Bobb?" I mumble a frightened "Yes sir"... him being a gazillion levels above me. Then he smiles. Scares the living shit out of me. He has a set of carnivorous teeth that make Vince Lombardi look like a breast feeder. As he smiles that carnivorous smile of his, inviting me into his lair, I notice a large framed sign in bright red letters high on the wall behind his desk. It says "RAW MEAT!". I kid you not... Raw fuckin' Meat! At first I think that Choppers uses the sign as a ploy to intimidate his visitors... overkill in my book... for his smile alone does the job... me being a prime example of such intimidation since I about pissed my pants at his first grin... but I later come to the conclusion that that sign is a kind of genetic marker for an alpha programming manager at KTI and probably for alpha programming managers the world over. Back to that blame pie meeting .

Oxbow Lake The 2nd

Jay McGonagall appears sober since he is sitting upright and speaks without slurring a word, but he is wearing sun glasses, for something he calls 'bad eyes'. Even back then I suspect that his eyes are bloodshot from the previous night's activities. Well Jay jumps up from his chair and yells, "It's your bag of shit. I'm here to tell you that Programming Development missed a key product schedule and you're already four days behind schedule. You guys work out your problems and get me three copies of that damn manual." Then he abruptly spins on his heels and high tails it the hell out of the meeting.

We all sit around the table pretty much staring at each other. Then Irr Irr Irv blurts out, "Where's the damn manual?" It is already November and Freddie, who has seated himself facing the conference room windows, keeps a sharp eye peeled on the clouds forming above the valley.

The Gooper turns to James, who says "As far as I know, it's in production. That's all I know."

Ol' Delmont puts on his glasses, looks down at a piece of paper, takes his glasses off, looks up and says, "According to the status report, the writer submitted several major changes late Thursday after the job has already been logged in by Harlan."

James yells, "That writer is me and I don't make those damn changes on my own. I get them from Freddie here and I must incorporate them."

Freddie stares intently out the window and says nothing. Irr Irr Irv jumps into the breach, "You never notify us that the requested changes in any way affect the schedule." Freddie continues his snow vigilance, unconcerned about the mere missing of a major product development schedule.

The humming bird, seeing immediately where the conversation is headed, flits into the fray with both feet and chirps away: "I-submit-the-changes-as-requested-by-James-to-Harlan-who-takes-them-without-notifying-me that-these-changes-would-in-any-way-change-the-scheduled-completion-date."

No Harlan is present to continue the circle jerk. The mental masturbation stops with him, him being the putative jerkee of last resort and absent. There is a long silence and then the Gooper gets up and draws this huge circle on the blackboard with great ceremony. He turns his head toward the meeting attendees while his body still faces the blackboard in one of his patented goops, "What we have here is a blame pie." He divides the pie into quarters and says, "Programming gets a quarter, tech pubs gets a quarter, editorial assistance gets a quarter, and scheduling and keypunch gets a quarter." He labels each piece of the blame pie as he speaks.

Even though Publications is accepting three quarters of the blame, Irr Irr Irv is having none of it, "Hold it, our piece of the pie is way too big. Hell, we shouldn't have any of that blame pie! We submitted changes to the writer following established development procedure. The changes are required to reflect changes in the design." He points at James and screams, "You never notify us that these changes in any way affect the scheduled completion date of the draft of the manual."

The Gooper redraws Programming's piece of the blame pie, reducing it to a mere sliver, and thus greatly expanding James's piece of that ol' blame pie. James, being no dope, yells, "Hold it, I submit those changes following established publications procedure to Popovich here. He takes the damn changes without saying a word to me about changing the schedule" and the Gooper dutifully reduces James's piece of the blame pie to a mere sliver just slightly larger than what is in actuality, Freddie's piece. Freddie continues staring intently out the window.

Popovich sees his piece of that blame pie expanding to almost three-quarters of the whole blame pie, is in no mood to eat that much blame pie, and says, in a staccato outburst, "I-follow-procedure-as-well-when-I-hand-the-requested-changes-to-Harlan-with-instructions-as-to-where-they-are-to-be-made-in-the-already-submitted-manuscript-listing-I-am-not-notified-that-the-requested-changes-in-any-way-affect-the-committed-schedule-for-the-work" and the Gooper dutifully redraws the Humming Bird's piece of the pie to a sliver slightly larger than James's.

It is now very obvious where the stink emanates from… that is, who is to blame for the missed schedule caused by large changes submitted late after the job is already accepted and a schedule already committed: none other than the absent and most likely inebriated, unaware and probably unconscious Harlan Gore. The Gooper writes Harlan's name across what becomes close to all of the blame pie. A look of great indignance spreads across Delmont's face as Freddie springs to his feet in great panic and rushes out the conference room door. All present realize that nature's first snow flake of the season has just fallen and our own Snowflake is out of here. Delmont's look changes to great anger and he mutters the words, "Harlan will pay dearly for this egregious misconduct."

Well Mr. Busy Body, where are your words of offensive wisdom now!

Blame Pie Redux

The fallout from the baking of that blame pie are many and prodigious. As I later learn through Bernstein's grape vine, Delmont takes his revenge upon the unsuspecting Harlan Gore, putting him on what's called a measured assignment and coming close to firing him for his egregious misconduct, making him a combination pariah and whipping boy forever after. For three months Harlan shuffles up to Delmont's now glassed in cube every Monday and every Friday morning at 8:12. He looks like a dead man walking. The walls around Delmont's cube shakes for an hour. Then hang dog Harlan emerges an even more thoroughly beaten man, if that is possible, and he slowly shuffles back to his cube with his head down and the weight of a vengeful KTI upon his stooped shoulders.

One result of the bi-weekly whipping of Harlan: all the schedules are met, for everyone now fears that Harlan is to be fired leaving an unassigned and very large chunk of blame pie to be consumed by one of the survivors. The unintended result: I believe that Smirnoff's stock takes a dreadful hit. And there are others, but for Harlan not all is lost. He plays his role of pariah and whipping boy so well that he becomes very important to Pubs management. He can be made to eat so much blame pie that he significantly reduces the portions the rest of Publications has to gobble. Most of the other participants get a sliver of blame pie to nibble on while ol' Harlan gets to gobble huge chunks of that KTI delicacy. None of the managers so much as sniff even a crumb of the stuff as long as Harlan dines. The ironical result: the self-effacing hang-dog Harlan inadvertently makes himself indispensible to Pubs management and thus Pubs management refuses to fire him.

Oxbow Lake The 2nd

The humming bird, not knowing of Harlan's recently achieved indispensability and fearing what a future without Harlan could portend, decides to go on the offense with a defensive action, for he cannot stomach even a sliver of that blame stuff. He designs a form in which he lists all the requirements that a writer is to meet in order to submit a job through him. I am still tagging around behind him when he flits into James's office to pick up the next update of James's book several weeks later.

The staccato humming bird: "Before-I-accept-this-job-you'll-have-to-sign-this-form-of-commitment."

James, after reading the lengthy document: "Form of commitment my ass. This is a list of all the things that I have to do and guarantee before you'll accept a job from a writer, namely me. Are you out of your mind?"

The humming bird: "This-form-designates-all-the-responsibilities-that-a-writer-must-and-should-perform-in order-to-insure-a-smooth-process."

James: "Where the hell are your responsibilities? I'm not signing this fuckin' thing!" I step outside of James's cubicle just in case the Polish Prince goes postal.

The hummingbird: "These-are-generic-responsibilities-necessary-to-make-the-process-run-smoothly."

James: "Generic responsibilities my ass. This is an 'I am not to blame' form. This form absolves you of any responsibility for anything." James rises from behind his desk and yells, "You can shove this fuckin' form up your fuckin' ass." At these words, the

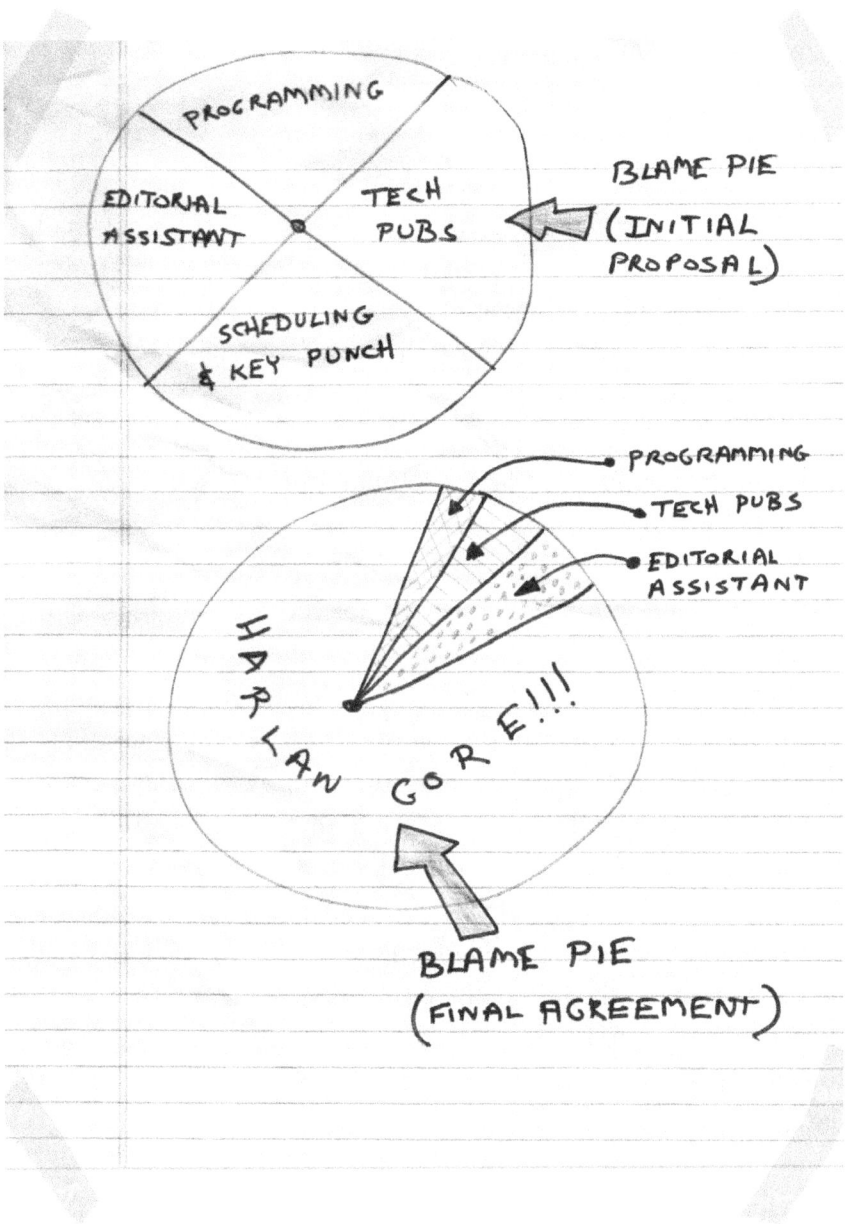

hummingbird flits an ASAP retreat from the ire of the Polish Prince as the following words blare behind us, "You'll have to sign my fuckin' 'I am not to blame form' before I'll sign yours."

The result… you guessed it… another meeting.
Again, I am a fly on the wall, as the tag team of the Gooper and our own Polish Prince and the tag team of rumpled ol' Delmont and his flitting Hummingbird meet… in mortal intranecine organizational combat. James, with the grace and charm of Godzilla, gets the match going. He points at Popovich and says, "What the fuck's wrong with that little twirp."

The Delmont, unfazed by James's initial foray, replies, "I assume you are referring to Joseph."

James: "Is there another little twirp in the room? Damn right I'm referring to Joseph." James shoves a thick document across the conference table. "Joseph here demands that I sign this document before he accepts a job from me. Jesus Christ, it even states that the committed schedule…" At this point James grabs the document back, flips it open and reads aloud while rhythmically smashing this index finger on the document as he reads, "A committed schedule must be renegotiated should inclement weather, illness or a change in priorities cause a reduction in the work week in which case the original schedule shall be considered null and void and must be renegotiated." With about as much sarcasm as is possible to cram into one sentence, James snarls, "Joseph here forgot to add anything about earthquakes."

The Hummingbird writes a note to himself which thankfully for all present, James does not notice, his focus at the time being on the document before him. James shoves the document back across the table at ol' Delmont, who, with great ceremony, puts on his glasses and reads the passage for himself, his lips moving as he reads.

When ol' Delmont's lips stop moving, he looks up, removes his glasses with great ceremony, and says, "I think that this document succinctly states the conditions under which jobs should be submitted to editorial assistants."

James fumes, "Succinct? If you consider this document succinct, I'd hate like hell to see the unboudlerized version. It'd give the fuckin' Manhattan phone directory a run for its fuckin' money."

A look of moral outrage spreads across ol' Delmont's face and he says, "There's no need to be vulgar. Please refrain from using such offensive words… there's no place for a word such as 'unboudlerized' in a KTI business meeting!"

James shakes his head in disgust and says, "OK. I'll refrain from using that fuckin' word in the fuckin' future."

Ol' Delmont smiles wryly having achieved what he considers to be a significant victory.

The Gooper pulls copies of another document from a folder he brings with him to the meeting and carefully places one of the copies of said document before each of the other attendees with the exception of me who remains a fly on the wall. In hushed tones, he says, "I agree that we should document all the conditions under which jobs should be submitted. We should also document all the conditions under which a job should be returned and James has prepared such a document. We believe that this document should be signed by an editorial assistant when that editorial assistant accepts a job. It states the conditions under which a job is to be returned, how schedules are to be renegotiated and what the accepted error rates are for a job to be returned. Appendix A lists definitions of all the possible categories of errors and the acceptable and unacceptable error rates. Appendix B is the Error Rate Reporting Form, the ERRF. Frankly, I'm a little surprised that there isn't an error rate standard and reporting structure already in place."

The negotiations grind on for hours as both warring parties carefully measure each word and parse each phrase and sentence of both documents. A number of changes are suggested and most accepted in a tit for tat negotiation… each tag team smiling wryly at each agreed upon change thinking that they are getting the better of their opponent. As a result of the agreed upon documents, a writer and his or her manager meets with an editorial assistant and his or her manager and formally signs both documents when a job is submitted by a writer to an editorial assistant. An average of two days are added to the schedule to accommodate the signing of these duel 'I am not to blame' documents, the Hummingbird's 'I am not to blame' agreement now teams with James's 'I am not to blame' agreement and thus cementing good relations between the writing and production departments, for as that old saw states, "Good fences make for good neighbors". A day is added to the end of the schedule to accommodate the work necessary to document the errors and calculate error rates with the possibility of adding yet another day or possibly days if the error processing data cannot be agreed to. But as a result of these momentous negotiations, Publications enters the golden age of blamelessness.

The Creep Sox March to Glory

Enough of that ancient history. All that bickering is meaningless now. From my room here, I can see the leaves on the trees beginning to turn in the valley. It's the first week of September. Back at KTI, football season is just around the corner if they still play touch football there. If I'm not sent here, I am most likely forming up the Creep Sox Football Military Drill Team… of which I am the drill instructor… for our annual Monday March to Glory… the Monday March to Glory being our march to the cafeteria and back… about a quarter of a mile each way… passing the techies in manufacturing who field our most hated touch football rivals, the Blue Shirts. The official opening kickoff for the Holmes Touch Football… A-League… is on the first Wednesday of September, but for us Pubs Creeps, it begins today, on Monday, two days before our first kickoff. Seven of us march to the cafeteria as the Creep Sox Football Military Drill Team. As the official drill instructor, I call cadence. We practice over the weekend in the Bridge Circle's parking lot, usually after a couple of pitchers of suds before and a whole bunch more after. We are sharp and ready if I do say so myself. Doc Frah-ken-steen's a member of the drill team. He just loves to march and actually enjoys the practices. Hell, he'd practice without the beer. I'm not so sure about the others.

Actually we don't march all the way to the cafeteria. We walk casually along the hallway treading ever so comfortably over the sainted P. T. Holmes Senior's wonderful wooden floors until we get to Building 006, the manufacturing building. Then the drill team forms up and I call cadence as we approach the so-called Hollywood and Vine intersection in the manufacturing area… Hollywood being the aisle bisecting the manufacturing building…

255

Vine being the main aisle to the cafeteria and other parts south. We form up in good order and I call cadence: "Hup... hup... March the best you can... Hup... hup... We're the Pubs Creep Band..."

The Flake, Magic Mike and the aforementioned Doc Fran-ken-steen are a part of the six man drill team as it marches smartly in lock step into the Hollywood and Vine intersection before the techies who are crawling all over the mainframes that line Hollywood.

The mainframes... and there are a bunch of them lining both sides of Hollywood... are in final test. Each mainframe has a sign hung above it with the customer's name in bold letters. The techies, faux engineers to the man, are crawling all over the mainframes like little techie ants with their white sox ablaze as they crawl and squat with Morlockian agility about the test machines.

I shout cadence "One, two... it ain't fair!... three, four... we have a pair!" The white-soxed techies are mostly from Pennsylvania escaping the coal mines through a rudimentary technical education, most of which they receive in one of the branches of the military, usually the Air Force as far as I can tell. A few graduate from two-year tech schools, but not many. The techies are very sensitive about their job titles and status. They consider themselves engineers who earn their self-proclaimed engineering titles by attending the school of fist-pounding hard knocks.

As we approach the intersection, I yell, "HALT... ABOUT FACE..."

The drill team halts and does a crisp about face so that the drill team now faces the techies who have gathered about the intersection.

I yell "GRAB PANT LEGS!" and the drill team reaches down and grabs the sides of their pant legs in unison.

I yell, "PANT LEGS UP!" and the drill team, while maintaining their formation and cadence, pull up their pant legs displaying wonderful argyle sox. The techies scream at us. It was hard to find six creeps who own or at least are willing to purchase a pair of argyle socks and then remember to wear them on the designated Monday before the football season kickoff, but those Pennsylvania boys don't know that.

Well as we bare our argyles, the techies start howling. They know that we're ridiculing their white sox and thus their claim to be engineers, a grievous insult to their believed, self-proclaimed status in a profession to which they actually don't belong. Those Pennsylvania boys start hurling insults: "Some pair? Pee Nuts... that's what!" "Wait 'til football season, you needle-dicked bastards!" We play them every year, twice, in the Holmes one-hand touch football league... the A-League. We make them nuts. The plan is to keep them in a frenzy so they lose their cool when we play them and it usually works. With the kickoff this coming Wednesday, their thirst for revenge will be fresh in their little minds. Pubs Creeps aren't overly gifted creatures athletic-wise. We're pretty good at a bunch of sports but we need every edge we can get, just like in softball. Making those Pennsylvania boys crazy for revenge is our edge in touch football.

I yell "ABOUT FACE! FORWARD MARCH!" and the drill team marches on to the shouted insults of those white-soxed techies. Mission accomplished!

I get to thinking about all those techie ants crawling all over those test mainframes and how they look an awful lot like a bunch of Morlocks in waiting. The thought strikes me: H. G. Wells may very well be writing metaphorically… a thought which occurs to me in the past… but the metaphor I now have in mind is of a different kind. If this different kind of metaphor is true, KTI is the perfect metaphorical front. It's a place providing technical services to all of society… to the entire world… making everyone dependant on them. The takeover and slaughter isn't literally as Wells writes. After all, he's writing prophesy and prophesy must be interpreted. Maybe the Morlocks and the Eloi are in an early state of evolutionary development. Maybe the Morlocks and the Eloi aren't fully differentiated yet which explains why the pre-Morlocks aren't harvesting thousands of Eloi.

But I've already seen two of the real Morlocks… big yellow frightening creatures. My money is on real Morlocks, like behind that steel door with the yellow symbol on it. And if these Morlocks are powerful enough, they'd just take over, but they don't. Must be, they aren't powerful enough yet. They must plan to take over gradually and maybe use surrogates or Judas goats to establish a beach head before they can take any action. Like I say, KTI is a good place to establish a such a beach head.

Preparing for the Inevitable

This whole beach head thing seems fantastic to me and not in a good sense. I pretend to myself that my thinking about those dreadful Morlockian creatures plotting behind that steel door at KTI… the one with the big yellow symbol… is just that… thinking… conjecture… that other kind of fantasy… the science fiction kind of fantasy. But I can't ignore the facts. I know in my heart of hearts that the threat is real and that I must be careful what I say and sometimes that's hard to do. Thank God, I'm not sitting in the Dance Hall anymore. Things could get dicey in that dungeon cell. Too much darkness… too much danger. I'd have trouble or at least difficulty controlling myself if I still sat there. There is a good chance that I'd act precipitously in that environment and blow my cover… thus giving those dreadful giant yellow creatures… that great threat to humanity… an opening to establish that KTI beachhead. Anyway, the image of those great yellow creatures slowly creeping pass my dungeon cell haunts me. I keep repeating to myself "Act normal!" And I do, that is as normal as is possible given where I work, with whom I work and the work itself. My intuition tells me that things are about to pop and the truth will out, as Willie S. says, vindicating me at last.

Things at home don't go so well. Because things at KTI are about to pop, I spend more and more time there since the crisis is about to come to a head like I say. When I am home, the little woman and kiddies seem more distant. I don't know why. I guess I just feel like that because I'm needed at KTI more and not there. So much depends on me at KTI… so much is at stake there… way too much. I must make sacrifices. Everyone must make sacrifices whether they know it or not, whether they like it or not. Even when I'm home, I concentrate on the threat… go over various scenarios in my head to prepare. All the talk in the house is insignificant muffled babble from the distant past. It's like they aren't really there. Then BANG! Last week, I come home very late after a long night observing the KTI parking lots looking for any suspicious movement… and they aren't. First, I fear that the Morlocks know that I know about them and their need for a beach head… that they've fooled me by striking on my home front first. I run through the house checking every room. Stuff is missing… clothes… personal items… all gone… The little woman, the kids, the stuff… all gone.

I sit at the kitchen table catching my breath… thinking. What are the chances that the Morlocks would stage their leaving to cover up the fact that they have taken them? Then I notice an envelope on the table… addressed to me and in her handwriting. I am pretty sure that if the Morlocks are clever enough to capture my family and stage their leaving, she'd have difficulty writing my name on the envelope in that even, ornate hand of hers. The facts indicate that they just plain absconded which greatly relieves me.

I stare at the envelope for a long time. I just can't pick it up, tear it open and read the letter. Then I realize that I can't remember their names and that I don't have the energy or time to even try. Too much is happening. I vow to read that note when the crisis passes and I have the energy and time to remember. Besides what is the sense of reading an intimate note from someone whose name you can't remember? I leave the envelope on the table unopened vowing to do so when time and circumstance allow and then I drive to the Bridge Circle and get very drunk.

That part of my life is still a blur. Now I have no house. Apparently it forecloses and the locks change. I don't think I'm divorced, but who knows. That note goes with the foreclosed house. I don't see her or the kids since that night… at least that I remember. No matter how hard I try now, their names still escape me but it doesn't really matter. I have more important things to think about… those fuckin' Morlocks. Losing the house from a mission standpoint doesn't matter that much since I know I am spending most of my time at KTI anyway where the immediate danger is…

where my great mission to save humanity takes me. Churchill probably felt this way too.

Before they leave and all that foreclosure business, I do take precautions to make my house as safe as possible for them knowing I can't be there much while keeping things at KTI as normal as possible… that is stay pretty much the same while still being very alert and cautious. Besides, it is easier for me at KTI where I think whatever I want and carry a flashlight as a precaution. No one there cares or even notices much. It's easier for me to fit in there. Maybe that's why I write about that part of my life and not about the other part. Besides, my entries about that other part would be rather short since I can't remember much about it.

I do remember trying to take certain measures to protect them before all that foreclosure business knowing I'm not able to spend much time there… but I just can't pull it off. I don't dare explain the dangers that we face, so I guess what I am trying to do there seems a little odd and unnecessary to her and even the neighbors… the Boughtons? … the Smiths? I try that once before and she goes bananas when we live in Albany… first floor apartment… Elberon place? Quail Street? It turns out to be a false alarm but I didn't know it at the time. I remember the landlord goes bananas when I request bars for the windows and a steel door. I can hear the little shit yelling "Are you out of your fuckin' mind! This ain't no fuckin' prison, you asshole." Shortly after this we move to a second floor apartment somewhere else… much safer. Washington Avenue? She tries to get me to see a councilor… I know what she means… what she means is a psychiatrist. I don't dare go there again. There is too much at stake. And then there is that incident in the teachers' lounge. That traitorous beast… Thomas fuckin'

Oxbow Lake The 2nd

Wolfe! That carnivorous, flesh-eating MAN-WOLF!

Just to be on the safe side, I install dead bolts on all the exterior doors of my house and exterior lights… very bright exterior lights… set up around our house on a timer. Bright lights bring safety from the potential danger. That word 'potential' scares the shit out of me. I even attempt to have bars installed on all the windows like I try to do in Albany. Unfortunately, the wife gets the work cancelled again. And then the neighbors get an injunction forcing me to turn the exterior lights off. The neighbors become hostile and I suspect why. I can't make that place safe. In retrospect, it was a good thing that the little woman and kids move out of there.

In my last act of desperation, I try to get the wife and kids to carry flashlights as a precautionary measure. Then she goes double bananas. That's probably the straw that breaks her camel's back. Anyway, I'm safe at KTI as long as I stay alert and away from the Dance Hall… and spend as little time as possible behind that first steel door and thus avoid being dragged behind that second one. It's easier to be safe at KTI because I know where the danger is coming from. Not passing through that first gate to hell is also pretty easy to do since KTI moves my subcontractor buddies to aisle 10… most of whom are long gone anyway… and now no one that I know or must work with sits behind that first steel door. The poor key punch operators… delicious morsels that they are… now occupy the dungeon and since the production process dictates that only Harlan interface with them… interface is a strange inhuman word to use when humans talk to each other… I rarely enter the place although the Dance Hall is still there. Management still uses that dungeon cell occasionally for what they euphemistically call their management initiated separations and for other cases where privacy is required for other reasons. Right, management initiated meals to go… Morlockian sacrifices. I know that if something happens to me, there's no one else. I am the only one who knows about the threat… the only one who can save… the rest humanity and I must do it alone… to stop the threat before it can develop. Nip it in the bud so to speak.

I keep things pretty generic when I talk with my fellow braves at KTI about the family taking off and the foreclosure and all… or is it a divorce?... and losing my house. All are very sympathetic. I talk in generalities and let their imaginations fill in the details. It's a good technique to use when you want to avoid details, particularly if you don't remember them. Let those with whom you talk fill in the blanks from that store of experiences that they keep in their heads… things from their past. Your rather cryptic story becomes instantly believable to those from whom you are seeking belief. If they happen to ask about details, use the 'it's too painful to talk about' ploy and they'll retreat out of consideration for your feelings and fill in those gaps themselves. Works like a charm!

I am in a tricky spot at KTI, but I must maintain my position here. After all, I am the only one who knows about the danger to humanity and the true nature of that danger. All else is irrelevant. Fortunately, that's easy to accomplish. But I must prepare for I'm sure something will break soon and the Morlocks will attempt to establish a beachhead.

I purchase a powerful portable spot light which I store in my office. I keep spare batteries in my desk too since I don't want to run out of matches so to speak. The spot light blinds the bastards, but that only momentarily paralyzes them. To finish the job, I purchase an untraceable Colt 45 from a guy that hangs around the Bridge

Circle… a guy everyone calls Tooch… I don't know his real name but like I said everyone calls him Tooch… for 400 bucks. He throws in a box of bullets. God creates men and Morlocks; Sam Colt makes them all equal! Rumor has it ol' Tooch is connected. Flake says he's a runner for a bookie… one Billy Teetock… who runs the local sports book. The Flake knows both of the bastards from high school, but he doesn't remember Tooch's real name… according to the Flake, no one does. He's always been just Tooch. Sounds fishy to me, but I test the Colt in the woods in Saugerties and it works fine.

I also have a Remington 870 12-gauge but a shot gun is hard to sneak into the building. Sneaking in the Colt 45 is a piece of cake. I keep the 12-guage in the back of my Auschwitz on Wheels. I have a lock box bolted to the floor in the cargo area where I store it. I always keep it loaded and ready for action… 12-guage shot, slug, 12-guage shot, slug until the damn thing is filled to capacity… I forget how many. The shot slows 'em down and the slug finishes them off. The locker serves as a seat in the cargo area for those unfortunate enough to be passengers number three and above. That's where I keep the 870 along with 11 boxes of shells and 7 boxes of slugs. Reminds me of a joke: why'd the Italians lose the war? Answer: they order spaghetti instead of shells. Well I order shells and fortify them up with slugs. I don't plan on losing this war. I plan to stop them on the beach before they can establish a KTI beachhead.

Where's Mr. Know-it-all? Pen run out of ink, you traitorous pussy!!!!

It Has Begun

I show up to work like always... that is a little late and hung over. I must file some forms with Personnel... EOP stuff... file them with our personnel rep, Mr. William Whitmore, the prick. Every six months I must fill in endless blanks with KTI drivel about the status of each female employee, each black employee, and each Hispanic surname employee in my department and send them to the Wet One. There is another form for disabled employees as well, but since I have no gimps in my department, I don't have to bother with this one... thank God. I think about this time they add Native Americans to the EOP list, ironically the tardy addition being its own justification for the need. However, that Native American EOP addition doesn't affect me much since all the Indians... ala the Sint Sinks... that lived in the Hudson Valley are considerate enough to disappear... die off...having been rubbed out... advertently and inadvertently... a long time ago, thus there aren't any of them around that the Wet One can make me hire and promote... consequently not requiring me to fill out any forms for them. Sometimes I wonder if the Morlocks aren't responsible for the extinction of Hudson Valley Indians. Maybe my Morlockian friends hunger for rare meat... have a real taste for the red stuff (a little levity here)... in which case having the added advantage of being able to blame aforesaid extinctions on white men such as me.

Get's me to thinking about this annoying EOP business as I stare down at the first EOP form before me. Suppose I'm the Supreme Morlock Commander in charge of the operation and want to infiltrate KTI's world of humans... that is today's KTI employees. How would I do it? What strategy would I develop? Then it strikes me like a 2x4 between my eyes! I use something already in existence and subvert it to my advantage... that's what I do.

Oxbow Lake The 2nd

That's how I'd get my Judas goats, who would look human and perhaps are human, into KTI. When I establish a beach head for my soldiers, I have a fifth column ready and waiting to support my soldiers at that beach head. The EOP program would be an ideal vehicle. The social and psychological dynamics within the organization that such a program creates would cause KTI to hire and promote individuals on criteria other than ability, talent and economic contribution to the success of KTI. The Supreme Morlock Commander could use the natural forces within the organization to his advantage. The task before me took on a whole new perspective... but a task that I still had to perform... particularly if I am to remain relatively anonymous.

This whole EOP process always pisses me off anyway... always has. Now it scares the shit out of me. The way the process works, if I want to hire or promote someone, I must fill out some more forms about why each of the available EOP candidates or employees in our group is not qualified to be hired or promoted. There's that organizational force at work. If that dufuss Igor has a management opening, he delegates the task of dealing with all the EOP stuff to me which means more forms. In both cases, if I can't come up with acceptable reasons of why a particular EOP candidate is not qualified, that EOP candidate must be hired or promoted. And if I say no to the candidates in our group, personnel sends me a list of EOP candidates from the lab... EOP candidates that they think are qualified and I must cull through that list, fill out another form for each of those candidates that I think are definitely not qualified and why I think that. Then I must interview the ones I think might be. I always interview at least one candidate from each list regardless of qualifications. If I don't, the Wet One comes down on me like a ton of bricks with insinuations that I am a prejudiced bastard unfit for management at KTI... AND ABSOLUTELY NO ONE WANTS

TO HAVE THAT LABEL STAPLED TO HIS FOREHEAD FOR IT PRETTY MUCH ENDS YOUR CAREER!!!!!!!! How's that for the Supreme Morlockian Commander's attack strategy!

The devil is in the details like all such corporate processes. The EOP program at KTI is no different, being complicated and subtle by its very nature. Although never stated and definitely never written, my department MUST have at least one EOP employee. If I don't, Personnel, in the guise of one William Whitmore, comes down on me like a ton of bricks. Although the KTI-EOP Gestapo denies it vehemently, I am pretty sure they have a point system to track me and my department's EOP status as KTI takes that great leap into performance-irrelevant equality and unknowingly opening that great steel door… that gate to hell. I can hear those EOP Judas goats braying now. Well in the end, I must have at least 1 point to my credit at all times. I realize that KTI has an even bigger Big Brother breathing down its infernal neck with a big ol' EOP enforcement cannon pointed at the back of its head… a cannon loaded with anti-business shrapnel… that is, Justice Department EOP lawyers who have the power to prevent the awarding of huge federal contracts and the power to tie KTI into court-induced and financially crippling legal pretzels for a decade, which for a high-tech corporation like KTI is forever and thus death. Supreme Morlock Commander has harnessed a powerful societal force… the bastard's smart, real smart.

In my naiveté, I actively seek what I call a 5-pointer… that golden EOP employee that ends all of my EOP woes… an employee who is a black female with an Hispanic surname whose mother was a Native American and who requires a wheel chair to mobilate around. Such an employee is pure gold and a smart five-pointer can negotiate a very sweet deal… for her qualifications meet all those EOP edicts… and very important qualifications they are organizationally within KTI... as important as performance and in many cases, more, depending on how many points a manager needs and what his rep is within the KTI-EOP Gestapo. I never find that golden 5-pointer. I often wonder if I find this golden EOP 5-pointer, must I fill out five separate forms for Miss EOP Gold in order to get credit for all 5 points?

Well, Bobbo me boy, that's the system. It pisses me off... always has... and it now scares the shit out of me but I just have to live with it as I watch my back, so my morning's work is cut out for me and my powers to write acceptable fiction are about to be tested yet again. Knowing what's behind this EOP process puts me on high alert.

At this moment in time, I am in pretty good shape EOP-wise, so it's unlikely I'll be forced to deal with more infiltrators. I have a 4-point department (although it takes two headcount to get there): one black female and one black male with an Hispanic surname. Thus I must fill out two forms. Filling out the forms for the black female, one Charlene... ironically surnamed White... she's my black female employee... poses several problems as I stare down at the form, pen in hand. She isn't really very black. She's more like Italian tan but she sports this huge Afro to solidify her blackness . She's tall, athletic and built like the proverbial brick shit house. The tribe refers to her as "the Octoroon"... never of course to her face. She is a very smart cookie and can do the job blind folded and do it well if she wants to. Unfortunately she doesn't always want to. She shows up to meetings late and when I ask her why in the most gentle of terms, she shoots back, and I quote, "I'm on CPT!"

I have no idea what she is talking about and innocently ask

"What's CPT?"

And she says, "Colored People Time, whitey."
Well the rest of the world runs on regular old Standard Time, the only recognized deviation being Daylight Savings Time which everyone else in the department pretty much agrees to. When she shows up to a department meeting on CPT, CPT being exactly one half hour later then the other two… interestingly enough, there seems to be a Standard CPT and a Daylight Savings CPT… she demands that I bring her up to speed on what happens at the meeting, thus forcing me to either argue with her about her being late in front of the rest of the department or repeating a lot of what is already said… again in front of the entire department… both of which pisses me off and pisses off the rest of the department, all of whom bother to show up pretty much on time. Once I schedule a department meeting for 9:30 but tell the Octoroon it starts at 9:00. She shows up on CPT which in this instance is actually the correct Standard Time which I guess would in Charlene's world be WPT or "White People's Time". When she walks into the conference room, 11 smiling faces greet her. At first she looks a bit befuddled, but being a smart cookie, she quickly realizes that she has been had... that is tricked into being on time. She spins on her heels and yells over her shoulder as she flees her surreptitious and inadvertent punctuality, "Excuse me, I've got to use the ladies room." She returns exactly 30 minutes later to the second by my watch and demands that I reprise what has happened in her absence. The trick gives me some pleasure but it is obvious I am in a battle I cannot win… my victory being quite pyrrhic.

There isn't much else I can do about it because Charlene knows she is a protected species. You gotta know when to hold 'em and when to fold 'em. In the case of Charlene's punctuality, I fold 'em and give a soured, highly condensed version of what has transpired at the department meeting during her absence. Everyone else in the department pretty much knows the score and puts up with it, grumbling about it to me privately from time to time.

And then I think of the incident that occurs last month during a meeting with her lead planner, the sainted Cardinal. She gets pissed off at the ol' Cardinal when he asks for more detail in her status report and she yells at him, "When the revolution comes, I'm going to personally shoot you in the head, whitey!" The Cardinal has the unmitigated gall to consider the remark both offensive and threatening and immediately informs me of the Octoroon's offensive threat. He is very pissed off. To keep him from going to personnel and causing a major stink, I give him two days of management directed time off. I originally offer one but he knows I'm in a tight spot and negotiates two. Claims the threat from the Octoroon causes a bogus on his logus or a logus on his bogus… I can't remember which… whatever the hell that means… and he takes the following Friday and Monday off for a long bogus-logus-logus bogus convalescing weekend, the prick.

Charlene is a major pain in my ass. Hers, however, is very nice to look at and she knows it in spades for she shows it off regularly wearing skimpy miniskirts to torture whitey… whitey being primarily me. She bends over to pick something up or leans over a desk or table with those long luscious legs of hers spread and… Bingo! I get flashed! I know it's intentional since she turns and with a broad shit-eaten grin spread across that beautiful face of hers, smiles at me, her flashee. Irrelevant… irrelevant… irrelevant, keep your focus on her EOP form and the threat. After some thought, I conclude that she's not a plant. No way… a plant would slide into the department and attract as little attention as possible… definitely wouldn't threaten to shoot someone in the head.

However, the more I think about her, the more pissed off I get anyway. Who the hell does she think she is! I can't flunk her totally since I need the points… there's that natural force of organizational dynamics doing its dirty work… so I decide to fill out two EOP forms for her: one because she is female and one because she is black. I fill out my female designated form giving her an 'OUTSTANDING' as a female employee since she is so good looking and is willing to show off that fine ass of hers. For her black evaluation, I give her a 'NEEDS IMPROVEMENT' since she runs on CPT and threatens to shoot fellow professionals… make that her non-fellow Caucasian professionals… in the head and for her use of what could be considered a racially charged and derisive term when communicating with said non-fellow Caucasian professionals… including yours truly… that term being, and I quote: "WHITEY". I think to preserve at least one EOP point by so doing.

I staple the two forms together and move on to my second and last EOPer, one Ziggy Gonzales. Ziggy's my Spanish surnamed black male employee, actually Ignatius Gonzales… Ziggy being his nom de plume. Ol' Ziggy's close to a midget… a veritable Mexican pigmy. But he earns his nom de plume not because of his physique but because of his rhetoric… Pubs Creeps being word people and all. He does so by never addressing a question directly… his method being to always first answer a question with an irrelevant question and then answer the original question as obliquely as possible, zigzagging about with his answer using a bunch of double negatives and other rhetorical pretzels… all while speaking painfully slowly. He is maddening to talk to. Basically he is a good guy but he does things so slowly that it is hard tell if he is doing a good job, a bad job or no job at all. He's an employment glacier. If there is a lot of time and he isn't working on project with another

271

writer, he gets the job done but it takes forever. My guess is his speech patterns reflect his thought patterns. That he eventually gets the job done is good enough for me and I give him a 'SAT' on the two forms I fill out for him. I figure that since I fill out two for Charlene, I might as well fill out two for ol' Ziggy… not wanting to show any prejudice for Mexican midgets… his EOP forms for being black and for possessing a Spanish surname. I figure giving him two 'SATS' preserves his 2 EOP points. I can't imagine Ziggy being a plant and if by some chance he is, he's obviously no good at it.

Department-wise I drop a point, but still have 3 points. True the trend is down, falling from a 4 to a 3, but a 3 is still pretty good. I take the forms over to James for his official approval before sending them to that prick Whitmore.

The Igor sits at his desk engrossed in the Daily News sports section when I enter. He puffs away on his maduro and waves me into his chair of subservience. "Have a seat. Did you see what Rutgers did last night? Lost another basketball game. Not just lost, but got slaughtered and by some dip shit school I never heard of… Acadia… ever hear of Acadia? Those Golden Knights ain't so golden this year. Slaughtered 63 to 50… by a no name college. I'll bet Simple Simon's going to be out of his fuckin' mind at lunch today"… Simple Simon being Simon Dansforth, a Rutgers graduate that Whitmore made us hire last year because of what he claims was some sort of recruiting screw up in Personnel, but that's a story unto itself. I remember the Wet One telling us we had to hire Simple Simon because someone in Personnel… and not him… had inadvertently sent the simple one an acceptance letter. By my calculations Simon's a god damn good candidate for a Wet Willie plant. I'll have to watch him carefully. He has perfect cover.

Thinking about him gives me the willies.

I slide the two stapled sets of EOP forms across the desk to Igor for his approval. As he reads the first page, I sit quietly waiting for him to approve the forms. I stare out his door at his secretary's desk and then it strikes me: no Phyllis. Another secretary is sitting at Phyllis' desk… someone I've never seen before. This stranger turns as I stare at her and she gives me the strangest look. In my hurry to get Igor to approve the EOP forms, I'd walked right by Phyllis' desk without noticing that a stranger now sits there. I ask, "Where's Phyllis?"

Igor keeps reading and mumbles, "She's taking a personal leave of absence. She leaves today. I think she's over in that empty cube over by the key punch pen. Wet Willie's with her processing her out."

I stammer, "What? She's with Wet Willie right now… taking an indefinite personal leave?"

Igor looks up from his reading and mumbles, "Yeah… she's taking an indefinite leave. Wet Willie called me this morning and this other secretary showed up… assigned by administration. She's a temp."

Igor flips through the EOP forms and his face turns beet red as he reads. I get a terrible feeling in the pit of my stomach and ask, "What's happened?"

He looks daggers at me and yells, "What's happened is you're out of your fuckin' mind. That's what's happened. I won't sign this shit. First, you've filled out two forms for each EOP. And then you

give the Octoroon an 'unsat' as an African-American. Jesus Christ, have you lost all your fuckin' marbles?"
I say, "I mean what's happened to Phyllis?"

He ignores my question, jumps up from his desk, runs to his office door and slams it shut. He turns and hisses, "And then you fill out two forms for Ziggy. Wet Willie's going to go ape shit if he sees these forms. And he's still over there looking for a reason to shove that KTI Management Manual up my ass sideways."

That yellow warning light flashes in front of me. I really like Phyllis and think she's in peril. I ask yet again, "What's happening to her? Why is she in the Dance Hall? Why is our Lady in Blue taking an indefinite personal leave?"

Igor is about to explode, "I don't know why the fuck she's taking an indefinite personal leave. That's why they call it personal... get it... as in it's none of your fuckin' business. All I know is she's not fuckin' here and if I approve these forms and you send them to Wet Willie, neither one of us will be either. You get your ass back to your cube, fill out two new forms, one for the Octoroon and one for Ziggy, give them both 'sats' and say they need more professional seasoning... more experience... and that we've got career plans in place to season the hell out of them, then bring the damn things over here for me to sign and hand deliver them to Wet Willie. And I mean now!"

I can't get the fate of our Lady in Blue out of my mind and that god damn turn coat traitor Mr. William Whitmore. Igor stands over his waste paper basket, takes the two sets of forms and slowly tears them into tiny pieces. As he does so, he stares at the pieces as they float into his waste can. He looks up at me and snarls "Do I have to repeat myself? Get your ass out of here and get those redone fuckin' forms to me to sign ASAP and hand deliver them to Wet Willie. Got it?"

I get up, slowly open his door and stare at the stranger sitting in Phyllis' chair who stares back with that same strange expression. Gotta be a plant. I walk past the stranger and a chill runs down my spine. Igor's been fooled… he's become an inadvertent fifth column for the fuckin' Morlocks… Then it strikes me… right between the eyes. Wet Willie in Personnel is the key… he's THE JUDAS GOAT! Then I realize... Our Lady in Blue has been lured into the Dance Hall by Wet Willie. She's the first sacrifice. That's where the beach head is. It has begun. It's time to act!

News Flash on the Nature and Ending of *Spanking Yesterday*

At this point the journal ends. We do not know where the story goes from here if this story is, in fact, a fictional narrative. We have attempted to contact Mr. Oxbow Lake and Mr. Ward Bobb to determine the true nature of this narrative and how it ends but have been unable to do so in spite of our best efforts. In fact, we have been unable to verify that Ward Bobb actually exists although it remains our distinct belief that his existence is a distinct possibility. As noted in previous News Flashes, I have hired the hard-hitting investigative reporter and scholar Dr. Kramer Killread the First, Esquire, to investigate what has become known as "The *Spanking Yesterday* Imbroglio". It is our profound hope that the good Doctor will be able to unravel this imbroglio and amongst his unravelings will be how this story, whether fact or fiction… or something in between… actually ends. A copy of Dr. Kramer's first hard-hitting investigative report appears below.

Robert A Ward III
Publishing Mogul & CEO
ShipWreckPublications LLC

275

The New Tampa Guide To Sane Automobile Repair

A JOURNAL DEDICATED TO THE PROPOSITION THAT ALL FICTION IS TRUE AND ALL NON-FICTION IS NOT

Kramer Killread Esquire, Editor In Chief

Investigative Report 1 Concerning the *Spanking Yesterday* Imbroglio

Note: The hard-hitting investigative reporter and scholar Dr. Kramer Killread the First, Esquire, is the Editor-in-Chief of *The New Tampa Guide to Sane Automobile Repair*, a journal based just north of Tampa, Florida, and dedicated to hard-hitting investigative journalism and profound scholarly articles about automobile mechanics, literary criticism, social commentary, and ice racing. His column "Exhaust Fumes" appears at irregular intervals quite regularly in that excellent afore named scholarly blog. Recently, Mr. Killread had an honorary doctorate of automobilean literary criticism and social commentary bestowed upon him by the prestigious *Factory Lane Automobile Institute of Very High Learning and Sane Automobile Repair* in Pine Plains, New York… which is why we are apparently legally required to refer to Mr. Kramer Killread the First, Esquire, as "Dr." according to the newly minted Doctor his very own self.

We at ShipWreckPublications highly recommend *The New Tampa Guide to Sane Automobile Repair* to the reader and believe that you will find the articles published there both edifying and entertaining like his first hard-hitting investigative report below on the *Spanking Yesterday* imbroglio written by the good Doctor his very own self. The Guide presents opinion and a view of the world which we guarantee you will find nowhere else. If you like the article below by Dr.

Kramer Killread the First, Esquire, you will love the Guide!

The New Tampa Guide to Sane Automobile Repair is only available electronically at http://guidetosaneautorepair.wordpress.com. If you'd like hard copy, you'll have to print it out yourself if you can figure out how to do it as this journal claims to be at the forefront of technology and eschews printed copy in all of its printed forms with the notable exception of dollar bills (preferably in the higher denominations) by its own admission. Dr. Killread's first investigative report, a preliminary conjecture on the question of the authorship of *Spanking Yesterday*, will be published next month in *The New Tampa Guide to Sane Automobile Repair* and appears below with the permission of that scholarly blog and the good Doctor his very own self in both written and orally recorded form as we know these guys like the back of our very own hands.

A candid shot of a surprised Dr. Kramer Killread the First, Esquire, while at work on his ground breaking investigative reporting "Who Really Wrote *Spanking Yesterday* (A Preliminary Conjecture)"

Who Really Wrote *Spanking Yesterday* (A Preliminary Conjecture)

By Dr. Kramer Killread the First, Esquire

New Tampa, Florida – Just to cover all the necessary investigative and scholarly bases, I have parenthetically subtitled this article "A Preliminary Conjecture" so that I can revise my claims later, if necessary, to come into line with other investigative and scholarly articles and thus remain in the respectable main stream so that I can continue to be invited to cocktail parties, get well-paying speaking gigs at colleges and universities, sniff young co-eds, receive gratuitous grants from all those foundations whose names appear in the credits for virtually all Public Broadcasting shows, and have my future investigative reporting and scholarly articles accepted by both the main stream media and other scholarly blogs and journals.

Before I continue, I'd like to apologize from the depths of my heart for any of the potentially wayward opinions that I may express in this critical article, for if they exist, they are the inadvertent residue of the devilishly clever, insidious and deleterious right wing propaganda of one of the Bush Administrations to which we all have been subjected. I will correct these opinions as necessary when those wayward opinions are pointed out to me by my journalistic and scholarly peers. Upon a potentially necessary revision of my opinions to align with the consensus of my peers, the parenthetical subtitle "A Preliminary Conjecture" will be removed from the article's title.

Now down to brass tacks as they say. The reputed single author of *Spanking Yesterday*, Mr. Oxbow Lake the Second, reminds me of Samuel Clemens in a number of ways. His hair is long, like Mr.

Clemens (even though, I am told, Mr. Lake gets it cut daily as did Mr. Clemens and as an aside, both men have obviously wasted a lot of money in so doing), Mr. Lake dresses quite distinctively (again as did Mr. Clemens), he smokes cheap, foul smelling cigars constantly (yet again like Mr. Clemens) and like Mr. Clemens, he writes what he believes to be, by his own admission, intentionally and uniquely American frontier humor ignoring the fact that *Spanking Yesterday* is set in upstate New York and that the true American frontier is now located in Hollywood, California, and not the location in which his latest novel is set or even Orlando, Florida, for that matter. While it must be admitted that *Spanking Yesterday* is very funny in an Animal House kind of way and I believe that it makes humorist Dave Barry the second funniest writer on planet Earth and possibly the third, the humor is hardly frontier in nature.

As to who wrote *Spanking Yesterday*, I look to Samuel Clemens as well for the answer. I believe that Mr. Lake, like Mr. Clemens, was, and possibly still is, a member of a writing team and does NOT write alone. In Mr. Clemens case, the other team member was Mark Twain. In the case of Mr. Lake, it is Mr. Ward A. Bobb the Third. I realize that my claim that Mr. Lake does NOT write alone may be controversial but the same was said for years about Mr. Samuel Clemens and look how that's turned out!

As the reader is probably aware, I have conclusively proven THAT negative in another of my ground breaking articles, "Samuel Clemens Wasn't Gay But He Did Have a Male Partner (Another Preliminary Conjecture)"… using as corroborating evidence the fact that even though Sam Clemens and Mark Twain never appeared on the same stage together at the same time, according to numerous play bills, they did in fact appear on different stages together at different

280

times… an undeniable truth and proof positive that they were in fact a writing team which is now the consensus opinion of all scholars.

In a companion article that I am presently writing which is also germane to the subject at hand… an article I have tentatively entitled "Why Samuel Clemens Intentionally Murdered Mark Twain (Yet Another Preliminary Conjecture)"… I am proving conclusively that Samuel Clemens had Mark Twain surreptitiously murdered to assume ownership of all the royalties for their jointly written works and got away with it by claiming that Mark Twain was a pen name that Mr. Clemens used to protect his anonymity. If I were a member of Mr. Oxbow Lake the Second's writing team, as is Ward A. Bobb the Third, I would not sleep well nor would I sleep often and I'd only meet with my writing team partner in open and very public places… but that's just me.

Even though Mr. Oxbow Lake the Second and Mr. Ward A. Bobb the Third have not been seen together on the same stage at the same time, they have been seen on different stages at different times together. Negative proven! Need I say more! Mr. Oxbow Lake the Second was part of a team which included Ward A Bobb the Third when Mr. Lake participated in the writing of *Spanking Yesterday* and he did NOT do so alone… contrary to his imputed claims.

POST SCRIPT: Contrary to claims to the contrary, it greatly saddens me to write that *The New Tampa Guide to Sane Automobile Repair* has proven well beyond a reasonable doubt that the beloved Mr. Dave Barry is in fact as well as opinion now the second funniest writer on planet Earth (and quite possibly the third) and only the untimely deaths of both Mr. Lake and/or Mr. Bobb could catapult him back to number 1. Mr. Barry now occupies a place with both factual and metaphoric meaning. Mr. Barry's close supportive friend, Mr.

Oxbow Lake The 2nd

Carl (stuttering a's) Hiaasen has dropped out of the top 10,000 behind an ethnic German graffiti scribbler named Sanas the Fakir from Jaipur, India, who spray paints jokes on bathroom walls about snake charmers who get bitten between their legs by their cobras!"

-- Dr. Kramer Killread the First, Esquire

An update to the biography of Oxbow Lake the 2nd

What follows is a copy of a letter signed by a Mr. Oxbow Lake the 2nd and written to Peter Q. Peckerwood, a literary agent, after the letter's author read Mr. Peckerwood's book entitled *How to Get a Really Good Literary Agent Who Really Cares About You* and subtly subtitled *The Story of an Agent Deserving of Your Sympathy.* I thought that the letter would illuminate the current views of the letter's author, possibly Mr. Oxbow Lake his very own self, on the publishing industry in general and literary agents in particular as these views will eventually greatly affect both and most likely influence the future of American literature regardless of the true identity of the author of the letter.

In the back of Oxbow Lake's first novel, *The Adventures of the Posse of Little Horses,* there appears a short biography of Oxbow Lake the 2nd entitled "About the Author and His Novel". In fact, now that I think about it, that biography may be, at least in part, autographical in nature. To better understand someone self-reputed to be Oxbow Lake, the man and the author, and his views of the publishing industry and literary agents as relates to his letter to literary agent Peter Q. Peckerwood, I suggest that you read that article first. Then read the publisher's note that appears in the front of this "novel" to clarify what you've already read. If you don't have *The Adventures of the Posse of Little Horses*, I suggest that you purchase a copy, read the novel and then read the biographical (and perhaps autobiographical) material at the back and then read the 'Publisher's Note' at the front of this 'novel'.

Since you're probably too lazy to bother with any of the above, you can still read the letter and get a pretty good idea of what someone reputed to be Oxbow Lake the 2nd thinks of literary agents in general and Mr. Peter Q. Peckerwood in particular. The letter follows.

A normal day in the life of Oxbow Lake the 2nd

April 1, 2012

Dear Mr. Peter Q. Peckerwood, Jr., AAR, etc., etc.

After reading your book How to Get a Really Good Literary Agent Who Really Cares About You, I've decided not to send you a manu- script, unsolicited or otherwise. Instead, I am sending you a pair of my shoes (actually my sneakers). No disrespect is intended, for I actually enjoyed your book, particularly the funny parts, although I must admit that some of it was a slog and quite discouraging. All in all, I took much of what you wrote to heart.

While I try not to spend too much time read- ing any chapter or page with a "13" in its number to reduce the opportunity for the transference of bad luck, a quote of yours on page 513 of your book caught my eye in your thirteenth interludinary chapter: "to know how hard it is to be an agent, try walk- ing in my seven-and-a-halfs and you'll have a lot more sympathy for all agents in general and me in particular." Well, Mr. Peckerwood, I did try walking around in a pair of seven- and-a-halfs and my feet hurt like hell, for as you can see, a likely outcome given that I wear a size 13 (which I believe may be the source of much of my bad luck and also why I love the song "A Man of Constant Sorrow").

No need to return my 13s. Keep them and do with them what you will. You can even try walking in them suckers to know what it is to walk in my shoes. As to not sending you a manuscript, I am not doing so (or should I say "doing so" to avoid a double negative?) because my favorite author is John Kennedy Toole, who, as it turns out, happens to be dead. (I discovered this after finishing his first novel A Confederacy of Dunces and eager-ly searching for his second.) Mr. Toole sub-mitted the manuscript for his first novel and, as fate would have it also his last, to a publisher (Simon and Schuster, I believe) who rejected it on the grounds that it was about nothing, a concept that Jerry Seinfeld proved to be not of great disadvantage in the cre-ative arts. The unpublished Mr. Toole, know-ing that he had written an American classic novel, apparently became very discouraged, lost his sense of humor, gave up writing and committed suicide.

Since I would like to keep my positive view of humanity, my sense of humor, and my de-sire to continue to write while avoiding Mr. Toole's self-inflicted final fate on this earth, I have decided not to send my manu-script to anyone, including you or your agen-cy (even though you seem to be a nice person

although given your above quote, somewhat
self-centered which I believe to be common in
your profession).

Besides, should I change my mind, I still do
not think that I could send my manuscript
to anyone living in San Francisco since I
have another criterion for an agent or publisher other than acceptance: any agent or
publisher that accepts my manuscript must
also have recently enjoyed a savory meal of
"Hoover pork". This criterion probably elimi-
nates many of the agents and publishers in
New York as well leaving me with a very small
pool of agents and publishers to accept my
manuscript, but a man has to live by certain principles and I have at least two (see
above).

I have the following suggestion for your
book, your agency and the publishing industry
in general. Not only should agents, editors
and publishing houses list the books that
they've accepted and that have become popular and, in some cases, classics. They should
also list the books that have become popular
and classics that they have rejected. It's
as American as baseball! Batters get statistics published on their strikeouts along with
their hits and homers as well as their bat-
ting averages, regardless of how low. Pitchers get statistics published on such things

as walks and balks as well as strikeouts, and the number of wins and losses, regardless of their winning percentage. And the record for each team is published daily during the baseball season, much to the dismay of such teams as the Houston Astros and, before last year, the Washington Nationals. To insure the accuracy and integrity of their performance measurements, Major League Baseball has an independent agency gather and publish their player and team statistics and so should the publishing industry.

I've included several recipes for Hoover pork below should your need arise for such information and the need may very well arrive given the state of the publishing industry in general and our economy in particular. I try to look at the positive side of the impending economic collapse of both: while such an event will decrease the number agents and publishers, it will likely increase my pool of acceptable agents and publishers.

Yours,
Oxbow Lake the 2nd
Proud member of the SFOLPMA

ARMADILLO AND ONIONS
1 armadillo
11/2 tsp. salt
1/4 tsp. paprika

1/2 c. flour
3 tbsp. fat
3 lg. onions, sliced
1 c. sour cream

Soak meat overnight in salted water (1 table-spoon salt to 1 quart water). Drain, disjoint and cut up. Season with 1 teaspoon salt, paprika, roll into flour and fry in fat until browned. Cover meat with onion, sprinkle onions with 1/2 teaspoon salt. Pour in the cream. Cover skillet tightly and simmer for 1 hour.

ARMADILLO MEATLOAF
11/2 lbs. ground meat
2 eggs, beaten
1/8 c. dry crumbs
1 c. evaporated milk
1/4 onion, minced or grated
1/4 tsp. thyme
1 tsp. salt
1/4 tsp. pepper
1 tsp. Worcestershire sauce

Soak meat overnight in salted water (1 table-spoon salt to 1 quart water). Remove meat from bones and grind. Mix thoroughly with other ingredients. Place in meat loaf dish. Place dish in pan containing hot water. Bake in a moderate oven, 350 degrees for 11/4 hours to

Unsolicited Praise for Oxbow Lake's First Novel *The Adventures of the Posse of Little Horses*

"I re-ckon Oxbow Lake is a pen name. Is that damned idiot Ward A Bobb the 3rd ashamed of his work?"
- Sam Clemens (channeled through Bob Dylan)

"If I were alive, I'd have written it myself, only differently and better!"
- Mark Twain (You Dead Tube)

"The Adventures of the Posse of Little Horses does not make me regret committing suicide."
- John Kennedy Toole (Giggle Beyond Internet Site)

"The bastard plagiarized my Ride a Cockhorse after I died so I know that at least part of it is good."
- Raymond Kennedy (scratched on a bar near Columbia)

"Worst punctuated novel I've ever read. The man's obsessed with ellipses... he's out of his freakin'... elliptical mind!"
- Lisa Lazzero (freelance professional punctuator)

"It has some damn short sentences which is damn good. Too bad they don't make any damn cents."
- Ernest Hemingway (channeled through Groucho Marx)

"He's my intellectual mini-me. Mr. Oxbow Lake the 2nd

knows how to really torture a thought."
- Marquis De Sade (channeled through VP Joe Biden)

**"To get this novel published, Oxbow will need at least two
sets of knee pads."**
- Senator John "Bluto" Blutarsky (Animal House séance)

**"I find Oxbow Lake's novel to be vulgar and despicable,
and I have only read the first page."**
- Charles Dickens (channeled through Hugh Hefner)

A Posse Teaser

Take a gander at the front and back covers of *The Adventures of the Posse of Little Horses* to whet your appetite, if those unsolicited praises didn't do the job, and if you're still not convinced, there's a wonderful excerpt awaiting you at www.shipwreckpublications. com for your perusal.

HUMOROUS CRIME FICTION   U.S.A $13.95

Why read this stupid novel? Because its funny and dirty . . . in the literary sense of both words. If you are titillated by someone else's ox getting gored, this is the book for you! It'll make your funny bone twitch at someone else's expense . . . provided you have a funny bone to twitch.
-- *Kramer Killread, The New Tampa Guide to Sane Automobile Repair*

Blackmail . . . Sex . . . Drugs . . . Tequila . . . Rock and Roll . . . and throw in a bunch of murders. . . Does it get any better?

Why would a Mexican drug cartel blackmail Jamie Steinkraus's father-in-law? Could it be to get possession of the mountain chalet Jamie gave to his young bride? Can detective Big Louie Fazzano solve the mystery?

Oxbow Lake the 2nd is a pen name used by **Ward Bobb the 3rd**, which is an alias. Oxbow claims that neither of them have been intentionally institutionalized although one of them may have worked at IBM for a considerable length of time.
The Adventures of the Posse of Little Horses, winner of the Costa Concordia, is Oxbow's first novel and his best to date.

Will Jamie and his Posse of Little Horses elude the cartel's hit men as they flee west on Route 66? Will their supply of Brand XXX tequila last long enough to get them to California?

What can modern psychiatry do to cure Jamie's young wife of her obsession to give herself to black men whom she believes are Zulu warriors?

Cover illustration by Karen Mathis
Author photograph by Lisa Lazzaro

If you don't laugh at our books, you're probably dead . . . or should be!

Visit www.ShipWreckPublications.com

ISBN 978-0-9839766-0-8
51395
9 780983 976608

293

How to Order Oxbow Lake's First Novel
The Adventures of the Posse of Little Horses

• To purchase the paperback ($13.95), order online at www.amazon. com or www.barnesandnoble.com .

• Kindle and Nook ebooks ($4.99) may also be ordered online at the Amazon or Barnes & Noble sites respectively and, we hope, respectfully.

• To purchase copies autographed by Oxbow Lake the 2nd his very own self... copies that will become collector's items and can be eventually auctioned off on eBay for great profit... send a good check for $19.00 per copy (includes shipping and handling), to:

ShipWreckPublications LLC
9745 Fox Chapel Road
Tampa, FL 33647

Please include your return address.

For quick links to make online purchases, go to www.shipwreck-publications.com and while there, check out our site... before we get shut down by the law... which contains lots of interesting stuff about the actions of our rogue publishing house and while there, read some free short stories by Oxbow Lake his very own self.

News Flash: The ShipWreckPublications site also contains links to Dr. Kramer Killread's investigative reports on the *Spanking Yesterday* imbroglio published online at *The New Tampa Guide to Sane Automobile Repair.* A copy of Dr. Kramer's first investigative report appears earlier.

www.ingramcontent.com/pod-product-compliance
Lightning Source LLC
Chambersburg PA
CBHW052015020726
47501CB00004B/1079